NO OTHER MAN

Her heart nearly pounded out of her chest. She could not believe he was bold enough to speak to her of so delicate a matter. Then it suddenly occurred to her that in a day's time she would belong to this man. He would have the right to possess her body. The very thought stole her breath. "If I'm to be your wife," she said, drawing in a deep breath, "I shall belong to you in every way."

"I shouldn't like for you to close your eyes and pretend I'm someone else, Fiona."

She trembled. He had called her by her first name—a gesture she found as intimate as a kiss. Just as intimate was his allusion to closing her eyes . . . closing her eyes while they made love. "There is no other man, Mr. Birmingham."

"Nick," he growled. "You're to call me Nick."

BOOK YOUR PLACE ON OUR WEBSITE AND MAKE THE READING CONNECTION!

We've created a customized website just for our very special readers, where you can get the inside scoop on everything that's going on with Zebra, Pinnacle and Kensington books.

When you come online, you'll have the exciting opportunity to:

- View covers of upcoming books
- Read sample chapters
- Learn about our future publishing schedule (listed by publication month *and author*)
- Find out when your favorite authors will be visiting a city near you
- Search for and order backlist books from our online catalog
- Check out author bios and background information
- Send e-mail to your favorite authors
- Meet the Kensington staff online
- Join us in weekly chats with authors, readers and other guests
- Get writing guidelines
- AND MUCH MORE!

Visit our website at
http://www.kensingtonbooks.com

ONE GOLDEN RING

CHERYL BOLEN

ZEBRA BOOKS
Kensington Publishing Corp.
www.kensingtonbooks.com

For my smart, savvy, funny,
overworked editor, Hilary Sares,
with gratitude for encouraging me to
"lighten up" my writing.

Chapter 1

Lady Fiona Hollingsworth felt wretchedly guilty for sitting there in her theatre box, and even more guilty for pondering a flame-haired actress, when her brother's very life was being threatened—not that Randy was likely to expire this very night. She had a week before the situation turned truly desperate.

"Who is that beautiful creature?" she asked her theatre companion.

Trevor Simpson screwed in his quizzing glass and, following Fiona's gaze, stared at the actress on the stage below. "Ah, that would be Diane Foley. Lovely, is she not?"

"She certainly is."

Trevor bent his head to hers and whispered, "Miss Foley's protector sits in the box opposite us."

"You are not supposed to discuss such matters with a maiden," Fiona scolded as she playfully swatted the flamboyantly dressed man beside her with her fan. Trevor's disregard for convention could always bring a smile to Fiona's lips. She did not know what she would have done this past year of overwhelming grief had she not had Trevor to cheer her. It was Trevor who had insisted she come here tonight. "Do you good," he had told her that afternoon, "to get your mind off the wretched business with Randolph." Though she had tearfully protested, Trevor's persistence eventually won out.

Curious to see the lovely actress's "protector," Fiona immediately swept her gaze to the lone man in the box across from hers. He was an extremely handsome man in his early thirties, tall and dark and exceptionally well dressed. She thought that even were he not possessed of such striking good looks, the man's haughty air of bored arrogance would have commanded attention. Only once before had she seen such a man. Her spine stiffened. She *had* met this man before. "Is that Mr. Nicholas Birmingham?" she asked her companion.

Trevor's eyes sparkled, and a grin pinched his slender cheeks. "He's utterly gorgeous, is he not?"

Fiona found herself smirking into her fan. Randy would be appalled over Trevor's blatant effeminism, but she had always found it rather amusing. "I don't think Randy likes Mr. Birmingham," she said.

"Of course not, my dear lady! The man's completely ineligible."

"Then why did Randy introduce him to me?"

"Can't imagine Birmingham being at the same gathering with a viscount's daughter. He's not of the *ton*, you know. Where could you have met the fellow?"

"Actually I persuaded my brother to allow me to go to Tattersall's with him. Once. Since Randy had been to Cambridge with Mr. Birmingham, he must have felt compelled to introduce us when Mr. Birmingham greeted him, but Randy was exceedingly cool to him."

"As well he should be! Even though they're wealthier than the Duke of Devonshire, Birmingham and his brothers are as ruthless as their late father—a man who was brilliant at banking and making money but who made a poor choice in a wife. The boys' mother's painfully crass. And . . ." Trevor lowered his voice. "It's said Nicholas Birmingham even has one of his bastards living with him."

Decidedly improper, she thought.

"He's the one," Trevor said authoritatively, "who's building that disgustingly opulent mansion on Piccadilly, you know."

No, she did not know, though she certainly knew about the Piccadilly mansion. London was agog over the palatial structure rising from the rubble that had been Lord Howard's townhouse. "It's said the man building it is the richest man in all of England."

Trevor examined his fingernails. "I daresay he is. Pity he's a Cit."

Throughout the remainder of the play Fiona watched Mr. Birmingham, who watched his beautiful mistress glide elegantly to and fro while saying the most suggestive things to the men who shared the stage with her. Once when Fiona was staring into Mr. Birmingham's box, his gaze flicked to hers. And held. Fiona quickly looked away.

Though she dared not risk staring at him anymore, she could not free her mind of the exceedingly rich Mr. Birmingham. During the final curtain call, she asked, "Is Nicholas Birmingham married?"

"No," Trevor said. "Deuced awkward for a man in his position to find a bride."

"I should think Mr. Birmingham could buy any woman in the kingdom."

Trevor shrugged. "The late Mr. Birmingham raised his sons to be gentlemen. Had the best education his wealth could buy, use only the best tailors, speak the King's English and all that. But they're still Cits. Too good for women of their own class and not good enough for women of our class, though I daresay their father had hoped for an aristocratic match for the eldest boy, Nicholas." Trevor's head inclined toward Mr. Birmingham's box.

While Fiona and Trevor waited outside the theatre for their carriage, shivering from the December night's frostiness, Fiona half wished to see Mr. Birmingham to confirm that he was as handsome as she remembered, as handsome as he appeared across a dark theatre, but he was nowhere in sight. She supposed someone of his vast wealth never had to wait for anything.

Once she and Trevor settled in her family's rickety coach she broached the subject that had dominated her thoughts all evening. "I'm planning to ask Mr. Birmingham to help me free Randy."

Trevor's eyes widened. "You cannot be serious!"

"Why?"

"Because the man's mercenary. He doesn't give away his precious hoards of money. You'll not be asking for a few guineas. What you need is a fortune. Men of Birmingham's ilk don't give away twenty-five thousand pounds."

Fiona squared her shoulders and spoke firmly. "I mean to strike a bargain with him."

"My dear lady, you have nothing left to bargain with. All your father's property—except that which is entailed—has already been sold off. You've nothing to offer as collateral."

"I do have something," she whispered.

Trevor spun toward her. "Pray, what?"

She took a deep breath. "Myself."

For once Trevor was speechless. When he recovered enough to close his gaping mouth, he said, "A viscount's daughter cannot marry a Cit!" His eyes narrowed. "Besides, have you not always said you would marry only for love?"

Her lips thinned. "I once believed in love, but you know what became of that. Since I shall never love again, why shouldn't I marry a man who can save my brother's life?"

"Randolph wouldn't like it above half if you was to throw yourself away on the likes of Birmingham. Even if the man is devilishly handsome."

A sudden rush of tears filled her eyes. "It's not as if I'm not already dead inside, Trevor, and if I were to be fortunate enough to tempt Mr. Birmingham, I would at least rejoice over saving Randy." Her voice cracked. "Do you know how long it's been since I had something to rejoice over? In the past sixteen months I've lost Mama, then Warwick, then Papa, then the family fortune." Her voice cracked. "I couldn't bear it if I lost Randy too."

Trevor took her hand and pressed it between his own gloved hands. "I know, my pet. Things have been dreadfully wretched for you. If I had a feather to fly with, it would be yours."

"But neither of us has a feather to fly with. That's why I must throw myself at Mr. Birmingham."

Trevor winced. "I beg that you wait, my lady. Surely we can think of something else."

She shook her head solemnly. "No, Trev. You said yourself twenty-five thousand pounds is a fortune. We'll never come up with that much money. And I only have until next week."

"I should like to wring your brother's neck," Trevor muttered in a guttural voice. "I told him he had no business rushing off to The Peninsula. Look what's it's gotten him."

"He didn't know Papa would die and leave his finances so muddled, and Randy couldn't have known those wretched bandits would abduct him."

"Still, he should have stayed here with you after that beastly business with Warwick."

"But he was as upset as I when Lord Warwick married. Randy had offered for the countess himself."

Trevor's lips stretched to a flat line. "He'd only known the countess a few days, certainly not long enough to form the kind of attachment to her that you had with Warwick. Pray, how many years had you loved Warwick?"

Her heart stung at the memory. "Thirteen," she said in a hoarse whisper. It was still difficult for her to believe the man she had loved since she was twelve and been pledged to for three years had married someone else. It was still difficult to imagine a future in which she wasn't Edward's wife, wasn't Lady Warwick. It was still difficult to accept that she would likely go to her grave without knowing a man's love.

"If I knew how to use pistols or swords I'd have called Warwick out myself," Trevor said.

The image of the milksoppish Trevor brandishing a sword brought a smile to her lips. She squeezed his hand even more tightly. For as many years as she had been in love with Warwick she and the diminutive Trevor Simpson had been the greatest of friends. "I don't think I hate him anymore, nor do I still love him," she said with resignation. "All that's left is a huge hole in my heart."

When the carriage pulled to a stop in front of Trevor's lodgings at Albany, he turned to her. "I beg that you don't do anything rash."

"Where does Mr. Birmingham live?"

"Doubtless in some unfashionable neighborhood you can't be seen in. Piccadilly won't be finished until the Italian painters complete the ceilings."

She lowered her fine brows. "Does Mr. Birmingham have offices in The City?"

"He's known as The Fox of the Exchange—but you must know women cannot go to the Exchange."

She smiled. "Women cannot go to Tattersall's, but I went there."

"Now see here, Lady Fiona! You simply cannot go into The City unchaperoned."

"I'm not, Trev dearest. You'll come with me. Tomorrow morning."

Nicholas Birmingham rose from his broad desk to greet the foreign secretary, Lord Warwick. Despite that he had not seen Warwick in many years, Nick had kept abreast of the peer's affairs, including his jilting of the lovely Lady Fiona Hollingsworth last year. How any man could reject such a perfect creature was beyond Nick's comprehension, and the fact that the most superior Lord Warwick humiliated the lady did nothing to endear him to Nick.

What a remarkable coincidence that Warwick should call the very morning after Nick saw Lady Fiona at the theatre. All morning Nick had been unable to purge his mind of the vision of the elegant blond beauty staring across the dark theatre at him. How lovely she had looked in her sapphire gown that matched her extraordinary eyes.

Nick was somewhat surprised that a man of Warwick's importance had sought him out. Though the two men had been at Cambridge together, their disparaging stations had prevented any sort of friendship from forming. "Your servant, my lord," he said. "Please be seated."

Warwick sat on a sturdy wooden chair that faced Nick's desk.

"What can I do for you, my lord?" Nick never wasted time on pleasantries. As long as the sun shone, he could make money, and every minute wasted was money lost.

The foreign secretary cleared his throat. "I'm here in an official capacity, Mr. Birmingham."

Nick's brows rose. "I am completely at your service."

A single corner of Warwick's aristocratic mouth

twitched as he somberly eyed Nick. "As you know, defeating Napoleon by any means is my objective in all that I do at the Foreign Office."

Why in the hell doesn't the man just get to the point? "As it should be, my lord."

"We've been bloody successful at sea, and our peninsular armies are making great strides in subduing the maniac Corsican, but there's one more area I wish to dominate."

He wants to crush the French treasury. Nick smiled. "Now I understand why you've come to me."

"There's only one man in England with the resources—and the knowledge—to manipulate the markets."

"What's needed is not a manipulation of the market but a devaluation of the franc."

The earl pondered this for a moment, then nodded. "At this point, such a devaluation can only be precipitated by someone possessed of a great fortune."

Nick laughed. "What you propose is that my brothers and I beggar ourselves in order to crush the French?"

"I'll admit there is a certain risk," the earl said, "but the English government is poised to enter into a contract with you. Should you fail—should you lose your vast resources—we would provide handsomely for you for the rest of your life."

"Then why doesn't the English government use its resources instead of mine to foil Napoleon?"

"Because the war's taking everything!"

Nick peered at the earl through narrowed eyes. "And if France wins this war?"

"That is an eventuality I cannot conceive of."

"You'd make a damned poor businessman, Warwick." Nick disliked the pompous foreign secretary even more now. It was bad enough that he had humiliated the delicate Lady Fiona, but now he was asking that Nick throw away his family's fortune on a poorly thought-out scheme that would in no way benefit Nick and his brothers and that the English government was not capable of funding.

There was a tap on his door, and his secretary entered the chamber, closing the door behind him. "A Lady Fiona Hollingsworth to see you, my lord," the young man said.

Nick and Warwick exchanged icy stares, then Warwick got to his feet. "I was just leaving. Oblige me by not mentioning this matter to anyone."

Nick nodded.

"And please, Birmingham," Warwick added, "I beg that you give the matter careful consideration. I shall call on you again next week."

As Warwick went to leave the office, Lady Fiona swept in. When she met Warwick's gaze, her face blanched. "Edward!" she said in a shaky voice.

He bowed. "May I hope you're as well as you look, Lady Fiona?"

Except for her ruffled composure, she did indeed look very well. The tomato color of her well-cut velvet pelisse perfectly matched the hue of her lovely mouth. The lithe, dainty blonde exuded more elegance than any woman Nick had ever seen. Warwick was an utter fool to have cast aside this beauty.

"I'm quite well," she answered. "And Lady Warwick?"

"She presented me with a son in September."

"Yes, I know. My felicitations."

After Warwick left, Nick crossed the room, bowed before Lady Fiona, then took her shaking hand and brushed his lips across it. "Allow me to say what a pleasure it is to see you again, my lady. Won't you have a seat?"

He pulled up an upholstered chair in front of his desk, and she sank into it.

Nick returned to his desk and faced her, for once not spurring on his visitor to get to the point. "My sympathies on your father's death last year," he offered. "I suppose Randolph is the new Lord Agar?"

Her pale blue eyes were utterly woeful when she looked up at him. "He is."

"I would be most happy to assist you, my lady, in communicating with your brother. My courier service is second to none."

"I do need your assistance, Mr. Birmingham, but not for that." She began to fumble in her reticule, then she removed a single piece of parchment and handed it to him.

"What's this?" he asked, his glance leaping to the masculine scribble on the page.

"A ransom demand I received yesterday. It was wrapped around my brother's signet ring—which I know he would never willingly part with. Randolph has apparently been abducted by Spanish bandits."

Nick took the letter and read.

> *We have in our custody the son of the wealthy English Lord Agar. If you wish to see Señor Randolph again, you must pay us twenty-five thousand pounds. We will give you a week to secure the funds, then we will be communicating with you once more. If you fail to comply, Señor Randolph will be killed.*

"Your brother was in Spain?" Nick asked.

She nodded.

"Why did you not take this letter to Warwick?"

"If you must know," she said proudly, "I'm out of charity with his lordship."

"So you expect a stranger to give you the twenty-five thousand pounds?" At the wounded look on her delicate face, he wished he could retract his insensitive words. Lady Fiona was under a great deal of strain. She was extremely close to her brother and quite naturally worried about him. "I'm sorry for being so brutally blunt, my lady. I'm flattered that you've come to me, but you must realize this is an exorbitant amount of money." He stopped short of reminding her that the Agar fortune had gone the way of powdered wigs. It was Nick's business to know everyone's financial business. The late Lord Agar had lost vast sums in African mines, and that loss was followed with a huge blow on the market. The man had been forced to sell all his ancillary properties and much of his renowned library and art collection just to meet present pecuniary demands.

"To me, yes, it's a great deal of money," she said. "To most people, it's a great deal of money, but not to you, Mr. Birmingham."

"If it's a loan you seek, you need to see my brother Adam. He's the banker of the family."

"I don't wish to speak with your brother," she said, her blue eyes glittering defiantly, her spine ramrod straight. "It's you I wish to deal with."

"Why am I to be so singularly honored, my lady?"

"Because you're not a complete stranger."

"You think one brief meeting gives you access to my money?" Damn, but he was behaving abominably to the poor lady! "Forgive me for my shockingly bad manners."

Two perfect, little white teeth nipped at her lip as she watched him. God, but she was exquisite!

But of course he wouldn't give her the money. "I must tell you, my lady, that in order to obtain a loan, one must secure it by pledging property or belongings of equal or greater value than the amount borrowed. What do you propose to use as collateral?"

She did not answer for a moment. Her hands folded and unfolded nervously as she stared at him. Then she finally cleared her throat, stared at his neck, and said, "I mean to offer myself as your bride, Mr. Birmingham."

Chapter 2

Never in his two and thirty years had Nick been more stunned. Never before had he dared even to entertain the unvoiced thought of marrying a woman of Lady Fiona's pedigree. As he sat there staring at her porcelain perfect face, at the wisps of silvery blond hair that escaped her Grecian coif, a feeling of profound elation swept over him. His gaze lazily traveled over her elegant figure, over her modest, heaving bosom and the graceful fingers that kept clasping and unclasping. He admired her proud effort at composure. God's teeth, but he envied the man who would possess this woman.

But that man could not be him.

He had no desire to spend the rest of his life with a woman who hated him, and nothing could rouse hatred more easily than a forced marriage. By her own offer, she had confirmed the deep disparity in their stations. Because she was the daughter of a viscount, she expected Nick to be so honored over her offer that he would be thankful to part with twenty-five thousand dollars.

The pity of it was that were it not for the class system, he thought Lady Fiona and he might have dealt rather well together. He would have enjoyed lavishing her with grand estates and fine jewels and beautiful gowns. He would have been proud to walk into a room with her on his arm, proud to have her bear his children. His attraction to her was impossible to deny.

That she had scarcely been able to remove her gaze from him last night at the theatre added some credence to the notion she found him not detestable. With all due humility, Nick was aware of his attractiveness to the opposite sex. And even though he and Lady Fiona were not really acquainted, she seemed to understand how utterly ripe Nick was for matrimony. Now that he had tripled the fortune his father left him five years ago, Nick was ready to set up a house with a woman of breeding and beauty— qualities this woman possessed in spades. His chest tightened. How could he ever settle for another woman now that he'd had a fleeting chance at Lady Fiona Hollingsworth? With bitter regret, he realized no other woman would ever do.

But he could not allow himself the sheer luxury of marrying her. She would never be able to forget that she had stooped low to marry him.

"I would be honored to have you as my bride . . ." Nick began.

Her solemn face brightened.

". . . were I inclined toward matrimony," he added, "which I'm not."

It pained him to see her proud countenance seep away, to watch as those rigid shoulders went slack, as the flicker of mirth in those steely eyes dulled. Her fingers laced together tightly, and she met his gaze with false bravado. "Forgive me for troubling you, then, Mr. Birmingham." She went to rise.

"Please don't go yet," he said in a gentle voice.

She slumped back into the chair, her eyes locked with his.

"I'd like to know why you came to me today," he said.

Her voice went cold. "Because you're rich."

"But you're acquainted with many wealthy men, men far more eligible to be your husband than I. Have you offered yourself to any of them?"

"Until today, Mr. Birmingham," she said in an icy voice, "I had offered myself to just one man—and he refused me."

Warwick. Damn the man! Had Warwick's perfidity driven her into the arms of an unworthy suitor? "I think, my lady, that one man's stupidity will be another man's greatest joy."

She gave a false laugh.

He picked up his pen and began to write. When he finished, he handed the letter to her.

She extended a shaking hand. "What's this?"

"I wish you to take this to my brother's bank. It instructs him to give you twenty-five thousand pounds."

Her eyes went from dull to fiery in the space of a blink. She snatched the letter and ripped it into shreds, then hurled the slivers of paper onto his desk. "I will not accept your charity, Mr. Birmingham!" She sprang from her chair and spun around to leave, but he rushed to stop her before she reached the door.

He reached her just in time to clasp both her shoulders and spin her around to face him. "What about your brother?"

She wrenched herself free. "Don't waste your concern on us. I'll find someone who's willing to accept the bargain I offer."

Then she stormed from his office.

After she was gone his pulses pounded with fury. *Arrogant, proud, maddening wench!* He sank into his chair and tried to interest himself in his ledgers but was unable to shake the delicate beauty from his thoughts. His stomach knotted as he realized that by this time tomorrow she might very well be pledged to another man.

He sent a fist crashing onto his desk.

As Fiona flung herself into the carriage outside Mr. Birmingham's Threadneedle Street office and swiftly covered her shivering limbs with the rug, Trevor sadly shook his head. "I perceive the Cit turned you down."

Fiona sighed as her eyes filled with tears. "I've never been more humiliated—even when Edward . . ." She need not finish. It seemed everyone in England knew about her failure to hold Warwick's affections.

Putting Warwick aside, she could not precisely determine which was the more humiliating—brazenly offering herself to Mr. Birmingham or his curt refusal. At least with Edward, she had saved face by crying off herself. Not that anyone would remember that. All that was whispered whenever she entered a room was that poor Lady Fiona had been spurned by Lord Warwick. Such a pity, it was said, after all those years of being promised to one another, and the poor lady wasn't getting any younger!

Of course Fiona didn't give a farthing what was said about her. She didn't even think it so utterly humiliating that she had brazenly offered herself to the dashing Mr. Birmingham—even if he was a Cit. What was humiliating was that the man had not been remotely interested in having her for his wife.

Her thoughts flitted to the beautiful Diane Foley. She wondered if Mr. Birmingham was actually in love with the actress who was his mistress. For some unaccountable reason, Fiona's heart thumped with an unexpected burst of jealousy. Not jealousy of Miss Foley but of envy to experience the fulfilling relationship the actress and Mr. Birmingham must enjoy, a relationship Fiona would never know.

Trevor scooted across the seat and patted her hand. "I simply must learn to become a swashbuckler so I can call out any man who dares affront you, but for the life of me I have no idea how one becomes a swashbuckler."

She giggled through her tears.

"I don't suppose," Trevor asked tentatively, "you asked who his tailor was?"

She giggled some more, and the tears that had been threatening to gush remarkably vanished.

"I honestly don't understand how the man could have turned you down," Trevor said with complete gravity. "You're absolute feminine perfection."

"I prefer to think his refusal had more to do with the fact he has no wish to marry than that he finds me repulsive." What she preferred to think and what constituted the truth, however, were two completely different matters. Deep in her breast she was convinced Mr. Birmingham was not in the least attracted to her. What a fool she had been to believe he would salivate at her presumptuous offer.

"The *R* word is never ever to be used in conjunction with you!" Trevor's voice softened. "Wish you'd have let me come with you to that awful man's office."

"He's not really an awful man," she defended. "He actually offered to *give* me the twenty-five thousand pounds." Oddly, she found Mr. Birmingham's remark about her being *another man's greatest joy* even more welcome than the fortune he offered.

Trevor gulped. "Give?"

She nodded.

"Surely you didn't turn him down?"

"Of course I had to turn him down! I couldn't possibly accept the arrogant man's charity."

Trevor's brows lowered. "Would that not have been preferable to marrying a man you don't love, a man you don't even know?"

Oh dear, Trevor was right. Why had she not considered Mr. Birmingham's generous offer in that light? She'd been so set on negotiating a reasonably fair exchange with him that she had been unable to leap on the alternate—far more palatable—scheme Mr. Birmingham had proposed. Her shoulders sagged. She found herself shaking her head. Never, though, would she have leaped on his charitable proposal. Fiona was incapable of accepting the man's pity. "I have my principles!"

Trevor lifted her chin. "Let me see if I understand this. You'd sell yourself but not accept a donation?"

"I know it sounds decidedly foolish, but I simply cannot accept the man's charity. Even for Randy."

"Then you're not going to try to save Randolph?"

"I didn't say that! I'll do anything to save him—or, almost anything." Her face brightened. "Mr. Birmingham said there must be any number of men of the *ton* who would wish to marry me."

"The Cit's right."

"Then I simply find another man. A wealthy man. Quickly."

"Now see here, I don't like this at all. Ain't right that you shackle yourself for life to some detestable man in order to come up with the funds."

"I told you, Trev, I don't mind. Truly. Since . . . since last year I've known I'll never love another man. I've come to accept that. So why not marry a man of wealth, a man who can save my brother?" *And why not a man as sinfully handsome as Nicholas Birmingham?* Her heart fluttered at the memory of his fierce black eyes lazily perusing her. She could not have felt more undressed had he stripped her bare. It was suddenly clear to her that a marriage to Mr. Birmingham would not have been so terribly repugnant.

"You don't need to marry at all. Go back to Birmingham and accept his offer."

Her brows lowered. "I can't do that."

He scowled. "You're being very obtuse."

"Help me think of wealthy bachelors."

His pointed chin thrust out. "Don't think I will!"

"Now you're being obtuse!"

Nick was in a foul temper. He had snapped at Shivers simply because his secretary had asked if Nick was going to the 'Change today. Nick always went to the 'Change. But not today. He was in such a bloody bad humor that even the prospect of making money did not satisfy him. He had torn up today's *Times* because it contained a lengthy article on Foreign Secretary Warwick. He had slung his teacup into the fire. And he had enumerated and cursed every eligible bachelor in the *ton*. Which of them would Lady Fiona offer herself to next?

Stalking angrily from his office, Nick gave Shivers the rest of the day off in a meager attempt to apologize for his sharp tongue, then he summoned his coach and headed to the West End. He felt like sparring with Jackson. At least to Jackson, his money was as good as the next man's.

But after riding for only a few blocks, Nick demanded his coachman turn around and take him to his brother's bank.

Adam, his brows dipping to a *V* with anxiety, leaped from his desk and sputtered forward when he saw his elder brother amble into his office. "What's wrong?" he demanded.

"Nothing's wrong!" Nick barked, plopping into a comfortable chair in front of Adam's desk.

"You *never* miss a session of the 'Change. Are you ill?"

"You sound like my secretary," Nick mumbled.

Adam moved closer and bent to look into Nick's pupils.

"I tell you I'm fine!" Nick hissed. "Can't a man take off a single afternoon without creating a commotion?"

"But you never take off! I've seen you propped up against the plaster pillar on the floor of the 'Change burning with fever, and still you wouldn't take to your bed. Something's wrong."

"Nothing's wrong," Nick insisted.

"Shall I ring for tea?"

"I don't want any blasted tea!"

"Mind if I have some, old boy?" Adam lifted a fine porcelain cup and took a drink, then sank into his own chair. "Something out of the ordinary has happened to you today," he said.

Nick watched his brother. It was somewhat like staring into a mirror, given that the brothers so closely resembled one another. To confound outsiders even more, there were but eleven months separating them. They were so close that Adam intrinsically knew Nick's every mood. "As a matter of fact," Nick said, striving for casualness, "I had two different callers today, both of them with rather bizarre proposals."

Adam raised a single brow.

"The first was our foreign secretary."

"Warwick?" Adam asked. "You don't mean to tell me the man came to you?"

"The man came to me."

"Why in the devil would he come to you?"

"He wants us to commit financial suicide in order to thwart the French."

Adam's scowl was identical to Nick's. "What kind of financial suicide?"

"I believe he would like for us to buy up all the francs our fortune could buy, then glut the market with them."

"That would most definitely be financial suicide. What did you tell him?"

"I told him he was a fool."

"Really, Nick, you could have tried to answer the man more delicately." Though Adam and Nick shared a strong physical resemblance, they were vastly different in temperament. Where Nick was brash and single minded, Adam was diplomatic and possessed of eclectic tastes that extended to art and music—two areas that Nick abhorred. "Did you not even try to be civil to the man? He's devilishly important!"

"I know he's important, dammit!" Nick said.

"So what else did you tell him?"

"Not much. I had another caller. Warwick asked that I think about his proposal. He'll be back next week."

"You really must apply your astute financial brain to the task. Having the foreign secretary in our laps could be extremely advantageous to our business interests."

Nick grinned. "Where's your patriotism? I thought you'd be urging me to jeopardize my fortune for the sake of crown and country and all that."

"It depends," Adam said shrewdly, "how much you'll have to stake. As it is, I know you too well to believe that you're not going to give the proposal careful consideration."

"It's rather fortunate that our younger brother has such a facility for languages."

Adam's chocolate eyes sparkled with mirth. "So you're already planning on dispatching him to other capitals to begin purchasing francs?"

"I never said anything of the kind."

"Tell me, who was your other caller?"

"You remember Randolph Hollingsworth from Cambridge?"

"I thought he was in The Peninsula?"

"He is."

"And I thought he was now Lord Agar. Wasn't he the eldest son and did his father not die last year?"

"Right on both accounts," Nick said.

"Then who in the devil came to see you today?"

"His sister."

A look of stark disbelief swept over Adam's face. "She came expressly to see you? To The City?"

"To see me and to ask that I marry her."

Adam spit his tea all over his snowy white cravat. "You're jesting me. I've seen the exquisite creature, and I know—even if you are considered irresistible to women—Lady Fiona Hollingsworth would never have to beg a man to marry her."

Nick shrugged. "It wasn't precisely me she wished to marry. She wanted twenty-five thousand pounds with which to pay off Spanish bandits who've kidnapped her brother and are holding him for ransom."

"She really offered herself in marriage to you?"

Nick would have sworn his brother gazed at him with wistful admiration. "She really did."

"Now I see why you couldn't go to the 'Change this afternoon. You're the victim of profound emotions brought on by your betrothal."

So Adam did not understand him as well as he thought. "There is," Nick said, a scowl on his face, "no betrothal."

Adam spun around in his chair. "You didn't turn down the lovely creature?"

"Of course I did! I couldn't take advantage of a woman in a time of such stress."

"How could you be so cruel to the lady? Do you realize how difficult it must have been for her to grovel to you?"

"Of course I realize it. That's why I went against my better judgment and offered her the damned money."

Adam spit out another mouthful of tea. "I don't believe you! I've known you all of my one and thirty years, and I've never known you to give away money—except, of course, to the orphanages and free schools you established, and I hardly think Lady Fiona fits in that charitable category."

"I did offer her the money. She refused it."

"Do you mean to tell me," Adam said, his face screwed up in disbelief, "that the lady was willing to sell herself to a strange man she'd never seen before but she was not willing to accept that same man's charity?"

"She had seen me before. Twice."

"I don't understand. Are you saying you and she have a tendré?"

Nick shook his head with exasperation. "Of course not! The first time I *saw* her was at Tat's—"

"Women don't go to Tat's!"

"This woman did. With her brother. He couldn't avoid introducing her to me, though it obviously pained him to do so."

"And the second time you saw her?"

"Last night at the theatre. Her box was opposite mine, and I believe she spent the better part of the evening staring at me."

"Good God! Do you think . . . ?"

"The woman is *not* enamored of me."

"I don't know how you could have turned her down. You've said yourself you're seeking a wife, and what woman could be more desirable than Lady Fiona Hollingsworth?"

"I can't deny her desirability."

"Hell, it's like guineas raining from the heavens, and you trod over them instead of scooping them up!"

That same feeling of elation Nick experienced with Lady Fiona this afternoon swept over him again.

It had been rather like guineas raining from the heavens. How could he have been such a fool? "Call me a fool," Nick said, shrugging, "but somehow I always fancied I'd wed a woman who was as attracted to me as I was to her."

"With your legendary bedchamber charms, I've no doubts the lady would have come around."

The sudden vision of Lady Fiona's bare body beneath him sent a painful throbbing to Nick's groin. "I shouldn't wish to take advantage of the lady's misfortune."

"You're too damn proud! Papa didn't rise from the gutter on pride. He made his fortune by humbly catering to the swells. Pride, dear brother, won't warm your bed at night!"

"The pity of it is," Nick confessed, "she'll make the offer to someone else. And quickly, too."

Adam uttered a curse. "Can you honestly tell me you would not want her for a wife?"

"Quite honestly, the lady's spectacular."

"Then push your pride aside. Go to her before it's too damned late."

Chapter 3

As he and Fiona settled into the carriage, Trevor swiped snowflakes from his greatcoat and screwed his face into a pout worthy of a spoiled princess. "Perfectly odious man, that bookseller! Offering you a piddly five thousand for your *pere*'s library. Daresay it's worth at least fifty thousand."

"It wasn't my father's library, actually," Fiona said with a shrug. "At least not originally. My grandfather's the one who built the collection, but remember, Trev, he was buying new. Since the books are no longer new—though I daresay most of them have never been opened—their value, quite naturally, plummets. And the bookseller has to make his money."

Trevor folded his arms across his chest and stomped his expensively shod foot. "You simply cannot give the books away to that thief."

"I won't unless I'm forced to," she said. "Tomorrow we'll see how much Mama's jewels will fetch."

"Nowhere near twenty-five thousand, I'll vow."

"You're likely right."

Her family coach, which should have been replaced a decade earlier, turned onto Cavendish Square and screeched to a halt in front of Agar House. The afternoon sun had almost shed its bril-

liance. Fiona sighed. Another day gone, and she was
no closer to raising the money to save Randy. "Come
help me draw up a list of well-to-do bachelors," she
said as they disembarked.

Trevor grumbled his dissatisfaction while he trailed
after her.

Fiona swept into her house, then stood deadly still
upon its marble entry hall, stunned. Bouquets of
sweetly pungent flowers crowded the entire hallway.
Roses reposed on the sideboard—six vases of them,
each sprouting roses of a different color. Fat arrange-
ments of marigolds and daisies graced the first half
dozen steps of the iron-railed staircase. Colorful posies
were strewn across the floor like a fragrant carpet.

"What the devil?" Trevor exclaimed.

Fiona's gaze flicked to the butler. "Pray, Livingston,
whatever is going on?"

"I couldn't say, my lady. A stream of urchins has
been delivering these for the past hour."

"Did the urchins say who engaged them?" she asked.

He thought for a moment, then strode to the sideboard where he extricated a letter from beneath a
vase of pink roses. "This note was delivered with the
first batch."

She eagerly snatched the now-damp missive and
nearly tore the page in her haste to read it. The note
was short:

My Dear Lady Fiona,

*I hope in some small way these flowers will express my
high regard for you more eloquently than can my
abominable tongue, and I beg that you will consent to
see me when I call upon you in the very near future.*

Sincerely,
Nicholas Birmingham

Trevor's impatience to read the note outweighing years of instruction in the art of good manners, he peered over her shoulder as she read. "Very nice, utterly masculine penmanship, don't you think?" he asked.

She turned and glared down her aristocratic nose at him. "I hadn't thought at all about the man's hand-writing!"

Trevor effected a contrite expression—for all of ten seconds, then his gaze circled the hallway. "You can't say Birmingham doesn't have a flair." His glance lit upon a basket of flowers all in hues of purple and lavender: pansies, violets, lavender, orchids, peri-winkles, and primroses. "I declare, this primrose is positively blue!" He withdrew it from the bouquet and inhaled it deeply. "I ask you, my lady, have you ever seen a primrose this color?"

She beat down the impulse to laugh. Trevor was surely the only man of her acquaintance who knew every flower by name. Her heart caught as she re-membered Randy taking a stab at naming a rose. "It's got thorns, must be a rose!" her brother had ex-claimed dubiously, anxiously watching his sister for confirmation.

"I refuse to discuss primroses or penmanship with you, Trevor," she snapped. "We've more important in-ferences to draw."

His expression suddenly less demented, he bent to her ear and spoke in a low voice. "Shall we repair to the library where we can speak in private?"

She slipped her arm into his. "An excellent plan."

Once they were in the library—which unlike Wind-mere Abbey's library, contained very few books—they dropped onto a fern-colored sofa.

"I perceive that Mr. Birmingham means to offer me the twenty-five thousand pounds again," she said.

Trevor's mouth puckered in concentration as he got up and went to pour himself a glass of wine. "Madeira would do your nerves good," he said, turning toward Fiona.

She favored him with a smile. "I believe I would like a glass."

He poured the two glasses and returned to sit beside her. "Daresay you're wrong about Birmingham."

"I'm rarely wrong about men," she argued. "My perceptions of men come from having an older brother and a younger one, neither of whose behavior ever surprises me."

"Be that as it may," Trevor said, his fingers flicking away lint from his golden breeches, "you've missed the mark this time."

She set down her glass and faced him. "What makes you think so?"

"The flowers."

Her brows lowered. "I don't follow you."

"A man don't send flowers when he plans to *give* away his money."

"Then?" Suddenly, Fiona understood. *A man sends flowers when he is courting.* God in heaven, did that mean Mr. Birmingham *was* going to accept her pathetic proposal? She spun to Trevor. "Surely you don't think . . ."

His slender hand holding the stemmed glass, his pinky finger extended, Trevor swished the wine around in his mouth. "Methinks the man has changed his mind about marrying you."

A pity the entire spectrum of emotions collided within her. Why could she not be perfectly blasé about Mr. Birmingham's probable interest in wedding her? Her pulse pounded, her chest tightened, her stomach sank—at the same time her heart was skipping with a lighter-than-air fluttering—all of this while picturing the darkly handsome Mr. Birmingham's black eyes regarding her. The very memory of him had the oddest physical effect upon her. Her meager breasts seemed to swell, and a tingling settled low in her torso.

Marriage to Mr. Birmingham, she decided, held far more appeal than marriage to bald-headed, pot-bellied Lord Strayhorn, whose fortune had placed him at the top of her list of matrimonial prospects.

Livingston tapped at the door, then entered. "A Mr. Birmingham to see you, my lady."

Her heart thumped as she and Trevor exchanged wide-eyed glances. "I really *must* be going," Trevor muttered. "The man can't offer for you when an-other man's in the room," he whispered.

She supposed he should go, though she was rather reluctant to face Mr. Birmingham alone. Not that the man was in the least bit terrifying. Fiona's apprehen-sion had less to do with Mr. Birmingham's presence and a lot more to do with her own embarrassment at facing him after this morning's fiasco. "Show Mr. Birmingham in," she told the butler.

She sucked in her breath as she watched the two men—Trevor quite short, Mr. Birmingham rather tall—exchange greetings. The top of poor Trevor's head came only to Mr. Birmingham's chest.

Once Trevor had departed, Mr. Birmingham came to stand before her, and she was powerless not to gape at his magnificence. From the tip of boots so shiny she could see her face in them, up long, sinewy legs to his trim waist and sloping upward to a manly, though not bulging, chest clothed in an exquisitely cut frock coat, she gaped, coming to settle on his sinfully hand-some face and the tuft of dark hair that carelessly spilled onto his forehead.

She offered her hand and prayed he would not detect its tremble when his enclosed it, and he bent to kiss it. Why had she never before noticed how completely provocative a kiss on the hand could be? "Please sit down, Mr. Birmingham. Won't you join me in having a glass of madeira?"

"An excellent idea, my lady," he said, his eye roaming to the decanter on a nearby table. "Allow me to get it myself."

To her utter surprise, after he filled his glass he came and sat next to her on the sofa. Her gaze dropped to his smoothly muscled thighs, which ran parallel to hers but were many inches longer than hers. Why had she never before noticed how utterly provocative a man's thighs could be? She quickly forced her gaze to his face. "I'm indebted to you for all the lovely flowers, Mr. Birmingham," she began.

"It seemed the least I could do after my shabby treatment of you."

Her heart fluttered as he nabbed her with those pensive black eyes of his. "Your idea of shabby and mine must be vastly different," she said. "I don't think offering me twenty-five thousand could be considered shabby."

He shook his head. "Not that. The other part."

The other part? Her heart thudded. Her marriage proposal. His quick refusal. Her complete humiliation. That "other part." She gathered her courage. "You've nothing to apologize for, Mr. Birmingham. You weren't interested in marriage. I was." She shrugged. "End of scenario."

"I'm somewhat distressed over your use of the past tense, my lady," he said.

Her use of the past tense? She thought back to try to remember her exact words. *I was.* She *was* interested in marriage. But no more? Is that what it sounded like to him? And that distressed him? How perfectly wonderful! "I still am," she said cryptically, hoping she would not once again be forced to brazenly declare her bizarre proposal to the almost-complete stranger.

"Then I must tell you," he said, not quite meeting her gaze, "that I regret my hasty refusal. Attribute it to my utter surprise and previous hostility toward matrimony—a hostility I no longer possess."

This was without a doubt the most deuced peculiar sequence of vague proposals she had ever heard of. What was needed at this juncture was a clear declaration, but far be it from her to set herself up for ridicule twice in the same day. No matter how much the man squirmed, she was not about to offer for him again. This time, he must do the asking.

So they sat there, as silent as a long-married couple in church, neither of them so much as glancing at the other. From the corner of her eye she saw that he took a long drink from his glass, then spent an inordinate amount of time twirling around his glass, the liquid swishing until it lapped at the glass's rim.

For some unaccountable reason, she pictured the beautiful actress who was his mistress. Was Miss Foley responsible for his reluctance to marry? For his reluctance to spell out his intentions toward Fiona?

No sooner had that thought taken root than he removed himself from the sofa, dropped down on one knee, took her hand in his, and blatantly met her gaze. "I would be the happiest of men if you would consider being my life's partner," he said, his thumb stroking sensuous circles on her palm.

"I will not refuse your generous offer, sir, but you must tell me why this change of heart."

He continued holding her hand but did not respond for a very long while. She was beginning to think he might reverse his reversal when he finally said, "It suddenly became clear to me that marriage to a woman of your . . . your background is precisely what I should like most in a wife—not that I ever would have been so presumptuous as to seek out one of your pedigree, you understand."

The tables had truly been turned. She fully understood how vulnerable he must feel at this moment, for she had been every bit as nervous this morning when she tossed aside her pride and begged him to marry her. "You may get up, dear sir! I assure you I have no intention of turning down your welcome offer, and there are many things we must discuss if we are to marry." She could scarcely credit her own words. Was this man really to become her husband?

Not without a trickle of affection, she watched as he returned to the sofa and took her hand again. "I won't expect any settlements," he said.

She chuckled. "Then you must know I'm dowryless. I daresay a man in your position knows everybody's financial affairs."

"Not everyone's."

"When should you like to be wed?"

He patted his pocket. "I've a special license. Would tomorrow be too soon?"

"But . . . tomorrow's Christmas Eve."

"Christmas is a time for giving. I can think of no better day to marry."

She closed her eyes. This was all so unexpected. "You really do have a special license?"

"I do."

"You were that assured I would accept?"

"I wasn't at all assured, my lady, but I've schooled myself to always be ready for any eventuality."

"Then tomorrow is agreeable to me."

"You know," he said with an atypical lack of confidence, "you don't have to marry me to save your brother. I could negotiate some sort of loan to secure his release."

She shrugged. "Marrying you is not repugnant to me, Mr. Birmingham. At six and twenty, I'm too long on the shelf not to leap at the chance of marrying—and I'm no longer the adolescent idealist who longs for a passionate love match."

His flashing eyes narrowed as he silently regarded her. She had the feeling he was carefully choosing his words. "You'll never convince me," he finally said, "that your being on the shelf is not of your own choosing. Any man in the kingdom would be only too happy to make you his wife."

"But not the one man I had hoped to wed," she whispered ruefully. She had to bring up Warwick. Everyone knew how thoroughly besotted she had been over the man, how humiliated she had been when he married another. If Mr. Birmingham was to become her husband, he had the right to know everything about her past.

Mr. Birmingham stiffened, and he spoke sternly. "I don't think I'd like being wed to a woman who's in love with another man."

"Please be assured, Mr. Birmingham, I'm no longer in love with Lord Warwick. I'm just wounded enough to be wary of giving my heart to another man."

His jaw tightened as his lazy gaze flicked over her. "And what of giving your body to another man?"

Her heart nearly pounded out of her chest. She could not believe he was bold enough to speak to her of so delicate a matter. Then it suddenly occurred to her that in a day's time she would belong to this man. He would have the right to possess her body. The very thought stole her breath and suffused her in a warm tingling sensation. "If I'm to be your wife," she said, drawing in a deep breath, "I shall belong to you in every way."

"I shouldn't like for you to close your eyes and pretend I'm someone else, Fiona."

Her insides trembled. He had called her by her first name—a gesture she found as intimate as a kiss. Just as intimate was his allusion to closing her eyes . . . closing her eyes while they made love. At the vision of their two bare bodies entwined, heated blood thundered through her veins. "There is no other man, Mr. Birmingham."

"Nick," he growled. "You're to call me Nick."

How intimate *Nick* seemed. Nicholas would not

have been nearly so personal. "I vow . . . Nick, I'll make you a good wife."

He began to slowly peel off her glove as she sat there stunned. Once it was removed, he pressed moist lips into her palm as his hungry eyes locked with hers. Liquid heat gushed to her core. "I hope you'll never regret your decision, my lady," he said in a deeply seductive voice. Then he settled an arm around her shoulders and gathered her into his chest. For a long time he held her before his lips eased lower until they softly touched hers.

The sheer delicacy of his restrained power snapped her own reserve. She opened her mouth to him as the kiss instantly transformed from sweet to potently passionate, the pressure of his lips from light to crushing. The firmer his pressure, the more intense her pleasure. Her arms circled his granite-hard back, and little murmuring sounds came from her throat. She experienced an aching, throbbing need to feel his hands stroke her in places no man had ever touched.

It was as if he were privy to her innermost thoughts, for his hand began to cup her breast, to knead it, his thumb feathering over her now-hardened nipple. Her moans grew deeper, the motion of her own hands tracing circles on his back, firmer. Though she knew her behavior utterly brazen, she refused to alter it for she gloried in this man's touch.

Yes, she told herself, Nick Birmingham was infinitely preferable to bald old Lord Strayhorn.

Then Nick Birmingham straightened up, gently cupped her face in his palms, and said, "Forgive me, my lady, for my presumptuousness."

When he went to get up, her cheeks grew hot. What an utter trollop he must think her! She eked out a feeble smile. "I'm afraid I was the presumptuous one, M-m- . . . Nick."

Her heart raced as he watched her with vivid intensity. "I think, my dearest Fiona, we may both be getting more than we bargained for—and for that I shall be exceedingly grateful." He moved toward the door, then turned back to her. "I shall call for you at eleven tomorrow morning. Is St. George's Hanover Square agreeable to you?"

Unable to summon her voice, she nodded. In less than twenty-four hours she would belong to Nick Birmingham. The very thought of it arrested her breath.

Chapter 4

He made it to the bank before it closed for the day, demanding that Adam—and not one of Adam's employees—personally handle his sizeable withdrawal.

"You want FIFTY thousand pounds?" an incredulous Adam asked.

"Half of it to secure the release of my future brother-in-law—"

Adam's eyes rounded. "Then . . . you're going to marry the lady?"

"Tomorrow. St. George's Hanover. You're invited."

A slow smile spread across Adam's admiring face. "I shall be there. Felicitations and all that, dear fellow. I'm convinced you've made the right decision."

"Would that I were," Nick mumbled. Of course, if Lady Fiona was half as passionate in bed as she was in the drawing room in a few minutes earlier, then he had struck a very fine bargain indeed. The very memory of her lips opening beneath his caused his breath to grow short.

Even when he had first taken up with Diane, her kisses had not affected him as profoundly as did Lady Fiona's. It suddenly occurred to him that bedding Diane would hold no allure after making Lady

Fiona his wife. "Actually," he added, "I'll need ten thousand more."

"Surely you don't mean SIXTY thousand?" Adam said.

Nick directed an impatient glance at his brother. "Surely I do."

"But I thought the ransom was for only twenty-five."

"My dear brother, I wish you wouldn't use the word *only* in connection with twenty-five thousand pounds!"

"You know what I mean. What's the other thirty-five thousand for?"

"Twenty-five for William to purchase francs when he travels to Portugal."

"So you're sending Will to negotiate with the bandits? And you've decided to help Lord Warwick after all?"

"Yes to both," Nick said. "You don't think I'd trust fifty thousand pounds with someone who wasn't family, do you?"

"Have you told Will yet?"

Nick flicked a glance at the clock on the wall behind Adam's well-ordered desk. His brother's business establishment with its fine walnut wainscoting, tasteful decor, and stunning brass chandeliers bore no resemblance to Nick's austere office that had been his father's before him and that Nick had no desire to change. "Not yet. I expect him here at any moment."

"What's the other ten thousand for?"

Nick's lips went taut. "For Diane's settlement."

Adam gave his brother yet another incredulous look. "You're going to spurn the loveliest actress on the London stage simply because you're going to marry a blueblood? How . . . puritanical."

"I don't take vows of any kind lightly."

Adam's eyes narrowed. "I believe you're smitten with Lady Fiona."

"Believe what you will," Nick said with a careless

shrug. "It's nothing to me. I merely felt I owe my wife-to-be a clean slate."

"Does she know about Emmie, then?"

Nick cursed. "I should have told her! I had so much on my mind I completely forgot."

"Yes, you should have told her." Adam eyed his brother warily, then shrugged. "I suppose you could send Emmie off somewhere."

"You think I should send the child back to the whore who gave birth to her?" Nick asked angrily.

"I know how distasteful that is to you. What about one of those girls' schools around Bath?"

"I should pretend my child does not exist rather than acknowledge her to my aristocratic wife?" This was the first time he'd voiced the word *wife* in connection with Fiona, and it gave him a not unpleasant feeling of possession.

"Now, don't get so ruffled! I'm only trying to prepare you, to warn you. Lady Fiona will not have an illegitimate child under her roof—much less take on the role of mother to the child."

His brother was likely right, Nick realized, his gut roiling. As far as the child was concerned, he had already gone over and above that which was expected of a gentleman toward his bastard. Still . . .

The door to Adam's office flew open, and the third and youngest Birmingham brother stormed in. It was as if the mold that created the two elder brothers had been retired when William Birmingham was conceived. Where the two elder brothers were tall and dark, William was only barely past medium height, with golden hair and a more muscular torso than his lean brothers. "What the devil was so important that you sent a messenger to Newmarket to fetch me?" William demanded. "Do you know how much I could have won on the final race?"

"You'll get no sympathy from Nick," Adam said.

"If you did a decent day's work," Nick chided, "you'd have no need to throw away your money at gaming hells and horse races."

Adam shrugged. "You know what Nick always says. His livelihood provides all the risks he needs."

"I don't believe Nick's ever thrown dice in his entire life," William said.

Nick's brows nudged down. "Why would I want to? I lose and win fortunes every day—no dice or pasteboards needed."

Dust still clinging to his Hessians, William sank into a chair. "What's so bloody urgent?"

"Nick's getting married tomorrow," Adam announced.

William bolted up. "The hell you say!"

"He truly is," Adam said.

"But tomorrow's Christmas Eve!"

"A perfectly good day for a wedding," Nick said.

"Who are you marrying?" William asked.

Adam met his younger brother's gaze. "Have you ever heard of Lady Fiona Hollingsworth?"

"I don't believe you . . ." William shook his head, his shocked gaze darting from one brother to the other. "She's a viscount's daughter. And she's beautiful. I don't care how legendary Nick's bedchamber prowess is, he couldn't coax an aristocrat—an aristocrat I'll vow he doesn't even know—into his marriage bed."

The very thought of sharing his bedchamber with Lady Fiona sent blood thundering to Nick's loins. Had someone told him yesterday that he would be marrying Lady Fiona Hollingsworth he would have thought that person a raving lunatic. Yet here he was on the eve of their wedding—oddly with no regrets. In fact, tomorrow couldn't come soon enough to please him.

"It wasn't his bedchamber charms—but his pockets—that attracted the lady," Adam explained.

"Why Nick?" William asked. "She could snare any peer of the realm she wanted—except Warwick."

Damn. Did everyone know of that scoundrel Warwick's mistreatment of Lady Fiona, Nick wondered. He did not at all like to be aiding the man. But Warwick was foreign secretary. And Nick was a patriot.

"Personally, I think she fancies our brother," Adam said.

Nick remembered how she had watched him at the theatre last night and wished to God what Adam was saying were true. But, of course, it wasn't. One had only to see her this morning with that damn Warwick to know it was that man whom she still loved.

"She fancies the twenty-five thousand I'll spend to free her brother." He turned to William to explain.

When Nick was finished telling him about the kidnapping, Will said, "So I'm to deal with the bandits?"

"You'll be well protected. You can ride your coach-and-four onto my yacht for the crossing, and on land you'll have four armed postilions, as well as four more armed men in and on the coach." That should sweeten the pot for his youngest brother, Nick thought. Will was happiest when operating under the threat of danger. No position in an indoor establishment would ever appeal to Will.

"Sounds very much like the time I smuggled bullion out of Frankfurt," Will said, his green eyes sparkling.

Nick smiled. "Let's hope you do as fine a job this time."

"No one at the bank knows of the substantial withdrawal since I'm taking care of it myself," Adam said, "so I wouldn't expect any trouble this side of the channel."

"What's the other matter you wish me to attend to?" William asked Nick.

"I wish you to begin buying up as many francs as you can."

William quirked a brow.

"The foreign secretary has asked for our assistance in crushing the French," Adam said. "Actually, he approached Nick."

Nick shrugged. "We were at Cambridge together, though not well acquainted."

"I never knew you had such aristocratic connections," William said. "How did you make the acquaintance of Lady Fiona?"

"Actually, I met her at Tat's."

"The hell you say!" William gave his brother an are-you-out-of-your-mind glance. "Women don't go to Tat's!"

"She was with her brother, who was rather forced to introduce us."

Adam directed his attention at William. "Methinks the lady was taken with Nick."

Oddly, Nick wished his brothers were right. "Hardly," he said. "I didn't see her again until last night, two years after the first meeting."

"You went to her last night?" William asked.

"No. She came to me. This morning."

Adam and William exchanged amused glances.

"It's NOT what you two think!" Nick said.

"Well, tell me this," William said. "Are you going to sleep with her?"

Nick's heart seemed to be racing right out of his chest. "Of course I'm going to sleep with her! This time tomorrow, she'll be my wife."

My wife. He still could scarcely credit it.

Dismissing a mistress was at the top of the list of Nick's most hated duties. Heretofore he had managed to sever these affairs in a most amiable fashion. He was still friends with Yvonne some six years after their parting. Of course it helped that as a parting gift he had purchased her one of the finest mansions on Paris's Avenue Foch. She had been so utterly grateful to return to the city of her birth she had pledged fealty to Nick for as long as he lived. "Nickee," she had said, "no matter how many years pass, if ever I can help you, you have only ask."

If only Diane would be as agreeable as her French predecessor. Diane's butler had admitted Nick to the Marylebone townhouse he had set her up in, and as he climbed the stairs to her bedchamber, a heavy sense of dread surged through him.

After he tapped on her door, he drew in a deep breath and entered. Standing before her dressing table, she smiled up at him. His gaze lazily traveled over the luscious curves of her body. She wore absolutely nothing beneath the sheer, snow white gown. Before today—before he had become betrothed to Lady Fiona Hollingsworth—the sight of Diane's rosy nipples beneath the gauzy fabric or the thatch of flaming hair between her thighs would have set his pulse racing. But not this evening.

He strolled to her dressing table and plopped two sacks of coins on its gilded surface.

"What's that, love?" she asked.

"Ten thousand pounds."

She whirled around to face him, her ruby lips lifting into a smile. "Pray, for whom?"

"For you."

Her hands flew to her breasts. "'Tis a fortune! Why do I merit so much?"

"Because I've been well satisfied with you." Would she notice his use of the past tense?

She moved to him, her eyes seductive as she began to snake her arms around him, the smell of her too-heavy perfume sickening. "I shall satisfy you tonight as you've never been satisfied before, Nicholas darling."

He removed her arms, quickly brushed his mouth

across the back of one hand, then dropped it. "Actually, the money's a parting gift, Diane."

She gasped. Her eyes watered. "Whatever do you mean?" she asked in a quivering voice.

"I'm getting married tomorrow."

"No!" she shrieked. Tears began to gush. "Why not me? Did I not please you?"

"You pleased me very much."

"But it's not as if you're some lord," she sobbed, "who must marry his own kind. I thought we s-s-s-uited."

"We suited very well, but I cannot continue with you, to hold my wife up to ridicule."

Diane launched herself at him, though Nick refused to put his arms around her. "I don't care about the money, my darling," she whimpered. "All I want is you." She draped her arms around him, planting soft kisses along his neck and moving up to his chin as he stiffened. "Can we not continue after you marry?" she begged. "I'll be discreet."

He clasped her shoulders and held her out at arm's length. "Tomorrow I take wedding vows—vows I'll not be breaking."

He had seen Diane cry on stage, but it was nothing like seeing her really cry. Her lovely face stained red, ravaged with tears. He had not realized the actress cared so deeply for him. To his amazement, she seemed more interested in *him* than in the ten thousand pounds.

"Who are you marrying?" she asked between sobs.

"Lady Fiona Hollingsworth." Acknowledging that Fiona really was going to become his wife brought back that odd feeling of well being.

Diane's sobs—a mixture of weeping and moaning—grew louder. "So that's it! I ca-a-a-an't compete with a fine lady." She swiped away her tears with the back of her hand and eyed him. "You've fallen in love with her, haven't you?"

"I'm not going to discuss my future wife with you."
Why, he asked himself as he took his leave, did everyone think he had fallen in love with Fiona?

That night—the eve of her wedding—Fiona's melancholy kept her from sleeping. Christmas without her family, the prospect of a loveless marriage, and worry over Randy all heaped upon her shoulders like a leaden mantle.

She had known spending Christmas at Windmere Abbey without her loved ones would not have been tolerable. Trevor had understood that, too, and had succeeded in persuading her that coming to London for Christmas would be far less depressing. Her little brother must also have realized how bleak Windmere Abbey would have been this year with Papa now dead and Randy gone, for he had opted to spend the holiday with the family of his dearest friend from Cambridge.

Now that Christmas was less than two days away, memories of the many joyous Christmases spent at Windmere flooded her. She and her brothers had always gathered up holly and mistletoe and helped Mama decorate the house with them. Randy helped Papa hang the kissing bough, and Randy and Stephen had taken great pride in finding and carrying in the huge yule log.

She fought back a sob when she realized this was her first Christmas ever that she had no loved one to whom she could give a Christmas present. At least she had contrived—through the greatest economies—to gather up enough funds to give her servants their Christmas "package."

Spending Christmas in foggy, gray London held no allure.

As she lay in the darkness listening to her sputtering

fire and the howl of wind outside her window, her thoughts turned to her marriage. She had told Trevor and Nick the truth when she said she no longer loved Edward, Lord Warwick. So why did she lay there in her bed thinking about Edward? She remembered how thoroughly she had loved him. How could she have so completely extinguished those profound feelings—feelings that had once stripped her of every shred of pride?

She recalled that blustery afternoon last year when she and Edward had walked the moors and she had ducked into an abandoned crofter's hut, begging him to make love to her. Only too vividly she remembered the humiliation she felt when he had rejected her.

She had so keenly wanted to lie with him that day. And now she had no feelings whatsoever for him, only a huge void in her heart, in the place Edward had occupied for half her life.

Only one other day in her life had Fiona been a captive to passions like those roused in her that day on the moors with Edward: Today. When Nicholas Birmingham had kissed her.

Mama would roll over in her grave if she knew what a strumpet her daughter had become! Was there some kind of prurient bent in her that made her behave so wantonly? So unladylike? What must Mr. . . . Nick think of the hungry way she kissed him?

When she recalled his satisfaction, her breath grew ragged. He had not seemed at all displeased over her passionate nature. Could it be that the man she would wed tomorrow was not averse to marrying a woman who so eagerly looked forward to learning about carnal pleasures?

Carnal pleasures Diane Foley would know all about.

For the first time in her life Fiona regretted she had been born an aristocrat. She envied the slack morals of a woman of Diane Foley's class, morals that smoothed the way for her to take Nick into her bed without the sanctity of marriage. Just thinking about Nick making love with the actress made Fiona's breath come hot and heavy, made her sting inside.

Then the sudden realization that Nick would continue sharing a bed with Diane Foley *after* their marriage sent Fiona into a deep funk. Not because she would be embarrassed for the *ton* to know of her husband's lady bird. And certainly not because she possessed any romantic feelings for Nicholas Birmingham herself. But because she was jealous.

She wasn't jealous for the usual reasons. Fiona was well satisfied with her own appearance (which she knew to be far above average), so she wasn't jealous of Miss Foley's beauty. She did not resent that Nick was likely in love with his paramour. How could Fiona possibly care when she had no intentions of claiming his affection for herself?

Her jealousy was for the affectionate intimacy Nick and Miss Foley were sure to share, an intimacy that would always be denied Fiona. She wanted affection, and she wanted intimacy—and she most especially wanted both those things with the same man, a man who would reciprocate her feelings.

She had hoped for such intimacy that day on the moors, but even if Edward had made love to her, the affection would have been only on one side: hers.

And now she would be intimate with a man who was a stranger, a man who had no more affection for her than she had for him. They would have the intimacy without the affection because his affections would be lavished on the beautiful actress.

So Fiona sulked.

As she lay there in her bed, the vision of Nicholas Birmingham, tall and lean and dark—and seductive—pushed every other thought from her mind, sent searing heat thundering through her, arrested the thin breath struggling through her lungs.

This time tomorrow night she would be lying with him, no longer a virgin.

Liquid heat pooled between her thighs.

Chapter 5

He had not expected to be so moved by his own wedding. When he saw Fiona solemnly strolling down the nave of the chapel in her pale pink gown, her eyes never leaving his, something inside him melted, filling him with an overwhelming tenderness for the slender woman who was going to pledge her life to his. She looked so forlorn it was all he could do not to pull her into his arms and assure her he would never let anything thwart her happiness.

Instead, he enclosed her trembling hand within his and gave it a reassuring squeeze. She did not let go as she turned to face the curate.

That fop Trevor Simpson stood up with her, Nick's brothers with him. Before the ceremony started, Nick turned around and winked at his plainly dressed daughter who sat with her governess on the third row. They were the only attendees.

Were he pressed to do so, Nick could not have recalled a single word uttered by the cleric. All his thoughts were on Fiona and the onslaught of powerful emotions she summoned in him. Most powerful of all was his need to take care of her for the rest of their days.

He fleetingly thought of how well pleased his father would have been today to see his firstborn marry into one of England's oldest aristocratic families. Two obsessions had guided the brilliant and ever-demanding man who had been Nick's father: making a vast fortune and grooming his son to tread where he himself had been forbidden. The relationship between father and son had been curiously cold. Though Jonathan Birmingham directed all his energies on Nick, Nick was merely an instrument Jonathan used to fulfill his own dreams. The father's fanatic demands alienated the son; the son's cultivated gentility later alienated the father. In the end Jonathan had been strangely in awe of the son he had created.

But never mind that today. Nick looked down at Fiona and swelled with pride. He had never seen a woman exude such grace or such delicate beauty. Everything about her was dainty, from her small stature to her slenderness to her exceedingly fair coloring.

He realized at once the ring he had brought was much too big for her slender fingers. Lacking the time to commission a special ring for the occasion, he had decided upon the simple gold band that had belonged to his favorite grandmother. When the time came, he slipped the ring on Fiona's finger and murmured, "This was worn by my father's mother."

Her eyes sparkled when she looked up at him and said, "I'm very touched."

He had been right. The band was too big. But no piece of jewelry had ever been lovelier. Of course he would replace it later with something more grand, something more befitting a lady of Fiona's stature.

After the ceremony he feted the guests to a meal at Claridge's, where he and Fiona sat together at the head of the small table that was squarely beneath a glittering chandelier.

"Your resemblance to my husband is remarkable," Fiona told Adam. "Are you sure you aren't twins?"

My husband. It had taken Nick a few seconds to realize she was speaking of him. Then a satisfying warmth spread over him.

"Nick's eleven months older," Adam answered.

"And would you look at the little one—though he's really not so little!" Trevor said, his glance whisking over William. "Pray, where did you get that luscious golden hair?"

William looked uncomfortable when he responded. "My mother's possessed of blond hair. At least it used to be blond before it turned gray."

"Then I take it your father was dark—like your older brothers," Trevor asked.

"Yes, my brothers resemble our late father," William said stiffly as he scooped prawns onto his plate.

Fiona turned to Nick. "Your mother's still alive?"

He nodded. "She hates The City, therefore she spends all her time in Kent."

"You have an estate there?" she asked.

"My mother and sister live at Great Acres, the estate my father built. I had the opportunity to purchase a neighboring estate for my own."

"What's it called?" Fiona asked.

"Camden Hall."

"I've been there!" she exclaimed, a smile brightening her face. "Was it not one of Lord Hartley's country properties?"

"It was."

"It's quite lovely there."

"I'm glad you like it. We shall honeymoon there."

Her brows lowered. "We're going today?"

Why in the deuce did she look so puzzled? "We are."

"But I thought The Fox never played when there was money to be made."

Of course she alluded to the fact the stock exchange

would reopen the day after Christmas. What other truths had she learned about him? He leaned toward her, settled an arm around her, and spoke in a husky voice. "That was before I was a married man."

A hint of a smile tweaked at her rose petal mouth. "I'm most relieved to learn you're not all business all the time."

"Don't be too relieved," Adam said. "Nick's incapable of turning his back on his business."

Nick wondered if Fiona's comments meant she actually wished to spend time with him. Had she not married him solely to secure the money to free her brother? "I must assure you," Nick said to his wife, "only half the things you hear about me are true."

"Do I believe the good half or the bad half?" she asked with a little half laugh.

"Oh, only the good."

A moment later, she asked, "How old is your sister?"

"Nineteen."

"Is she out yet?"

Did this wife of his not realize that the daughter of Jonathan Birmingham couldn't just *come out* like women of Fiona's class? Besides, like him, Verity straddled two worlds and wasn't fit for either of them. He shrugged. "No, she hasn't."

He looked into Fiona's pale blue eyes and saw a flicker of dawning alight them. "I would be delighted to sponsor her," Fiona said. "Actually, I've already promised to bring out Miss Rebecca Peabody, so the two can come out together. I should love it above all things."

"Who, pray tell, is Rebecca Peabody?" Nick asked.

She stiffened. "The sister of the new Countess Warwick."

"They're from the colonies," Trevor added.

Nick had a difficult time believing Fiona was friendly with the woman who had stolen Warwick from her. "I didn't know you and Lady Warwick were friends."

"I haven't spoken to her since . . ." She faced Nick and gave a hopeless shrug. "Well, I expect you know all about it. But I am rather attached to Miss Peabody, owing to the fact that she resided with me at Windmere Abbey for half of the last year."

"Pray, why did a colonial reside with you?" Nick asked.

"Because she was mad to catalogue our library," Fiona said.

Trevor, who seemed to hang on Fiona's every word, nodded. "The girl absolutely adores anything to do with books."

"So you're close to the girl?" Nick asked his wife.

She appeared to give the matter consideration. "Not really. I doubt anyone's close to Miss Peabody. She's entirely too enamored of books to be companionable." Fiona gave a little laugh. "She doesn't really wish to be presented, either, since she doesn't think she's interested in men."

Nick hiked a single brow. "And how old is Miss Peabody?"

"Nineteen," Fiona said.

"She'd be quite lovely," Trevor said, "if she didn't persist in wearing those blasted spectacles."

Fiona nodded. "Her sister had hoped to present her last year, but Miss Peabody would have nothing to do with it."

How different the two sisters must be, Nick thought. Not only had the new countess been married once before she married Warwick, but it was said she had turned down a half a dozen marriage offers from men she had bewitched. "Why does her sister not present her?"

"The countess is not well acquainted with the *ton*— because she's a colonist and because she's been breeding ever since she wed Warwick. In fact, I've heard that she's breeding again."

Nick lowered his voice as he addressed his wife. "Will it not be difficult for you to present Miss Peabody since your relationship with her sister is somewhat strained?" He eyed his brothers who were courteously listening to Trevor rhapsodize about the sauce drizzled on the asparagus.

"Actually, it would be very good for me to sponsor the countess's sister. That—and being married to you—should convince everyone that I've forgotten all about Warwick."

Would that she *had* forgotten Warwick. Nick's stomach dropped. Now he understood her other reason for marrying him. She wished to assure the *ton* she was no longer in love with the earl who had rejected her. *Damn Warwick!* "About presenting my sister . . ."

"What's her name?" Fiona asked.

"Verity." He lowered his voice again. "How do you know Verity won't be an embarrassment to you?"

"No sister of yours could ever be an embarrassment, Mr.—" She caught herself and smiled. "Pardon me, Nick."

He was oddly pleased that she did not find him offensive.

"Your brothers are perfect gentlemen, too," she whispered.

"The younger one will take the money to Portugal."

"You've got the money, then?"

He nodded. "I await instructions."

"Are you not worried about your brother's safety?"

"He's an old hand at this sort of thing."

"With ransom demands?" she asked incredulously.

"With safely delivering large sums of money."

"I thrive upon danger," William said, watching Fiona with dancing eyes.

Her gaze met William's. "I'm persuaded you must know how to defend yourself?"

William looked from one brother to the other,

then addressed Fiona. "All of the Birmingham brothers have been schooled in fencing and pugilism."

"Though, thankfully, we've never had to defend ourselves," Nick added.

"How I admire you manly types," Trevor lamented, his affectionate gaze leaping from one brother to the other.

Nick's brothers went deadly silent. "I daresay fencing is not a skill one needs in Mayfair," Nick said, giving his wife's friend a feeble smile.

Champagne was served, and everyone toasted the bridal couple before the gathering broke up.

"Where are we going?" she asked her husband as she settled into his luxurious carriage.

He tucked the rug around her. It was beastly cold today. "To Piccadilly. To see our new house."

Our. How odd it seemed to be on the verge of sharing this stranger's vast wealth. "I've admired it from the street," she said, thinking of its Palladian elegance. "It seems rather . . . well, rather large for a bachelor."

"I knew I wasn't always going to be a bachelor."

Her heart drummed. No, he wanted a family. Hadn't he made that clear to her? "When will it be ready to move in?"

"That's hard to say. Most of it's finished now. It ought to be, considering that construction began three years ago. The Italian artist who's painting the ceilings has rather delayed things."

"Temperamental?"

A lazy grin lifted a corner of his mouth. "Exceedingly so. He repainted the dining room three times because his first two efforts didn't satisfy."

"What did you think of the first two efforts?"

"I thought they were magnificent. Everything the man paints is magnificent."

"Otherwise you wouldn't have had him, I gather." The little she had seen of Nicholas Birmingham had convinced her that he was possessed of excellent taste. The rich fabrics and demure styling of his clothes could only have been tailored by London's best. His carriage was fit for a duke, and the house he was building on Piccadilly would be the most elegant address in London.

"I am rather demanding," he confessed with a smile.

Good Lord, would he expect her to be perfect? "I sincerely hope you won't be disappointed in me, then."

He turned to her, taking both her hands in his while those black eyes of his studied her. "I could never be disappointed in you, Fiona."

She felt his heat, smelled his faint sandalwood scent, and was blatantly aware of how close they were.

Then the carriage came to a stop.

She withdrew one hand and lifted the velvet curtain to peer out the window. "We're here," she murmured.

The coach door swung open, then Nick was assisting her from the carriage. He continued to hold her hand as they walked through the front courtyard, up four steps, and through double doors into the mansion. It was hard for her to believe it was not finished. From the vast entry hall she could see four rooms, one with scaffolding erected beneath a clouded ceiling of nymphs and seraphs. Though she could not see the artist, she knew that was the room he was now finishing. Highly polished marble floors stretched as far as the eye could see, and an array of huge crystal chandeliers suspended from every ceiling except in the room with the scaffolding. The walls were painted in vibrant colors and trimmed in stark white with heavily gilded cornices and pilasters.

When Trevor had called the mansion disgustingly opulent, he had once again exaggerated. It was tastefully opulent, she decided. She could not wait to show it to Trevor, who would be sure to appreciate its classically elegant lines. It reminded her of Lord Burlington's house in Richmond, but on a larger scale. "It looks ready to move in," she said.

His hand settled at her waist. "It will need your touch, Mrs. Birmingham. We'll need furnishings and draperies and . . . well, you'll know. Vases and such."

Mrs. Birmingham. She could scarcely credit it! She really was this man's wife. "You will permit me to make the selections?" she asked.

"I'll be grateful for you to make the selections. I rather fancy architecture, but I assure you I'd be hopeless at selecting draperies and things."

As would most men. Except for Trevor. Trevor was devilishly clever about decorating. In fact, she would value Trevor's help. "Then I think I would need to start immediately. It takes time to fashion draperies and build furniture."

"How lucky that I've taken you for a wife, then."

"Oh, somehow I think you would have managed with Mr. Sheraton or some such authority had you not been saddled with me."

"I'm not saddled with you, Fiona," he said in a serious voice, gazing down at her. "I'm a most fortunate man to have wed you."

Her heart fluttered. "It's I who am fortunate," she whispered.

He showed her all the entertaining rooms on the ground floor, then paused to speak to the Italian painter who told him he would be finished by week's end.

Smiling, Nick turned to her. "Then we can begin moving in as soon as we return from Camden Hall."

She smiled back at him. "This is very exciting."

Together she and Nick walked up the broad terrazzo

stairway to the second floor, where high-quality oak floors replaced the marble floors that were downstairs. An asparagus green drawing room was at the top of the stairs. The hallway was studded with classically pedimented doorways, the middle one opening to Nick's bedchamber, which was painted royal blue. To one side of his bedchamber a study was located, on the other, a dressing room. They walked through the dressing room and found themselves in another dressing room that was all ivory and gilt. "This one will be yours," he said.

She had never given much thought before to her parents' dressing rooms being adjacent, but that hers and Nick's were next to each other sent the blush to her cheeks.

They continued through the dressing room and came to her bedchamber, which was also painted in ivory and gilt. "Feel free to change it," he said.

"Ivory's perfect! I can bring another color in with the draperies and bed coverings." She wondered if they would make love in her room or his.

And her cheeks turned even more scarlet.

After he completed the tour she said, "The house is truly wonderful, Nick."

"Not *the* house," he said, squeezing her hand. "Our house."

"Perhaps one day I'll be able to think of it as ours, but now it speaks of your magnificent vision. You should be very proud of yourself."

He shrugged. "I'd best get you back to Agar House so you can pack for Camden Hall."

So he did not like to be praised.

Once they were back in the carriage for the short ride to Cavendish Square, she asked, "Did you know that little girl who was at St. George's today?"

He did not answer for a moment. Then he said, "That was my daughter."

"I didn't know you'd been married—" She stopped as if she'd been stung by a wasp. Of course he hadn't been married before! Hadn't Trevor said Nick allowed his bastard to live with him? Only Fiona had not thought that a bastard would be a little girl. A lovely little girl with plaited brown hair, a much lighter shade of brown than her father's.

"She's my illegitimate daughter, Fiona."

Fiona studied the lapels on Nick's frock coat. "And she lives with you?"

"She does."

"That seems rather . . . unorthodox. Her mother has died, then?"

"As far as I know, her mother's alive."

"Then why . . . ?"

"Because her mother would not have been a good influence on a daughter I had come to care about."

"Then I cannot help but to wonder if the mother was so inferior why you would have . . ." *Have been attracted to the woman, have made love to her?*

He raked his long fingers through his thick, dark hair. "I've asked myself the same question thousands of times."

"Why does the child not reside with your mother?"

He stiffened. "My mother, being religiously evangelical, vehemently disapproved of my daughter."

"Her own grandchild? That doesn't seem terribly Christian to me."

He shrugged.

Fiona tried to remember what Trevor had said about Mrs. Birmingham's origins. Oh yes, he had said she was crass. Fiona could not in her wildest dreams believe a gentleman as fine as Nick could be the spawn of a crass woman.

They sat in silence the next few minutes, her thoughts a jumble. She was disappointed that Nick had been involved with a woman who must have been a

whore, yet she was oddly pleased that he had risked
personal censure for the sake of rescuing an innocent
child. She sucked in her breath. If they were to have
children together—and she did so desperately want
to have children—Nick would be a fine father.

But surely he would not expect her to be a mother
to his illegitimate child! Her hands dug into the
plush velvet seat. She wasn't ready to discuss this further with him. It would take time for her to adjust to
the disappointing reality.

They spoke hardly at all during the three-hour
ride to Camden Hall. His bride was obviously distressed to learn of Emmie's existence. Perhaps he
should have taken Adam's advice and stuck the child
away in a boarding school. Such an action would
have indicated his wife was more important to him
than his own child. He had not wanted to live in a
world where he would have to rank those he cared
about, where he would have to choose one loved
one over another. Nick was a great believer in harmony. Why could Fiona not embrace his daughter?
Surely she could repay him in some way for the fortune he was putting up to make her his wife.

Then he remembered she planned to repay him
tonight. A smoldering heat began to burn inside
him as he thought of what lay ahead for them that
night. He lifted her hand and began to peel off her
glove, finger by agonizing finger until the glove was
removed. He filled with pride as he eyed the golden
ring, then pressed a lingering kiss into the cup of her
palm as his fiery eyes met hers.

"Nick," she whispered softly as her other hand
lifted to stroke his face.

He pulled her into his arms for a hungry kiss. The
kiss was harsh and wet and unbelievably intense as her

lips parted beneath his, as she began to make little whimpering sounds. His hands began to move possessively over her, stroking her creamy shoulders, splaying over her back, then cupping her small breasts, his thumb feathering along the tip of her nipple.

Who would ever have thought his delicate little wife capable of such passion? Her reaction to him was more intoxicating than an entire bottle of champagne.

The coach lurched to a stop, and he lifted the curtain. He had not been aware that it had turned dark outside or that they were already at Camden Hall.

Chapter 6

He was hungry, but not for the food served to them shortly after they arrived at Camden Hall, which his servants had thoughtfully strewn with Christmas greenery. As he and his bride sat facing one another across the dinner table, he was unable to remove his gaze from her. It seemed almost incomprehensible that this exquisite creature was his wife, that in a few hours he would completely possess her. He drank in the way the candlelight played on her delicate features as she sucked a spoonful of turtle soup into her mouth. Good Lord, it was hot in here!

Remembering the taste of her tongue mingling with his, he grew winded and began to tug on his cravat. Once more he began to get aroused. As he spread the butter on his roll he thought of slowly stroking every inch of her smooth flesh. His lids lifted and he hungrily watched her tongue nip at her lower lip. He was not at all sure he could make it through the dinner without leaping from his chair, hauling her into his arms, and carrying her upstairs to his bedchamber.

"Is your cravat too tight?" she asked. "I must say they look beastly uncomfortable."

How could a cravat that had fit perfectly since ten o'clock this morning now be so wretchedly uncomfortable? "Indeed they are," he said. For the first time he noticed the metallic glints in her blond hair. She really was exquisite. Warwick was an idiot. "You looked lovely today, my dear," he said. "You still do." She wore the same pink gown she had married in that morning. It displayed her creamy shoulders and swept low at the bodice to reveal her delectable decolletage.

When he had filled his hand with her breast, he had been pleasantly surprised that someone as slender as she possessed any breasts at all. Remembering the feel of her plump little breasts thinned his breath.

"Thank you, Nick," she said, then she sipped her wine, her long lashes lowering seductively.

On her lips, his name became an endearment. Did she have any idea how acutely she aroused him? Could she possibly understand how tormented he was, how desperately he wished to peel off her clothing, spread her legs wide and embed himself within her?

Would this blasted meal ever come to an end?

"Did you find your chambers satisfactory?" he asked.

"Yes, they're very nice. It was as if they were just awaiting your wife."

"Thanks to the previous occupant, Lady Hartley," he said. "Of course, you're welcome to change anything you like."

"Will we be spending much time here?"

"Not really."

"I didn't think so," she said. "I know The Fox does not like to be away from his den."

The nickname he'd been proud of now took on almost sinister overtones. "I beg that you and I not discuss my business. We'll get on better that way."

Her blue eyes regarded him with puzzlement. "I want to make you a good wife, Nick. If you don't wish to discuss business, I promise to never bring it up again." She nibbled at that lush lower lip of hers. "I shouldn't like it if we didn't get on well."

"Nor would I," he said solemnly.

It was too soon to tell how they would get along with one another, but he was convinced that on the physical level they would be highly compatible. He had been stunned over the depths of her passion, and he had not yet penetrated her simmering veneer!

As much as he would like to bury himself within her, he cautioned himself to be mindful that she was a virgin, to hold back from devouring her.

Perhaps if she imbibed great quantities of wine, the losing of her maidenhead would be less painful, more pleasurable. He lifted the decanter and refilled her glass. "Drink up, my dear. It will make our . . . consummation easier on you."

His throbbing intensified as he watched a rosy hue climb into her cheeks. Though she was obviously embarrassed over his reference to their lovemaking, she lifted her solemn gaze to his, then sipped the wine.

The candles weren't the only thing in the room giving off heat. Never breaking eye contact with her, he loosened the cravat even more. He had the damnedest feeling he and Fiona were surrounded by flames.

Still watching him, she took another sip.

He refilled his own glass and drank.

"I feel guilty for robbing you of the bachelorhood you so cherished," she said. "I will try to please you in the bedchamber, but I shall have to be schooled. I'm told you're exceedingly knowledgeable about such things."

"By whom?" he demanded.

"Trevor. He knows everything about everybody."

"I told you this morning," he said in a husky voice, "to believe only half the things you're told about me."

"Then you're not skillful in the ways of . . . love?"

He burst out laughing. Actually, he thought lovemaking one of his areas of expertise, but he wasn't about to admit that to his bride. It was bad enough that she knew about Emmie's mother. He wondered if Trevor would have told her about Diane. "I know enough to . . . to teach you all you need to know, my dear."

The firelight danced in her simmering eyes. "Will I be able to learn all I need to know tonight?"

Every minute he sat there talking about making love to her was sheer torture. "You'll learn enough tonight, but I shall look forward to . . . expanding that knowledge every night." Had he known marriage would be this intoxicating, he would have taken the plunge years earlier. But then he wouldn't have won Fiona's hand. And somehow he did not think marriage to anyone else could match having Fiona for his wife.

She stared at him. He felt deuced awkward. He did not know her well enough to know if this was a good stare or a bad stare. When she spoke, that question was answered.

"Could we skip the sweetmeats," she said in a wispy voice, "and go upstairs now?"

He began to tremble and could barely find his voice. "An excellent idea." He shoved away from the table and came to settle his hands on her smooth shoulders, dipping his head to nibble at her graceful neck. She bent toward him and began to make little whimpering sounds. In one sleek move he scooped her up into his arms and strode from the dining room to swiftly mount the stairs.

Lit by wall sconces, the second floor was eerily quiet. He came to his bedchamber and kicked open the door, pleased to see that servants had built a fire and left a candle burning at the bedside table. Her arms clasped behind his neck as he crossed the room and set her down on the bed. "Should you like me to send for your maid?" he murmured.

When she shook her head, her eyes looked glazed.

"Will you allow me to assist you in removing your clothing?" he asked in a husky voice as he came to sit beside her.

Her eyes widened as she met his somber gaze, then nodded.

Though the idea of allowing him—a virtual stranger—to strip her bare must have shocked her, it did not repulse her. *Thank God*. He wondered how many virginal daughters of the *ton* would be as precocious as the beautiful woman he had wed. God, he was pleased he had married her! "Should you like me to fetch the wine?" he asked.

"I had three glasses." She began to untie his cravat. "I never have that much."

"Does that mean you're feeling mellow?" he asked, his lungs feeling bereft of air.

"I feel as if I've drunk an entire bottle of champagne, Nick." She sounded unbelievably provocative when she said his name. "I feel all tingly inside. And breathless."

He moved closer to her. "That's perfectly normal. I feel the very same." His lips lowered to gently touch hers. He heard a jerky intake of breath as her lips parted beneath his and she sucked his tongue into her mouth. He tasted the wine she had drunk, smelled her lavender scent, and thought he could explode with joy.

As the kiss intensified, his hands began to glide over her back, to cup her buttocks, to mold her small breasts. He gloried in the sound of her whimpering.

Her dress was easy to unfasten. He pushed it down to her waist and looked at her. "The stays will have to go, my love." He began to unlace them, and when her breasts sprang free he almost lost his breath. "So beautiful," he murmured, filling his hand with one, flicking his thumb over the rosy nipple, then bending down to take it into his mouth. She began to arch into him, her breasts flattening against his face as he sucked at one, then the other.

Over her skirts, his hand cupped her mound, squeezing at it, rubbing his wrist against her pelvis as she squirmed into his palm, moving from side to side and up and down and beginning to make moaning sounds that heated his blood.

Mindful that she wished to be taught all there was to know about lovemaking, he drew his face away from her breasts and spoke throatily. "When a woman is sexually aroused, the tips of her breasts harden into erotic points." He throbbed as he watched her gaze drop to the nubs in the center of her nipples.

"And when a man is sexually aroused," she asked in a low voice, lifting her smoldering gaze to him, "does something on his anatomy change?"

Good Lord! Did his wife not know about erections? He took her hand and held it to his crotch. "A man's . . . member enlarges and becomes stiff. Feel me, Fiona. Curl your hands around my shaft."

At first her fingers were stiff, then they began to gently coil around him. "You're so . . . so big. I don't think—"

He held an index finger to her mouth. "Don't think, love. Trust me on this." His hand went back to cupping her between her thighs, applying pressure that made her rhythm accelerate. "What you've got down here *will* accommodate my size," he said. His other hand went beneath her skirts and inched up to her smooth thighs as he lowered her onto the bed. "One other change occurs to a sexually aroused woman," he whispered.

"What?" she asked, her voice winded.

His voice was low when he asked, "Do you feel wet?" The hand beneath her skirts nudged up between her thighs and dipped into her slick folds. "Here?"

She looked like a woman drugged when she nodded and raised her hips into the movement of his fingers.

"This is nature's way of lubricating you for my entry." God, he wanted to enter her this second! She was so blessedly wet. Not able to wait much longer, he sat up and began to tug her dress all the way to her ankles, then she kicked one leg free.

Like everything else about her, her body was exquisite—tiny and milky white with little fluffs of breasts and a tuft of golden hair between her thighs. Had his life depended upon it, he could not have found a voice with which to spew on ad infinitum of her beauty. But it was a beauty that would forever be emblazoned upon his memory. And on his heart.

He stood and blew out the candle, then threw off his shirt and breeches. The hearth provided enough light for him to see her as he came to lie beside her, this time tenderly settling his lips over hers. "Are you ready, love?" he asked.

"Yes, please," she said, sifting her fingers in his hair.

"You'll need to widen your legs," he whispered as he began to move over her.

She did as he told her, and he came to settle between those luscious lily thighs, his thumb pressing the pearly bud in the center of her, then easing one finger back into her slippery opening. "Oh, Nick," she said with a sigh.

"I'm coming, love." He tucked the head of his shaft into her, just until the head disappeared, then he stopped. "Are you all right?" he asked in a gentle voice.

"Yes," she whispered as her hips raised up to accommodate even more of him.

He gently eased himself in farther. "All right still?"

She raised her head until her lips met his and spoke breathlessly. "Don't stop."

He forced himself in still farther, this time he came up against a barrier. *The maidenhead.* He drew in his breath. "This may hurt. I've got to break through your chastity."

Her head fell back against the pillow, and she nodded.

He was not sure what he should do next. Should he ram himself in so the unpleasantness would be quickly over? Or should he gently ease forward?

The decision was taken out of his hands when Fiona began to pulse against him. No pleasure he had ever known could equal this. She was so wet and warm and tight. And utterly willing. But his powerful emotions encompassed far more than just the physical.

When he tore through her barrier, she winced.

He stilled.

"Don't stop," she urged hungrily, moving against him.

He gradually regained the rhythm until the rhythm itself became the master and he its slave. They were both caught in the maelstrom, carried to a place where thoughts were fleeting fragments, where intense physical pleasure leaped at them like a raging fire, consuming them. Then she arched and stilled and began to tremble as her breath became ragged. He held her tightly as the orgasm rolled over her, lapping at her like an angry tide as she clenched him tighter and made throaty exclamations.

She pressed her lips into his, her fingers digging into his back as his seed began to fill her, as the rest of his length plunged into her.

How, she wondered, could such an uncomfortable action bring her such delirious pleasure? Would she always be this sore, or would the discomfort diminish with practice? Nick would know. If she had the brazenness to ask him. And, Good Lord, how could this bedchamber be this hot in the dead of winter? Were she wearing something it would have been completely drenched. Like her. Even her hair was damp and clung to her head.

When she felt Nick's seed seeping through her, profound emotions swept over her. She really was his wife. She could quite possibly bear his child. Something in her heart rolled over at the thought. A very pleasant thought, to be sure.

From this moment on, there was no turning back. She was irrevocably bound to the enigmatic man whose shaft was buried in her at this very second.

Like she had done, he stilled, then began to tremble. Only he called out her name. "Oh God, Fiona!" At first she thought something was wrong with him, then she realized he was not dissatisfied. Not dissatisfied at all.

A moment later he slipped from her and rolled to her side, his body sleek with sweat. His gentle hand swept the moist hair from her brow, and he bent to press a soft kiss there. "There's one other thing I neglected to tell you about being sexually aroused," he said.

"What is that?" she asked in a breathless voice.

"After the deed is done, one feels as if one's just run uphill."

That explained the sweating. And the breathlessness. So far all of her reactions had been perfectly normal. Even the pointed nipples. The thought of her breasts being erotic sent pulsebeats of pleasure licking at her.

She lay there in the darkness, Nick tugging her to his chest, and she felt completely blissful. Except for the devilish soreness.

"Oh, love," he murmured, "we are so good together. I couldn't ask for a better wife."

Her smile went deep as she buried her head into the crevice between his shoulder and chest. She could not have been any happier. Nick had called her *love*. Once tonight he had even said *my love*, which was infinitely better—considering the intimacy they had just shared. He was pleased with her. She truly believed he did not resent that she'd robbed his treasured bachelorhood.

And she truly hoped they could make love several times a night.

"Are you all right?" he asked a moment later, his voice gentle as he dropped soft kisses into her hair.

"I think so."

He went suddenly stiff. "What's the matter?" he asked in a concerned voice.

"I've heard that when a woman loses her chastity, there is blood?"

He drew in a deep breath. "There is."

"Is that why I . . . experienced discomfort? Is it only for the first time?"

He held her tightly. "I'm not an authority on women's virginity—you're my first virgin—but I believe you may experience soreness for a week or so—until your . . . anatomy gets used to my invasion."

"Will you answer me truthfully if I ask you a personal question?"

He did not answer for a moment. "Yes," he finally said.

"Do the women you bed usually experience pain?"

"Never," he said with authority. Then he sighed and tenderly stroked her back, her arms, her buttocks. "If you'd like, I won't . . . enter you again until the soreness goes away."

That's not at all what she liked. She stiffened. "Is that what you wish?"

"You want the truth?"

She held her breath. "Yes."

"No."

"I'm very glad to hear that for I'd like to do it all over again."

He gave a husky chuckle. "There's another thing you need to know about making love, my dear. Men are rather different from women. After a man has spilled his seed his size diminishes and he experiences a profound sense of exhaustion."

She rather thought this lovemaking would be more pleasant if a man's size was diminished! "Can a man not make love when he's not so 'expanded'?" she asked.

"He cannot!" he said with a laugh. "He needs to be quite hard in order to . . . slide in properly." He pushed her over on her back and settled his lips on hers for a heated kiss. "However, Mrs. Birmingham, just speaking about being rigid seems to have made me hard."

"Then we *can* do it again?"

"And again and again and again if you continue to have such an effect on me," he growled as he covered her body with his.

Chapter 7

The sudden burst of light awakened her the next morning. For several seconds she lay there, her eyes closed, suffused with a deep sense of well-being, despite the soreness in a place whose existence had been unknown to her before yesterday. Gradually, she came fully awake and recognized her surroundings: her husband's bedchamber. With glowing pride, she watched Nick—fully dressed and freshly shaven—move along a bank of tall windows, drawing open the blue silk draperies that had cloaked the room in darkness.

When he turned to face her, a crooked grin lifting one corner of his sensuous mouth, her heart leaped.

"Merry Christmas, Mrs. Birmingham. I've brought you breakfast," he said as he went to the table, collected the silver tea tray, and brought it to her.

She sat up and pulled the sheets to cover her nakedness. "Merry Christmas to you, Mr. Birmingham." She took the steaming cup of hot chocolate he offered. "You look so clean and well groomed, and I'm such a mess."

He leaned over to kiss her forehead, then sat on the

bed beside her. "You've never looked lovelier. I take it you slept well."

"Like the dead. At least . . . after . . ."

"After a night of wildly passionate lovemaking." His voice was a satisfied growl.

She wondered if all married people indulged in the activities she and Nick had last night. How did married people ever get any sleep?

A flicker of embarrassment leaped over her. She and Nick had behaved so very brazenly throughout the night. There was not an inch of her body that his mouth had not touched. Only his deep satisfaction had erased her embarrassment. Her brothers had told her that men were possessed of a strong need for sexual gratification. Her complete compliance in that area had definitely pleased her husband.

But the memory that Diane Foley had often assuaged Nick's needs definitely displeased Fiona.

"I have a Christmas gift for you," he said, withdrawing a small, red leather and gilt book from his pocket and handing it to her. "I had no time to buy anything so I decided to give you something that is very special to me. It's William Blake's poems. You'll find the pages much dog-eared. I only recently had the book rebound."

Her mouth dropped open. It was really extraordinary. *Songs of Innocence* was her favorite book. Tears gathered in her eyes.

His brows lowered. "What's the matter, love? Do you not like it?"

"Oh, Nick, I adore it—so much so that I gave away my only copy to Randy as a parting gift when he left the country." She clutched the book to her breast. "You could not have given me anything I would value more." She carefully thumbed through the pages, then gazed up into his face. "I feel wretched I have no gift for you."

He burst out laughing. "You've given my *everything* this day. No Christmas could be more wonderful." He lifted her left hand and kissed it. "By the way, the gold band is only temporary. I plan to have a more suitable wedding ring made for you. Do you like emeralds?"

She scowled. "A gold band perfectly suits me. I infinitely prefer something that has been passed down in your family over something purchased."

He fingered the golden ring. "You won't be embarrassed over its plainness?"

"Of course not!" Her gaze scanned her fully dressed husband, and color came to her cheeks as the grip on the sheets she held to her breast tightened. "How long have you been awake?"

He shrugged. "About an hour."

"What time is it?"

"Noon." His entire demeanor toward her had changed. His eyes positively glowed when he looked at her. His voice was like a tender caress. She suddenly came to understand how women throughout history— women like Cleopatra—had been able to wield such power over men. They did it with their bodies. With their bodies, they captured hearts. Her heartbeat drummed.

She could scarcely believe the day was half over. "Will we go to see your mother today?"

"Later. For Christmas dinner. Do you ride?"

A smile curved her mouth. "I adore riding."

"Then I'm looking forward to riding with you. It will be a good way for you to see all of your new country home."

"*Our country home,*" she teased. She decided she liked being a married woman. She liked sharing her life with someone else. And she especially liked sharing her body with that someone else.

His eyes glittering, a devilish smile on his face, he tugged at the sheet that covered her breasts. She concentrated on watching him when she really wanted to gaze at her uncovered breasts, wishing they were bigger. Their small size did not seem to repel her husband, who eased his head down and drew a nipple into his mouth. "Very nice," he murmured. She remembered what he had told her about the nipples turning rigid, and she stole a peek. They had indeed hardened.

She wondered if he had hardened, too. Her gaze flicked to his crotch, and she could not suppress her smile. His crotch resembled a tent. A tent with a pole in the middle.

A bizarre idea suddenly popped into her head. "Dearest?" she asked. It was the first time she had used such an endearment, but it seemed appropriate after what had occurred between them the night before.

He had switched to her other breast. "Uh huh?"

"Can people make love in the daytime?"

He burst into laughter as he straightened up, then gave her a solemn look. "They most certainly can, and we most definitely will. But not now. We've only a few more hours of daylight, and there's much I wish to show you."

She decided this man she had married must be possessed of a great deal of self-discipline. Which she found rather admirable.

No stable in all of England could exceed her husband's in grandeur or in horseflesh. "Oh my!" she said when they began to stroll the center aisle of the long, two-story building, where stalls on either side were filled with fine Arabians. "I don't remember Lord Hartley having such a fine stable."

"Actually, his stable's been torn down. I built this one three years ago."

"Not only is the facility first rate," she said with

awe, "but the horses! How can a man who spends so much time in The City have amassed such wonderful creatures?"

"It's my one weakness."

She fleetingly thought he might have another weakness. A weakness for women. Women like Diane Foley. "You go to Newmarket?"

"Rarely," he said. "I don't fancy wagering. I enjoy breeding—and collecting the cups my horses win. If there's an especially big meet—like the One Thousand Guinea Classic or the Derby at Epson—I'll go to a race meeting for the joy of seeing one of my horses win and collecting the prize money."

She thought all men wagered. Especially men with large pockets, men like her husband. But she was coming to realize this man she had married was not like the men of her class, though one not familiar with his background would never believe Nick had not been born to the same privilege she had been born to. His cultured voice, his remarkable taste in clothing and houses and carriages and horseflesh, bespoke a man of aristocratic origins. The differences were subtle. Nick did not like being idle. Nick did not wager. Trevor had even told her Nick was not enamored of strong drink.

Her heart clenched. He was enamored of actresses. Like the men of her class.

"Which is your horse?" she asked.

A smile came over his handsome face. "Midnight." He strolled two more stalls and directed his attention at a magnificent black horse.

"He's a beauty," she said.

"He's descended from the Gondolphin Barb."

She moved closer to stroke the animal's nuzzle. "I'm impressed."

"Which one would you like?"

"What a wonderful Christmas!" she squealed, then

she began to stroll up and down the length of the mews. The decision was not easy, given that they were all such fine beasts. But she came to stand before a stall holding a chestnut mare with white markings. "This little filly speaks to me. What's her name?"

"Feel free to name her. She's yours."

Fiona threw her arms around her husband's neck and kissed his cheek, then she stood back and stared at the mare's sleek lines. "I believe I should like to call her Missus B."

Her husband came to stand beside her, draping an arm around her as his head dipped to hers and she felt the brush of his lips on her cheek. "That pleases me, Fiona," he said in a husky voice.

The haystack seemed suddenly appealing. This man's touch had the most devastating effect upon her.

"I'll have Jeremiah saddle her," he said.

A few minutes later they were galloping across the gently sloping meadows left colorless from winter's cold. It was obvious to Fiona that her husband had the best riding instructors, too. She gave up a silent prayer of thanks to the father who had molded this man who was now her husband.

They rode from one end of his property to the other, very few words exchanged. Though the sun was high in the sky, it was an extremely cold, breezy day. Eventually they turned onto a fairly well-traveled road and slowed to a canter.

He eyed her, his gaze lazily skimming over the navy blue velvet of her riding habit. "I like you in that color," he said. "It makes your eyes a deep blue."

"You're remarkably observant for a man."

"There's much to appreciate when a man looks at you, Fiona."

That fluttering he always seemed to elicit returned. "Thank you, Nick."

A moment later he asked, "Is the cold uncomfortable for you?"

"For one accustomed to Yorkshire winters, I assure you the weather in Kent's most tolerable."

After they rode over a gentle hill, she slowed and asked, "Will Verity be at your mother's tonight?"

"Yes, and my brothers too. I'm hoping you and Verity will have some commonality."

Not nearly as strongly as she hoped. A moment later she asked, "Your mother knows about our marriage?"

"I dispatched a letter to her at the same time I put the notice in the *Times*. The afternoon before our marriage."

She had been so busy and so rattled the morning of her wedding she had not read the newspaper. It never occurred to her that Nick would have the presence of mind to insert the notice in the *Times*. She wondered what it said. But she was even more curious to learn what he had told his mother. "Did you tell your mother I asked you to marry me?"

His eyes narrowed. "Of course not! I wouldn't tell anyone that." He paused a moment. "Except for Adam. And the only reason I told him was because I saw him directly after I had turned down your generous offer. I was agitated, and he knew it."

Had his brother persuaded him to marry her? Her stomach sank. Would a marriage between the house of Birmingham and the Viscount Agar's family be beneficial to the family businesses? Was she merely a business acquisition? She drew in a breath. "Then your brother urged you to marry me?"

Nick slowed beside a copse of birch trees and gave her a solemn look. "I'm the eldest, Fiona. My brother doesn't tell me what to do. He merely asked if I found you attractive." His dark eyes swept over her. "Which I do. Very much. As I thought about it, I realized I would never find a woman possessed of more qualities I seek in a wife than you." He lowered his voice almost to a growl. "And that was before I knew of your passionate nature, my sweet."

Relief washed over her.

Great Acres was not furnished as tastefully as Camden Hall, but it was a very grand place surrounded by a lush park and built in a stately Tudor style.

As the butler escorted her and Nick to the drawing room, Fiona's gaze traveled over the Christmas garlands strewn over every window and doorway.

"I see my sister's shown no restraint in her Christmas decorations," Nick said with a chuckle. "'Tis a miracle if there's a single holly bush that was spared her ax."

Fiona's eyes suddenly watered as a powerful rush of emotions surged through her. Like Verity, Fiona had always adored gathering Christmas greenery to decorate Windmere Abbey. When she'd had a family to enjoy her efforts. How she envied Miss Birmingham, whose mother was still alive, whose three brothers would spend the holiday with her. Fiona would give all that she possessed to see Randy again. Her chest tightened. She had given all that she possessed in the hopes of once again seeing her eldest brother. How she missed him! How she missed Mama and Papa and Windmere Abbey, and how she longed for those happy Christmases spent with her own family.

Despite Nick's comforting arm looping around her, Fiona grew nervous as the door swept open and she got a glimpse of the woman she presumed to be Nick's mother, though the two looked nothing alike. Until his mother looked up. And glared. There was an unmistakable resemblance around the prominent cheekbones.

Nick kept one arm around Fiona as they entered

the room. "Mother, I should like to present you to my wife. Lady Fiona, my mother, Dolina Birmingham."

Mrs. Birmingham was close to sixty. Fiona could not say what color the woman's hair was because it was stuffed beneath a mobcap, but she immediately saw a resemblance between Mrs. Birmingham and her youngest son. Both had eyes the same shade of green, and she was also stocky like William. But unlike her sons, Dolina Birmingham had no fashion sense. Her kelly green dress, though of a high-quality fabric, was a decade out of date and exceedingly tight on her—which was not flattering, given the woman's girth. The band around the sleeve of her dress squeezed her flabby arms, and her bosom was positively indecent for the amount of it which was *not* concealed beneath the low neckline.

The woman did not smile as Fiona stepped forward and curtsied. "Please don't address me as 'my lady,'" Fiona said. "Call me Fiona, and I hope you won't object if I call you Mother."

Still glaring, the woman shrugged, then snorted. "Now why would Quality like yerself go callin' me Mother? People would think I was trying to be too high in the instep."

"I don't care what others think," Fiona said. "You will be as a mother to me, for you gave birth to my dear husband."

The "dear husband" seemed to please Mrs. Birmingham, for she finally allowed a sliver of a smile. "Sit down," Mrs. Birmingham commanded.

"Where are my brothers and Verity?" Nick asked after he and Fiona sat at a brocade sofa across from his mother.

"Yer brothers are riding." Mrs. Birmingham rolled her eyes. "Yer sister's off at the vicar's, and ye'll never guess what that peculiar sister of yours is doing there."

Nick arched a brow.

"She's payin' the vicar to teach her Latin!" Mrs. Birmingham faced Fiona. "Have you ever heard of a woman who wanted to read and write Latin? I'll wager even a fine lady like yerself don't speak Latin."

"My brothers learned, but I confess I never did," Fiona said.

"Why does she wish to learn Latin?" Nick asked.

"Something about wishing to read certain authors at the 'source,' whatever that means."

Smiling, Nick shook his head. "A pity the poor girl had no sisters. I'm afraid three brothers weren't the best influence on a young lady."

"There ye go, wantin' to make yer sister a lady, like that high-flying wife of yers."

The lady they had been discussing strolled into the room at that moment. Had Nick been a girl, Fiona thought, he would have looked exactly like Verity. Like him, his sister was tall and lean, and her hair was the exact shade of brown as his—a deep mahogany. Even her eyes were so dark they looked black. Just like Nick's. Her dress was of excellent quality but exceedingly drab, a deep beige with no trim. Only her hair separated her from the average country miss. Cut in the latest fashion, it was short and curly and very attractive. Already Fiona could picture her in a stark white ball gown. With her height, she would cut a dashing figure.

When Verity saw Nick, a smile lighted her face and her step quickened. "Nicky!"

He stood up and came to brush his lips across her cheeks. "You're looking fit, Verity," he said with affection.

She clutched his hand, then turned to Fiona. "Your wife?" she asked shyly.

"Indeed it is. Lady Fiona, allow me to present my sister Verity to you."

Fiona stood and curtsied. "I am so very happy to

make your acquaintance—and so very happy that at long last I shall have a sister."

A smile tweaked at the corners of Verity's mouth. "You, too, have only brothers?"

Fiona nodded. "Two brothers. No sisters." She hoped Verity would share her enthusiasm for finally having a sister, but Verity said nothing as the three of them sat down.

The butler brought tea, and Mrs. Birmingham served.

Verity obviously did not possess her brother's self-confidence, Fiona decided. As they sipped their tea and spoke of village occurrences, it occurred to Fiona that Verity's reluctance to embrace Fiona's idea of sisterhood stemmed from her perception of the disparity in their ranks. That wouldn't do at all. Verity would be a sister to her, and Fiona was willing to do whatever it took to force the notion on Verity.

"We've a fine goose for Christmas dinner," Mrs. Birmingham said. Turning to Fiona, she added, "Don't expect one of those fancy meals like fine lords and ladies are used to. We're simple country folk."

"Then you must know," Fiona said, "I've spent most of my life in the country, too. In Yorkshire."

Mrs. Birmingham glared some more.

Verity, obviously embarrassed over her mother's rudeness, said, "I'm so happy Nick's brought you here, my lady. I was dying to meet you."

"Please," Fiona said, "call me Fiona. Sisters have no need to use titles."

Verity's cheeks flushed.

"Nicky?" Mrs. Birmingham said.

"Yes, Mother?"

"Do you think I could steal you away from yer bride for a few minutes? I've been going over some of yer father's papers, and I need you to tell me what needs keeping."

Nick flicked a glance at Fiona.

"I would love to take a walk with Verity through the park," Fiona said.

A few minutes later the two ladies had donned their hats, cloaks, and muffs and were strolling across the broad lawn. "Nick and I would like nothing better than for you to come live with us in London once th—our house is finished," Fiona said. "I'm going to be presenting Miss Rebecca Peabody, who is your age, and I'd like to present you at the same time."

Verity stiffened. "That's very kind of you, my lady . . ."

"Fiona."

"Fiona. But you must know I cannot be presented."

There was no reason an attractive young lady of wealth could not be presented. "Then, you've married?"

"Of course not!"

"Then why do you say you cannot be presented?"

Verity came to a stop. "Because I'm not of the *ton*."

"But I am, and you are my sister. Besides, you have a large dowry, and I assure you men of the *ton* are always seeking ladies possessed of large dowries, my viscount brother included!"

"I shouldn't like to marry a fortune hunter."

Now the blush rose to Fiona's cheeks. She did not wish for people to think she was a fortune hunter— after Nick's fortune. Even if it was true. Nick deserved better than that.

She could see she was going to have to be very blunt with the proud Miss Birmingham. "You must know, Verity, that—like Nick—you would be marrying beneath you should you marry a man of the class you were born to."

Verity nodded shyly. "But I have no aspirations of marrying into the aristocracy as my brother has done."

"You don't have to marry a peer, goose. There are any number of gentlemen in London who would make you an excellent husband." She remembered Verity's hunger for learning and added, "Learned men. Men with whom you would have a great deal in common."

"Then I vow to give consideration to your offer."

They walked in silence for a few more moments. By now they had strolled the park's perimeter.

"You must see our parterre garden," Verity suggested. "Papa had it built just before he died."

"I should love to."

The two ladies began to stroll along the paths of the parterre that was located directly behind the house. Pebble paths crossed through the raised beds, most of which were barren this time of year.

"This reminds me of Lord Culbertsen's garden that was designed by Inigo Jones," Fiona said.

"Papa had an affinity for Inigo Jones's work and hired a garden designer who had extensively studied Jones's gardens."

Fiona wished she could have met Jonathan Birmingham. "I look forward to seeing it in the spring."

"You'll have to coerce Nicky. He gets so carried away with his work he forgets to come here."

It seemed incomprehensible that she could ever coerce her husband into anything. Nick was a very strong-willed man.

Verity cleared her throat and said, "I must apologize for my mother. She is neither possessed of social graces nor happy that Nick's married an aristocrat. She thinks you'll keep Nick away from the rest of us. And even if she's incapable of showing her affection—to any of us—Nicky's her favorite."

"Please assure your mother that I will look upon her as my own mother." Fiona's shoulders sagged. "Nick's been so wonderful to me, I would never slight his family. Though Nick's not from an aristocratic background, I know no man in the *ton* who's a better prize."

Now Verity turned a full smile on Fiona. "I am so happy to hear you say that! It's no secret that Nick's my favorite brother, and I had so feared you were a fortune hunter who would not love him as he should be loved."

Fiona hadn't said anything about love. It would never have occurred to her to use such a word in connection with their marriage.

After dinner when they all gathered around the still-glowing yule log to exchange Christmas gifts, Fiona's heart ached for the loss of her own family, for the loss of the Christmases that had once brought her such joy.

Mrs. Birmingham and Verity exclaimed over the Kashmir shawls Nick gave them, and his brothers were delighted with his gift of French brandy.

"Where in the devil did you get this?" Adam asked Nick.

Nick smiled sheepishly. "I cannot divulge my source."

Verity presented each of her brothers with miniatures of herself and her mother. "I know this makes me look exceedingly vain," she said, "but it all started when I decided to help out an itinerant painter."

William stared at his pair of miniatures. "The artist is quite talented. These likenesses are almost lifelike."

"I'm very glad to have them," Nick said.

Fiona stole a peek at the miniatures her husband held in his hand. "I know your brothers will treasure their gifts," Fiona said to Verity. "I always carry with me the miniature of my dear brother." Just speaking of Randy was like reopening a gaping wound.

"Where is your brother this Christmas?" asked

Verity, whose somber demeanor indicated she sensed Fiona's moroseness.

Nick clasped Fiona's hand. "Her brother's an officer in The Peninsula."

"How you must worry about him!" a sympathetic Verity said.

"I beg that you not discuss it," Nick said. "I wish for my wife to have only happy thoughts this Christmas night."

"I'm so dreadfully sorry I have no present for her," Verity said.

"Then we are equal," Fiona said, attempting gaiety, "for I have none for you, either. But I did receive a most precious gift from my husband."

"Jewels, no doubt," Mrs. Birmingham said with a snort.

Her eyes dancing, Fiona shook her head. "Something much more useful and enjoyable than jewels. He gave me his favorite volume of poetry—which is also my favorite but which I no longer possess because I gave it to my dear brother when he left England."

Verity looked from Nick to Fiona. "How fortuitous that you two enjoy the same things. That bodes for a most satisfactory marriage."

Nick squeezed Fiona's hand and peered at her. "I feel rather like the man who won the Irish Sweepstakes."

His comment made Fiona feel even more jubilant than the man who won the Irish Sweepstakes. And more than that, she suddenly realized she belonged to a new family. Nick's family. From now on, she would share all her Christmases with him.

She only hoped that one day she would be able to recapture the Christmas magic.

Chapter 8

As they drove back to Camden Hall, Nick settled into the squabs of his carriage and tugged his wife close. Today had been the best Christmas of his life. He could not have been prouder of Fiona. He was proud of her beauty and breeding, but most especially he was thankful for her tolerance of his family. It was now clear to him that his wife and sister would get along very well with one another. Fiona was possessed of the ability to appreciate his modest sister. Thank God.

He was also grateful to Fiona for her extreme courtesy to his brash mother. Now that Fiona had conversed with what must be the most ill-mannered person she had ever spent an evening with, his wife had every reason to regret this marriage, but to his dismay she seemed not to give their disparity a second thought. Which was a relief to Nick. Crass his mother might be, but he loved her. As he was coming to love Fiona. Thank God there would be harmony among those he cared for. Now . . . if only Fiona would embrace Emmie.

A whisper of a yawn escaped from his delicate wife. "Tired?" he asked.

She nuzzled her face into his chest and sighed. "Very."

Of course she would be tired. Their vibrant love-making throughout the night had stolen away most of their sleep, and the day's constant activities and the tension of meeting her new family would be sure to have taken their toll on her. "Since I'm incapable of sharing your bed without ravaging you," he said with a little laugh, "I'll offer to stay in my chamber tonight so you can get a good night's sleep, my dear."

Her face lifted, and she met his somber gaze. "I should like to share my bed with you, Nick."

He drew her into his swaddling embrace and dropped a kiss on top her head. "I'm very happy to hear that."

As they mounted the stairs inside Camden Hall, their hands clasped, his breathing accelerated. She dismissed the maid who waited in her bedchamber, then she turned to Nick, flowing into his arms like butter to a mold and settling her face against his shoulder.

She felt so damned good. Though she was smaller and less buxom than the women who had been his lovers, this woman he had married was sheer perfection. It seemed almost incomprehensible that four days ago he had never shared a private conversation with her, that four days ago marriage to her had seemed as unobtainable as the stars in the sky, that four days ago he had thought himself satisfied with a woman who was not a tenth the lady his dearest Fiona was.

It seemed incomprehensible, too, that he would ever wish to lie with another woman after making love to his very own wife. She was so much more than he had bargained for. The very thought of her passionate nature sent heated blood thundering through his veins, sent blood rushing to his groin.

Whimpering seductively, she lifted her face to his. Stirred by her simmering eyes set in a flawless face and by the feel of her body nestled against his, he lowered his head to hers for a kiss that was at first tender, then passionate. Her mouth opened to his for a wet, breathless, thoroughly wrenching kiss. When he finally managed to stop and hold her at arm's length, she surprised him by untying his cravat, then moving deft fingers to the buttons of his fine linen shirt, never removing her sultry gaze from his.

Her back was to the fire, and the firelight glancing off her hair looked like a halo. He drew in a deep breath and cupped one of her breasts, bending to kiss it reverently. Then he cupped the other.

And she began to moan, arching toward him.

The very idea of stripping her bare in front of the fire sent his pulse pounding. He came closer and gently lowered the bodice of her dress, skimming its shoulders over her arms and allowing it to pool on the floor. With trembling hands, he began to unlace her stays, and when her smoothly rounded, little breasts sprang free, he growled his satisfaction and stepped even closer. Her breasts brushed against his shirt as he cupped her derriere, urging her against his erection in a staccato rhythm.

The sound of her harsh breathing was an aphrodisiac. A sudden need to free her of those silky drawers, to trace his finger against her moist seam, consumed him. He began to lower the drawers slowly, and when they slipped over her smooth ivory curves and revealed the golden curls guarding her entrance, he nearly lost his breath. "So lovely," he murmured like a man drugged as he scooped her into his arms and carried her to the turned-down bed.

She scooted to its center as he flicked off all the bed coverings. "We won't need these tonight."

As he had done the night before, he gazed at her while he stripped himself bare, but unlike the night before, tonight she lazily perused him with simmering eyes—from his shoulders, skipping down his chest to his waist, and lower still. The way the corners of her sweet mouth almost imperceptively lifted with satisfaction heated his blood.

This night he left the candle burning. He could not deny himself the pleasure of feasting on her luxurious body.

She whimpered as he stretched out beside her and began to trace feathery kisses from her ear down to her delicate neck. When he went lower and drew a nipple into his mouth, she let out a breathy sigh and arched into him. He felt like a unencumbered child frolicking in a field of lavender. Fiona's scent. And he felt unbelievable pleasure.

He strayed from her breasts and pressed a trail of kisses along her silky flesh as he came to settle himself between her legs, widening them still further with his shoulders as he nudged his head down to taste her fruity essence.

At the first thrust of his tongue, she nearly came off the bed. "Nicholas Birmingham!" she called in a shrill voice.

He lifted his head and gave her a sheepish grin. "Yes, love?"

"What are you doing?"

"Nothing I've invented, my love."

"You mean . . . ?" Her eyes rounded.

He nodded. "There may even come a time," he said in a husky voice, "that you will put me in your mouth." As he spoke, his finger replaced his tongue. She watched him with heavy-lidded eyes and spoke in a quivering voice. "People . . . other people really do that?"

"They do."

"Then continue. Please."

Once more he parted her with his tongue, flicking and thrusting as she squirmed into the pressure of his mouth. Closing his eyes, he imagined her warm mouth closing around his shaft.

Spasms of pleasure rocketed through her. She gasped. She moaned. She trembled violently. A fine mist slickened her smooth body.

Deeply satisfied at how easily he could bring her to climax, Nick eased his body over hers and plunged into her in one sure thrust as she arched her hips to meet him, thrust for thrust. "Oh, Nick," she whispered, her hands digging into his back. "How can you keep making me so crazy for this?"

He stilled, then shuddered as his seed came bursting into her, as he soared to a place he'd never been, a place of swirling motion and sparkling lights and almost unbearable pleasure. A place inhabited only by him and his precious wife. "Oh God, Fiona," he finally sputtered as he sank back into the soft mattress, "I could die right here in your arms."

She gave a satisfied little moan and snuggled up against him, her head pillowing in the dark hair that centered on his chest. "You, my dear husband, make me a wanton woman." She still struggled to breathe.

His hand splayed over the soft, smooth sphere of her buttocks, and he groaned. "But I have the pleasure of knowing you're *my* wanton woman. And I couldn't be happier." *My woman.* The words were like a soothing balm. No possession could ever be more precious.

He offered up a prayer of thanks to the bandits who had brought her into his life.

Despite her exhaustion, she could have made love to him all night long again. But tonight his soft snore told her he had gone to sleep immediately after their lovemaking, his hand still splayed over her bare hips. She truly did belong to this man, but instead of resenting his possession, she found it strangely satisfying. A contented smile on her face, she sighed deeply, snaked an arm around his rock-hard back, and lay in the darkness, listening to the steady thump of his heart.

How could she have lived six and twenty years and have no clue about what went on in a married couple's bedchamber? And how could she have gone six and twenty years without the lovemaking she had begun to crave so thoroughly?

She wondered if she truly was a wanton woman. Would she have been so ripe for any other man's possession? She fleetingly thought of Edward. Just a year ago she had wanted him to make love with her, but those feelings she had felt for him were not as powerful as what she felt for Nick. Not that she loved Nick, of course.

But the very idea of Edward lapping at her body as Nick had done was repellant. The idea of Nick burying his shaft within her made her glow. Like a candle in the dark.

She pressed soft kisses into the mat of dark hair on Nick's sturdy chest and went to sleep with a smile on her face.

Still naked, still linked to one another like a pair of doves, they woke the next morning and made love once again before dressing for their morning ride. Nick had instructed the groom to have Midnight and Missus B saddled so they did not have to wait when they arrived at the mews.

After a quick gallop over the rolling meadow behind Camden Hall, Nick reined in at the top of a gently sloping hill. "I wish we didn't have to leave today," he said as she drew up beside him.

Her face fell. So did her heart. She did not want to return to London. Once they returned to The City, her husband was sure to obsess over his beastly business and exclude her from his life. He wouldn't even allow her to speak of his wretched business. She wondered if they would still share a bedchamber in their London home. Would they continue to make love every night? Good Lord, was she becoming an absolute slave to passion? "Must we return so quickly?" she asked, trying to rein in her disappointment.

He grimaced. "I'm afraid so."

She stopped short of cursing his business. Hadn't she promised him she would not speak of it? She proudly flicked up her chin. "I shall miss Camden Hall."

He brought Midnight up beside her and leaned over to kiss Fiona's cheek. "So shall I, but we must return. The kidnappers will be trying to communicate with you."

How could she have forgotten all about Randy's wretched circumstances? Was she that self-absorbed? Perhaps she *did* need to return to London.

"Where did you receive their last letter?" he asked.

"At Agar House."

"Did you learn who delivered it?"

She shook her head. "It was brought by a lad who'd been given a shilling. That's all I know." It suddenly occurred to her that she did not know where they would live until they moved into the new house on Piccadilly. "Will we stay there until the new house is ready?"

"We'll live at my house," he said sternly.

"The new one?"

"The new one's *ours.*"

He was behaving most arrogantly. "Then where is *your* present house, sir?"

"Actually," he said with a softening in his voice, "I live in my father's former lodgings south of the Thames."

South of the Thames? She had never known a single Londoner who resided *south* of the Thames. And she was not at all sure she wished to reside there, even if it would be for only a few weeks until they could move into the new house. Good Lord, would gin-stupored prostitutes and pickpockets be running amuck there?

He eyed her with amusement. "I assure you it's a most proper neighborhood. Not Mayfair, but nice."

She was ashamed of her initial reaction. Of course Nick wouldn't live in a hovel. "I'm sure it is."

A lazy grin spread across his face. "And why are you so sure?"

"Because you're possessed of remarkably good taste."

He leaned over and kissed her again. "Especially in wives."

Oddly, she thought that was the nicest thing anyone had ever told her.

The first thing Nick and Fiona did upon returning to London was to query the servants at Agar House to see if a second ransom note had come, but after questioning them and rifling through the posts she determined there had been no word from the kidnappers. His brows lowered with concern, Nick faced his wife and drew her hands into his. "Don't worry, my dear. We'll have Randolph safely returned in no time. My brother's ready to be dispatched to Portugal at a moment's notice."

How could she not worry? True, a week had not yet passed since she received the first letter, but she still feared the silence. Could Randy have been gravely injured? She squeezed Nick's hand. "Though I can't *not* worry, I'm grateful that you're helping me shoulder this. It truly does help."

He gave her a lopsided grin before confronting the butler. "I wish for you to write down my address," Nick told the servant, "and see to it that any correspondence for Lady Fiona is dispatched there at once."

After giving the direction to the butler, Nick offered

his arm to his wife. "Come, love, let's go see if our new house is indeed finished."

Fiona felt wretchedly guilty that the prospect of seeing her new house relieved some of her glumness.

When they arrived at the Piccadilly mansion she was surprised that not a single worker was there, even though it was three in the afternoon.

"They really are finished," Nick said as he strolled over the threshold, his hand set possessively at her waist. "Now you will need to get busy."

Her admiring gaze swung from the gleaming marble floors to the gilded cornices and over the heavenly ceiling. "I'll begin contacting the various tradesmen this afternoon while you go to your office."

"And what makes you think I'm going to my office today?" he asked, peering down at her with a devilish grin.

"Because I've been your wife for three days. Give me credit for knowing something about the workings of your mind." She had the oddest desire to tell him she would know him as no other woman ever would but realized Diane Foley might have the advantage over her. How long had the two of them been lovers? Good Lord, would Nick go to the actress now?

Fiona's heart sank. She knew most married men had their lady birds, but she didn't like to think of her husband as being one of those men. She didn't like to think of his bare, smoothly muscled body poised over the actress's, of him intimately caressing her as he had caressed Fiona. She visualized the flame-haired actress and was filled with intense jealousy, a jealousy even more profound than what she had once felt toward Edward's countess.

As they swept from room to room she marveled at how easily she had begun to picture each of them with the proper furnishings. "I think the drawing room would look perfect with pale yellow damask wall coverings and gold silken draperies," she told her husband.

"I shall have to trust you on that, my dear. I haven't a clue what damask is."

"Well, I do, and I shall adore making all the selections—with Trevor's help, of course."

Nick rolled his eyes and muttered something about Trevor she could not understand.

"You are aware that most women have a best friend?" Fiona asked.

He eyed her curiously for a moment. "Do you mean to tell me Trevor Simpson is your best friend?"

She nodded.

"Bloody hell!"

"Once you get to know him, you'll love him as I do."

Nick's eyes narrowed. "I don't know how I like my wife loving another man."

Her heartbeat skipped. Love was never part of their bargain. Could Nick wish for her to fall in love with him? Her shoulders sagged. Of course Nick—the great accumulator of possessions—would wish to possess her heart, soul, and body. Marrying her had been rather like acquiring the crowning piece of his vast collections. She shrugged. "I suppose Trevor's the only man I know with whom I can be alone without having to worry about the damage to my reputation. Surely you'll not object if Trevor's forever in my pocket?"

His grin pinched one cheek. "I don't like sharing my possessions."

She stiffened, then began to mount the central stairway. Of course, that's all she was to Nick. A possession.

They strolled down the broad hallway to his bedchamber. "We'll move in here first," he said, his voice husky, his jet eyes glittering as he watched her. "And I don't give a damn if your bed ever arrives."

Her gaze flicked below his waist. He was aroused.

A feeling of power, of sheer lust swept over her. She moved closer to him, lifting her arms to circle his neck as his head bent to taste her lips.

He crushed her to him, cupping her hips and grinding her into his erection. Her breasts felt heavy, her breath seemed nonexistent, and she tingled low in her torso. She had never been so sexually aroused. She thought she might die of excruciating need if he did not take her right here in this huge empty room.

Nick had the same idea.

He backed her into the door and began to lift her skirts. She fumbled to free him of his pantaloons. When she saw his engorged need jut out over the lowering waistband, her breath caught.

"Widen your legs," he rasped.

As she did, he stepped between them and eased himself into her. Almost instantly, spasms began to rock through each of them as they bleated heated exclamations of pleasure and murmurs of affection.

Fiona was vaguely aware that sunlight from twenty casements poured into the big, echoing chamber. She was vaguely aware that they were alone in the large, empty house, rutting like dogs in heat. But all else was a blur of excruciating physical pleasure.

A moment later it was all over and, drenched and panting, she sagged into her husband. "You do seem to bring out the trollop in me," she murmured. She thought she should be ashamed over her behavior, but the pleasure far outweighed any embarrassment.

He wiped her brow, set gentle lips to it, and said, "Precisely what I wish for in a wife: a trollop in the bedchamber and a lady in the drawing room."

The sudden memory that men suffered acute exhaustion after lovemaking made her happy. Surely now he would have no desire to find and bed Diane Foley. Perhaps if she could keep her husband sexually sated, he'd never return to the actress's bed.

"Oh, dearest," she said with a sigh, "will we always take such pleasure in each other's bodies?"

He held her close and let out a long sigh. "It's unlikely."

She pouted.

"You vixen!" he growled. "Do you realize if we continue at this pace, neither of us would ever get anything done?"

"Because we'd never get out of the bed!"

They crossed the Thames at Westminster and a few minutes later were entering his house. "Allow me to present you to your new mistress, Mrs. Birmingham," he said to the butler, housekeeper, and downstairs parlormaid who gathered in the entry hall. Introducing Fiona as his wife filled him with pride. "Mrs. Hill is the housekeeper." He nodded at the middle-aged woman. "Biddles is the butler, and . . . ?" He eyed the housekeeper for assistance in naming the maid.

"Lottie," Mrs. Hill said.

Fiona nodded to the curtseying girl.

"My wife," he said proudly, "may be referred to as Mrs. Birmingham or as Lady Fiona."

"Mr. Birmingham has assured me of your great competence," Fiona said to the group.

"By the way," Nick added, flicking his gaze over his servants, "we shall be moving shortly. The new house is finally ready." Then he turned to Fiona. "Allow me to show you around, my dear."

She placed her arm in the crook of his as they strolled each of the spacious rooms on the ground floor, and as they returned to the stairway, she asked, "Where is the child?"

His breath hitched. "Should you like to meet her?" *Please say yes.*

"Of course."

"The nursery's on the third floor," he said as they began to mount the stairs.

"How old is she?"

"Eight."

"Then you were . . ."

"Four and twenty when she was born." Old enough to take responsibility for his actions.

"An how old was she when she came to you?"

He shrugged. "Three or four months." He had never told anyone of the harrowing act that had precipitated his removal of Emmie from Ruby's home. From a friend of Ruby's who was out of charity with her, he had learned that Emmie was not the first babe Ruby had given birth to—even though she was but eighteen when she came under Nick's protection. Her first child—a healthy son—had the life strangled out of him by his own mother a few minutes after his birth.

Nick's ever-expanding knowledge of his mistress convinced him the only reason Emmie was still alive was because Ruby planned to use the child as her milk cow to drain Nick's pockets. Not that money entered into his decision to take the child. The very notion of the volatile Ruby losing patience with the babe and killing her in a sudden fit of anger preyed on him so heavily he could not sleep until the babe was safely under his roof, her mother happy to collect a lifelong settlement from Nick.

"What's her name?"

"Emily, but she's always been called Emmie."

They began to mount the stairs. "What shall the child call me?" Fiona asked. "She can hardly call me mother, and Mrs. Birmingham's much too stuffy."

They reached the landing and began to mount a second stretch of stairs. "What about Lady Fiona?" he asked.

Just then, Fiona's foot slipped. Her scream was followed by the sickening thump of her body tumbling down the stairs.

His heart thundering in his chest, he whirled to her and lunged, hoping to stop her descent.

He watched in horror as she bounced down half a dozen steps before her left leg jammed into the space between the banister's spindles, jerking her to a painful stop—right after he heard the harrowing sound of her bone snapping.

Chapter 9

Floating between dream and reality, Fiona was not precisely sure where she was when she heard her husband barking orders. "You will use a sedan chair to convey Mrs. Birmingham anywhere she desires to go, inside the house. Under no circumstances is she to put weight on her leg."

Had Nick's mother injured her leg? Fiona wondered.

"And Biddles," he said to the butler, "see to it that the laudanum stores are replenished. She took a devilishly large amount of it."

"As you wish, Mr. Birmingham."

Laudanum? Fiona had only taken the opiate once before, and she had felt . . . exactly as fuzzy as she felt right now. She suddenly remembered stumbling down the stairs. She also remembered the stab of pain so excruciating that unconsciousness was the only relief from it.

She tried to move her injured left leg and found that not only was it immobile but it was also considerably heavier than it had been earlier that afternoon. She lifted her head to look at it. The movement attracted Nick's notice. He rushed to her bedside, clasping her hand within both of his. "How do you feel, love?" he asked in a gentle voice.

"Woozy." It was difficult to get the words out, and when she did, her voice seem strangely detached. In her mind's eye she saw elongated letters forming the single word she had uttered.

"The surgeon's just left," he explained. "He set your leg and cautioned me to see that you stay in bed at least for the first week."

Her swirling sense of well-being was punctured by something dark and menacing. "But I've got to . . ." She could not remember what it was she had to do, but she knew whatever it was could not be done from this bed.

This bed . . . Where was she? Her eyes coming fully open, she looked around the green bedchamber that was unmistakably feminine. "Where am I?" she asked groggily.

"In Verity's room. I thought it would suit you better than Mother's."

She collapsed back into the pillows. So she was at Nick's house. South of the Thames. "My leg?"

"Is broken," he answered, squeezing her hand. "Are you in pain?"

"No. I perceive that laudanum has been administered."

He tenderly swiped at her brow. "You're to take it whenever you feel the need."

"But it makes me so . . . slow. How ever will I see to furnishings for the new house?"

"I'll send for Trevor Simpson. He'll be able to carry out your orders."

A slow smile spread over her face. "Now I see why you're so good at business. You're able to adapt instantly to changes."

There was one other matter that concerned her, but

she was not able to remember what it was. Something important, she was sure.

"The surgeon stressed that for the first few days you mustn't get out of bed. To do so would cause more swelling."

Bed! That was it! How was she to share a bed with her husband? Even worse, how could they possibly manage to make love when she could not even move her leg? Her insides clenched. Her husband was a most virile man. Quite naturally, he would return to Miss Foley to satisfy his bedroom needs. The idea of him slaking his need between the actress's thighs caused Fiona more pain than her broken leg. A tear began to seep along her cheek.

"What's the matter?" Nick demanded. "Are you hurting? Shall I procure more laudanum for you?"

She swatted at her glistening cheek. "I'm distressed, dearest, because I do so want to share my bed with you."

He sighed with relief and bent to brush a gentle kiss over her lips. "Perhaps by next week," he murmured, "we'll be able to resume some of those . . . activities— if I'm very careful."

The memory of everyone she had ever known who had suffered a broken leg flashed through her mind. Once the leg was properly set and once the swelling had gone down they had been able to resume limited activity. She recalled how surprised the surgeon had been when Stephen, her younger brother, fully recovered from his broken leg in a mere six weeks. Of course Mama had been alive then and had seen to it that he did not put his weight on the leg for the entire six weeks—and forbade him to ever climb another tree.

Six weeks. Were the time in the past, it would seem fleeting, but in the future it seemed to stretch on endlessly. And she had so much to do to ready the new house and to begin planning the come-out ball for Miss Peabody and Verity.

And then there was her fledgling marriage to consider. She did not at all like to think of Nick rushing to that odious actress.

So she pouted.

"What's the matter, love?" he asked.

"I don't wish to sleep away from you."

"But we can't—" He paused. "I understand your reluctance to sleep alone in a strange room. Would you like me to have a cot brought in so that I can sleep beside you?"

She shook her head. "This bed's big enough for both of us."

"I can't risk that. My movements might harm your leg."

"It's been splinted properly, I'm sure. Knowing you, I would say you procured the services of the finest surgeon your money could buy."

"Of course, but I can't sleep in this bed, Fiona," he said sternly. "Were I to bump your leg in my sleep, it could cause you excruciating pain—and it might even reinjure it."

"I'll sleep on the left side of the bed. You'll be on my good side." She met his unwavering gaze. "Are you not strong enough to lie beside me and not wish to . . . ?"

"That's not it! I'm not so shallow that I wouldn't put my wife's welfare above my own fleeting pleasure."

Fleeting pleasure? Was that all their lovemaking was to him?

Another tear sprouted.

And Nick sighed. "I can see the laudanum's making you maudlin. Very well, I'll sleep with you. But no kissing. No touching. Do you understand?"

She favored him with a broad smile as she nodded.

Balancing a cup of warm milk in one hand while easing open her door with the other, Nick came to her bedchamber that night. "I've brought you warm milk," he said, moving to the bed and setting the cup on the night table. "Allow me to help you up."

When he closed an arm around her and began to lift her upper torso, she winced.

He froze. "Am I hurting you?"

She sank back. "I believe I'll have some more laudanum, please."

He cursed under his breath, berating himself, if she wasn't mistaken. "If I put it into your milk, will you promise to drink all of it?"

She answered him with a wan nod.

He mixed the drought and offered it to her. "Perhaps it will be more comfortable for you to prop yourself up on your right elbow. I'm devilishly afraid of hurting you."

It took her a full minute to raise herself enough to sip the milk. After three swift sips, she stopped and met his concerned gaze. "Did you heat the milk yourself?"

"I did."

"That was very thoughtful of you, Nick."

"I didn't do it out of thoughtfulness. Guilt, more likely. I should have had your arm when we mounted the stairs."

"It's certainly not your fault your wife is so clumsy." She did not like that her voice resembled that of a person in a drunken stupor.

"My wife most certainly is *not* clumsy. You're the most elegant woman I know."

This husband of hers was most charming, especially given the fact that any physical attributes she might have possessed were sadly lacking at the present. Not only was she slurring her words, but her hair was a tangled mess, and her clothing was hopelessly wrinkled. She had no wish to peer into a looking glass. "I can't stay in this wretched dress. Did you know there's dried blood on it?"

He nodded. "As much as I disliked another man seeing your body, I asked the surgeon if we should remove it, but he said it wasn't necessary."

"Perhaps not then, but now. I can't receive visitors like this."

He stood up straight and glared at her. "You're not going to be receiving visitors."

"What about Trevor?"

"I forgot about him," Nick said with a frown. "So you fancy getting pretty for that milksop?"

"And for you." Dear God, what was she saying? The laudanum had the same effect on her as the overindulgence of liquor. She was babbling on to this man she had married—and quite embarrassing herself.

"You don't have to wear anything to please me," he said.

She gave him a seductive grin. "Yes, I know."

"That's not what I meant."

"Nevertheless, I desire to put on a light muslin morning dress. One *without* blood, if you please."

"Should I send for your maid?"

"I don't trust her not to hurt me. I know you'll not hurt me, Nick."

"Very well. I believe your maid unpacked your things before . . . the accident." He walked to the linen press and opened it. "Which do you desire, my lady?"

"The one with little lavender buds."

He took the dress and came to set it on her bed. "I'm beastly afraid of hurting you."

"I thought perhaps you could pull me up, and I could lift away the skirts. Then you could set me back down and remove the entire gown."

He winced. "Let's try," he said, bending to her and cupping his hands under her arms, "but we stop if it hurts you." Then he lifted her as easily as he would a piece of parchment.

She fumbled with her skirts, pushing them clear of her hips before she plopped back down. "Painless," she assured him.

"I hope the laudanum's not masking your pain to the point where you'll hurt yourself."

She fell back into the pillows. "I'll have some more. Please."

He stood over her while she finished the cup. "Let's try removing the dress now."

Once she had eased herself back up, he was able to remove the dress and the chemise in mere seconds.

"You can't possibly sleep in those stays," he said in a low voice, coming closer and beginning to untie the laces. The proximity of those long fingers of his so close to her breasts sent her nipples puckering— and sent a blush to her face. Once the laces were loosened she raised her arms, and he lifted off the corset. Her gaze flicked to the pointed nubs in the center of her breasts, and her blush deepened. Nick was sure to notice.

She was powerless not to remember the feel of him weighing her breasts, of him taking them into his mouth. Perhaps it was the laudanum that magnified her sexuality. She began to throb between her legs. A pity neither of them could act upon her seductive mood. She found herself wishing the week were behind them, wishing they could lie together again as man and wife. Her gaze lifted to him, but he directed his full attention to the fresh garment.

"Raise you arms," he instructed.

Her arms held high, she stayed as still as a rock while he assisted her into the muslin dress, then he stood back and gazed at her. "Lovely. Now, my dear, you need to go to sleep." He moved to the bedside table and extinguished the candle.

She lay back and watched as he stood there and removed all his clothing, the firelight flickering on the solid planes of his utterly masculine body. This was the first time she had seen him naked when he was not aroused, and she admired him all the more for his self-discipline.

He slowly eased himself onto the right side of the bed. "Are you all right?" he whispered.

"I assure you I didn't feel the movement at all." Each word she had uttered had been a struggle, like swimming against a swiftly moving stream.

He kissed the air. "Go to sleep now, love."

Love. She liked the way that word sounded on his lips. Even though he couldn't possibly mean it.

While she waited for sleep to envelop her, she recalled how patient and loving he had been with his mother, who was not an easy woman to admire. He was a good son. A good brother. And now a good husband.

Nick lay still beside her long after she'd slipped into a deep sleep. He was afraid to move for fear of hurting her leg, afraid to go to sleep because she might need him. A thousand times today he had cursed himself for allowing her to fall. For as long as he lived he would remember the sound of her delicate body thumping down the stairs, the horrifying sound of her femur snapping in two.

And he would never forget the paralyzing seconds when he feared she was plunging to her death. Even now as he thought about it, his stomach twisted.

She was so very precious to him. Last night he had offered up thanks to the bandits that had brought her into his life. Tonight he offered up thanks that her life had been spared.

There was no other place on earth that he would rather be than beside her, his cherished wife.

* * *

"A Mr. Trevor Simpson to see you, madame," the butler announced the following afternoon.

Shutting her eyes against the pain, Fiona pulled herself into a sitting position. "Show him in."

Trevor rushed into the room, practically dressed for court in pumps and silken finery—including a bright violet satin vest. She was awfully glad Nick wasn't here to poke fun of him.

"Oh, my poor darling!" Trevor shrieked as he hurried to her bed. "I shouldn't have let you marry that beastly man. It's bad enough that he has you living *south* of the Thames, but now he's gone and allowed you to break your leg." He pulled a chair up to her bedside and sat down. "I brought flowers. The maid's fetching water for them."

"That was most kind of you, but I must ask that you not malign my husband. He's really quite a dear, and he's dreadfully upset that I've broken my leg."

"As well he should be. The beast."

Her brows lowered. "I'll not permit you to speak of my husband in such a way."

Trevor studied her through narrowed eyes for a moment. "It's beastly unfair that one man be so blessed. That demmed Birmingham's not only handsome and muscled and *tall*, but he has quite a way with the ladies. I believe you've fallen in love with the fellow."

"Love was never part of the bargain I struck with Nick." She was almost sorry there had been no time for a courtship for she wondered if she and Nick might have fallen in love. But if she had to choose between a courtship and being pleasured in his bed, she was ashamed to say she would take the bed. Still, love *and* sublime sex would be the only ingredients needed for a perfect marriage. A pity she and Nick had only one of the ingredients.

"You can't fool me," Trevor said, folding elegant hands in his lap while avoiding her gaze.

While Trevor did know her better than anyone, he was wrong this time. She couldn't possibly be in love with Nick. She had only known him for a few days. Not like with Edward, whom she had known almost her whole life—and loved for half her life.

"Now tell me how this wretched accident happened," Trevor said.

"There's little to tell. I slipped and fell down the stairs, and the pity of it is that my wretched left leg jammed between the bannister posts and snapped in two."

Trevor grimaced and held out the palm of one hand. "I beg that you not say another word about the ghastly incident, or I shall faint straight away."

She thanked God Nick was not so squeamish. "You can't faint, for I need you desperately."

He leaped from his chair and outstretched an imaginary cape as he fell to one knee. "I am at your service, my lady."

Fiona giggled. "I shall need your help in decorating the new mansion on Piccadilly. It's finished now, you know."

He smiled like a drunken sailor. "I'm quite dying to see it."

"Good. I'll need you to go there this afternoon. We'll need to procure furnishings and draperies and objets d'art."

His positive glow had her grinning. "I've just the cabinetmaker for you! He's from the Sheraton school and does the most stunning work."

"Then see if you can get his catalogues for us to study."

"Will your husband wish to incorporate any items from this residence?" There was disdain in his voice when he alluded to "this residence."

"He says I've carte blanche to procure all new furnishings."

"Then his pockets are even deeper than has been speculated."

She shrugged. "He has the most wonderful stables down at Camden Hall."

"So he's the one who bought Lord Hartley's place? A scrumptious estate."

"Indeed it is. I didn't want to return to London."

Trevor's nose wrinkled. "Especially to *south* of the Thames."

With a haughty lift to her chin, she said, "This is a perfectly lovely home."

"I'll grant," Trevor said, flicking lint from his charcoal breeches, "the man has exceedingly good taste."

"As do you. That's why I need you to help with the new house."

There was a tap at her chamber door.

"Yes?" Fiona asked.

The parlormaid opened the door. "Your flowers, madame."

Trevor got up and took them.

"Oh, Trev! They're lovely," Fiona said, eying the nosegay of violets and primrose. "Thank you."

He placed them beside the bed. "I'd best be off now to see the showplace. I'll also try to see the cabinetmaker today. We can dive into the project tomorrow."

Nick left the Exchange early that day. He couldn't dislodge Fiona from his thoughts. Was she in pain? Would she be lonely in the strange house? What if she needed something and no one helped her? He had instructed his servants to see to her every need and had asked her maid to sit with her, but Fiona had insisted she didn't need a companion. "I have a book to read," she had told him. "Go now. I'll be fine."

But as the day wore on, his worry for her mounted. So he stormed from the floor of the Exchange, called for his gig to be brought around, and hastened home to his ailing wife.

Relief rushed over him when he saw her sitting up in Verity's bed, her head bent to the book in her lap, sun from a half-dozen casements dappling over her as she looked up at him and smiled.

God but she was lovely! And delicate. And so very dear to him. He rushed to her side and pressed a kiss to her cheek. "How are you feeling, love?" he asked as he stood gazing down at her fair countenance.

"Much better now that you've come." She patted the mattress beside her.

"Are you sure my weight won't disturb your leg?"

"Yes, I'm sure, silly. I've actually succeeded in lifting the leg off the bed today."

"I wish you wouldn't."

"I vow it didn't hurt."

"Still taking the laudanum?"

"I've been able to reduce the dose by a third. My mother was exceedingly wary of the overuse of laudanum. In fact, she refused to take it when . . . she was dying."

His poor Fiona. She'd lost so many loved ones. And now she could possibly lose Randolph. "Wretched losing both your parents, but I vow to care for you as diligently as they would have." What had possessed him to make such a telling declaration? His wife didn't want his love. She wanted his money. And perhaps his body.

But not his heart.

There was a rap at the door.

"Come in," Nick said, turning to watch Biddles stroll into the chamber holding a letter. "A page from her ladyship's former house just delivered this."

Fiona and Nick looked at each other. "The kidnappers," they both said at once.

Chapter 10

His face grim, Nick handed the letter to Fiona, who quickly raised up from the bed and tore it open. When she peered at the writing, her heart skidded. The letter was in Randy's own handwriting. As her eyes skimmed over the single page, she was at once elated that he was still alive at the same time a knot of worry lodged in her chest.

My Dearest Sister,

It's devilishly distasteful for me to have to write you, knowing that Papa could not have left much money, but my captors have instructed me to pen this letter to instruct you or your agent to deliver the twenty-five thousand guineas to Figueria, a village just north of Portugal's Mondego Bay. You or your agent are to arrive at the St. Michael's Inn on January 8 and use the surname Hollingsworth. Further instructions will be forthcoming.

I beg that you are successful because I have no doubts these vile creatures who've already treated me so cruelly will kill me if you're not.

Her heart caught painfully at the last sentence, and tears brimmed her eyes. With a shaking hand, she handed Nick the note.

He nodded as he read, and when he was finished, he met her gaze. "Don't worry. We'll free him."

"What do you do now?" she asked in a forlorn voice.

"William will be dispatched within the hour."

"But we've got eight more days until the eighth. I wouldn't think he'd need more than three days to reach Portugal."

He did not answer for a moment, and she knew her pragmatic husband was analyzing the situation and developing a strategy. "It's vital to my plan," he finally said, "that William arrive early."

Her brows dipped. "Why? What plan?"

"William will arrive in Figueria several days early, take rooms under the name Hollingsworth, and instruct the innkeeper—with a generous bribe to ensure compliance—to give his own letter to whoever delivers a message to Mr. Hollingsworth. I'm counting on the fact that the innkeeper will alert his staff to be expecting a letter for Hollingsworth and be prepared to conduct the exchange of letters."

"And what will William's letter say?"

"It will demand that the exchange be made in the village plaza. Being fairly certain the exchange would occur in Portugal, I've taken the liberty of studying all the coastal towns. Figueria, like most Portuguese towns, is possessed of a central plaza."

"You're worried about William?"

"As you are worried about Randolph. I have no desire for William to be robbed and killed in some remote mountain area. His letter will explain that he'll have the money in a wagon in the plaza for the captors to examine before turning over your brother. The letter will warn them that until the time of the exchange—the time to be set by the captors—the wagon will be guarded by heavily armed men day and night. At the time of the exchange our men who are manning the bell tower of the plaza's church will disperse."

Her eyes rounded. "Heavily armed men?"

Nick nodded. "The Birminghams are used to conveying large sums of money across the continent. We have our own small, well-trained, well-armed guards. A dozen experienced men will travel with Will."

She slumped. "I'm afraid the captors won't comply. Why should they allow you to make the decisions? Won't they fear being ambushed upon entering the city?"

"An ambush would only result in your brother's death. I'd much rather have him than the twenty-five thousand guineas. The letter will convey that Lord Agar's safety is our first concern."

"How will they know that after Randy's turned over, your men won't massacre them?"

"Because—as the letter will convey—our men will lay down their arms before Lord Agar can be freed."

She closed her eyes and spoke in a fragile voice. "It's all so terrifying."

He set a sturdy hand over hers. "I know."

She knew he was as terrified for his own brother's safety as she was for Randy's.

"How can William be sure the released man is my brother?"

"Have you a likeness of him?"

A gentle smile lifted the corners of her mouth. "I have the miniature he had made for Mama, but it's quite outdated. It was painted nearly ten years ago, when he first reached his majority."

"Where is it?"

"In my reticule. I carry it with me wherever I go."

Nick stood over her bed, looking down at her. "You miss him that much?"

"All I have left are my two brothers."

"You have me," he murmured.

She understood that Nick's assurances had not been made out of jealousy toward her brothers but out of consideration for her, to let her know there was one more person now in her family who cared about her. And even though she knew he didn't love her, she was beginning to believe he would have the same loyalty toward her that he had for his mother and Verity and his brothers. "You've been an enormous comfort to me," she said. "I cannot bear to contemplate what would have become of Randy or me had you not come into my life."

A smile curved his lips. "You would have married some old peer who wouldn't have pleasured you in bed as I have."

"Nicholas Birmingham! How can you speak of *that* at a time like this?"

Chuckling to himself, he crossed the room and found her reticule. "Is this where you keep your brother's miniature?"

"Yes. I'll get it."

He shot an amused glance at her. "You don't want me sifting through your reticule?"

"As a matter of fact, I don't!"

He brought her the beaded bag, and she removed her brother's likeness and gave it to him. That she carried a vinaigrette—which she never had occasion to use—embarrassed her. She did not wish for Nick to think her some weakling prone to fainting fits.

Before he left, he bent down to press a kiss to her forehead. His masculine scent was a blend of sandalwood and exotic tobacco. "You're not to move at all while I'm gone," he cautioned.

After he left she became more acutely aware of the throbbing pain in her leg but decided she would see if she could go without the laudanum—at least until

Nick returned. Her eyes shut tightly against the pain, she settled back into the mound of pillows. Were she to break all her limbs, the suffering could not compare to the agony of losing her brother. She hoped to God Nick was dealing with Randy's captors in the right way—if there could ever be a right way to deal with criminals like the brutes who had abducted Randy.

Randy's admission that his captors had abused him disturbed her deeply. Had he suffered any broken bones? Were they starving him? Her chest tight, her stomach tumbling, she did not know how she could stand it until her brother returned safely. She lay there for a long time, steeped in gloom, then she finally forced herself to use the bell Nick had left on her bedside table to ring for a servant.

Biddles came. "Yes, madame?"

"I wish to speak with the governess. What is her name?"

"Miss Beckham."

Ten minutes later a woman who was a few years older than Fiona hesitantly entered the room. Fiona was immediately relieved that the governess was not even tolerably pretty. The notion of Nick living under the same roof with a pretty unmarried woman—before he was married—had caused Fiona considerable trepidation. Why anything that happened before they were wed should matter to her, Fiona could not understand. Nevertheless, her jealousy was a fact.

She perused the woman for a moment. Dressed quite properly in gray bombazine, Miss Beckham presented a most tidy figure. Her black hair was swept back so tightly that not a single strand dared stray loose. She was rather taller than average and rather thinner than average, with a somewhat gaunt face which had as its only distinguishing feature a pair of brilliant blue eyes. "Mrs. Birmingham?" the governess said tentatively.

"Please sit in the chair by my bed," Fiona said. "Forgive me for not sitting. You've heard the particulars of my foolish accident, have you not?"

"I have, madame, and I'm very sorry for your misfortune."

Miss Beckham's voice was genteel, and her manners were all that could be expected. After she sat, Fiona asked, "I wish for you to tell me all about your pupil."

Not replying for a moment, Miss Beckham seemed taken aback. "Miss Emmie," she finally replied, "is not as enamored of books as I would have liked, though she is a most capable reader. I've found that she learns more quickly than other pupils I've taught in the past. Her greatest talent is in mathematics—and she seems to love working with sums."

"Like her father," Fiona said with affection. "What of the more feminine pursuits you've been instructing her in?"

"She's coming along nicely at the pianoforte, and her French is tolerable—for one who's studied it but for two years. Her penmanship and artistic talent, I'm afraid to say, are quite deplorable."

Fiona laughed. "I daresay she should have been a boy."

"Miss Emmie, I think, would rather have been a boy. She's happiest in the country. She loves being outdoors, and she loves riding and being around animals."

It was no surprise to Fiona that the child loved animals. After all she had neither siblings nor intercourse with other children. *She's probably lonely*, Fiona thought with a flicker of pity.

Fiona wondered if the child ever rode with her father. "Does the young lady, my stepdaughter," she managed in a wobbly voice, surprising herself that she would even consider accepting the child of a whore as her very own stepdaughter, "ever ride with her father?"

"Oh, yes, madame. Often. He taught her to ride himself."

The image of Nick patiently riding alongside the child warmed her. His heart was so big, with room enough for all the people who mattered to him. "Would you say Miss Emmie is fond of her father?"

"I would say she thinks he hung the stars in the sky."

For the briefest of seconds, Fiona wondered if Miss Beckham might share her pupil's admiration for Nick. He *was* so devilishly handsome. And he was nice, too. She wondered if he was nice to Miss Beckham. "Does Miss Emmie have any friends?"

"No, madame."

A child without friends? How unfortunate. Then Fiona realized even in the country, the child's only neighbor would be her own grandmother, who abhorred the child. Since none of Nick's siblings had wed, there were not even any cousins with whom the little girl could play. "Poor Emmie."

"Miss Emmie is certainly not a poor little girl. I've never seen a child as indulged as she. I daresay no little girl in the kingdom is possessed of more lovely dresses or dolls than she."

Things money could buy, not things the child truly needed, things like friends—or a mother. "I suppose it's her lack of a mother that has made her a bit of a tomboy," Fiona said.

Miss Beckham shrugged. "She's always been cared for by women. First, her nurse, Winnie, whose marriage resulted in my hiring."

"Do you think the girl was attached to her nurse?"

The governess's face turned hard, her mouth thinning with disapproval. "She was far too attached to that Winnie."

Was Miss Beckham jealous? "Does she still see her nurse?"

Miss Beckham's stiff posture reminded Fiona of

her own governess, who had unfailingly instructed Fiona to pretend there was a pole fused to her spine. "No, madame," the governess replied. "Winnie returned to her village and has never returned to London, having her own babes to care for now—though she corresponds with Miss Emmie, and Miss Emmie eagerly looks forward to receiving her letters."

I suppose those are the only letters the child has ever received. Poor child.

Fiona sighed. "Thank you, Miss Beckham, for answering my questions. You are, no doubt, aware that we will be moving in the near future?"

"Oh, yes, madame. I've seen the new house from the outside. It's magnificent."

Fiona, having developed an affinity for the place where she and Nick would officially begin their married life, swelled with pride. "Your chambers there," Fiona said, "will, quite naturally, be larger than what you have here. Is there any particular request you wish to make for furnishings?"

"The furnishings in my chambers at present are quite adequate, but I thank you for inquiring," Miss Beckham said as she moved to get up.

After she was gone Fiona pondered the child, the child she had just claimed as her stepdaughter, the child Nick obviously cared about. How could Fiona not accept the little girl when Nick had been so generous to her and her family? After all, it wasn't as if she had to appear in public with the little girl. Nick had obviously married a viscount's daughter in order to heighten his station in life, and trotting out an illegitimate child would threaten the shaky foundation of that newfound station.

Fiona considered summoning Emmie but decided to wait until her leg began to heal. Were the child to see her now, she might be frightened, or she might develop the impression that her new stepmother was frail, neither prospect acceptable to Fiona.

As they sped to the Thames dock where Nick's yacht was harbored, Nick imparted his instructions to his younger brother. "Your letter must stress three things: first, that Lord Agar's safe return is your uppermost concern; second, that the exchange must take place in the plaza; and third, the wagon with the money will be guarded around the clock until the time set by the captors for the exchange, at which time your men will disperse from their stations and lay down their arms."

"Then I'll need another contingent of men to guard the other twenty-five thousand guineas you're making me bring for the purchase of francs," William said.

"I've already thought of that. Instead of the usual eight, you'll find twelve men waiting at the *Athena*. Is the money concealed at present below the false bottom of the storage space beneath your coach seats?"

William nodded. "Yes, under the false bottom of the seats. It has been guarded around the clock since the day before your wedding. By the way, felicitations on your wife. She's remarkably beautiful." His green eyes flashing good-naturedly, William inched back and directed an amused glance at his brother. "How are you recommending matrimony?"

"Zealously," Nick said with a chuckle.

It was dark when they reached the dock. Nick got out of his coach and, bracing against the cold wind, stood on the weathered dock to watch as Will's coach was brought aboard the *Athena*. His glance flicked to his little brother, who was dressed for traveling in Hessians, buff breeches, and brown topcoat, his carelessly tied cravat a stark contrast to his tanned face. As his glance trailed over William's muscular body,

Nick was dismayed that this capable man was his baby brother. Heaven help Nick if anything ever happened to the lad.

Once everything was loaded onto the ship, William turned to Nick, smiling cheerfully.

"Take care," Nick said, a gnawing ache in the pit of his stomach.

"I always do."

Long after William boarded the vessel, Nick stood beneath the lantern light and somberly watched as the yacht began to power down the Thames.

Chapter 11

Fiona was feeling decidedly sorry for herself. It had been two weeks since she had broken her leg, and she was coming to think of Nick's house as her prison. Not that it wasn't a perfectly nice house. The rooms were well appointed and relatively spacious, and since the first week she had not been confined to just her bedchamber, or, rather, Verity's bedchamber. The servants carried her in a sedan chair to any room she desired. But she was getting devilishly tired of the same set of rooms and the same set of faces—mostly servants, except for Nick and Trevor, both of whom were exceedingly solicitous of her.

Trevor had been an enormous help in readying the new house. He'd brought her catalogues and assisted her in making selections. And because her husband's pockets were deep, they had been able to jump over the cabinetmaker's waiting list and been assured they could procure all the furnishings they desired within the next six weeks.

She hoped her leg would be entirely mended in six weeks. As much as she hated the forced inactivity, she hated even more the ugly leather sheath she wore from the base of her hips to her ankle. Even though

her dresses covered the ugly brown leather of the surgeon's bonesetting apparatus, Nick viewed it nightly
when he helped her dress for bed. She felt less than
attractive.

But her husband did not seem to find her unat-
tractive at all. After the first week they had resumed
intimacies—not the same intimacies as before, for
Nick refused to mount her. But oh how he pleasured
her! Using only his wondrously deft hands, he had
brought her to climax more times than she could
count. He had paid homage to her body, reverently
kissing along its pulsepoints, precisely where the
erotic effect was greatest.

And she had often curled her greedy hand around
his stiff shaft and pulsed it until she brought him to
his deliciously groaning release.

The resumption of his normal business activity
kept Nick away from the house until nightfall and left
her irritable in his absence.

Being irritable was not the way she wished to be
when she met her stepdaughter. Though Fiona would
rather have waited until she was completely mended
to meet the child, she knew that delaying the meeting would send the wrong message to Emmie. The
little girl would be sure to think the woman her papa
had married had no interest in her, which was far from
the truth.

So this morning Fiona had instructed Miss Beckham that she wished to have a private nuncheon
with Emmie, then remembering how fond children
were of sweets and suspecting that Miss Beckham
was unlikely to indulge that particular appetite, Fiona
ordered that a tray with a variety of sweetmeats be
brought. When the time for the nuncheon drew
close, Fiona was carried downstairs to the gold dining
room, which was flooded with light from a half-dozen
tall casements, and she tucked herself up to the table,

hoping the child would not notice her use of the invalid's chair.

She had requested that Miss Emmie have a demi-tasse cup, which turned out to be identical to Fiona's eggshell-thin cup in every way except its smaller size.

Fiona found herself growing nervous as she waited for Emmie. If she were this nervous, how must the poor child feel? Really, she cautioned herself, she must quit using the word *poor* when thinking of Emmie.

The dining room door creaked halfway open. Fiona looked up to see Emmie standing there, half in the room, half out, a somber look on her lovely little face. She wore a freshly starched, white muslin dress that stopped just above her pale blue satin slippers and was caught below the bodice with ribbands in the same shade of blue as her slippers. Her clothes were so scrupulously elegant she looked like a miniature lady of the *ton*.

She was an extremely pretty child with fair skin, a dusting of light freckles across her nose, and long curls the light brown Fiona imagined would result from blending her father's dark hair with that of a blond woman. In Emmie, Nick's and his mother's high cheekbones had found their way to still another generation, and eyes the same shade of green as Dolina Birmingham's shone from Emmie's worried little face. How could Nick's mother not embrace this child?

"Good afternoon, Emmie," Fiona said cheerfully. "Won't you please come sit by me?"

Not removing her frightened gaze from Fiona, the child crept closer.

"Here, love," Fiona said, patting the chair at her right. Why, Fiona wondered, had she gone and called the child *love*? They had never even met before. But something in the little girl's petrified demeanor had coaxed the tender word.

Fiona suddenly recalled a distant memory of herself as a frightened seven-year-old shipped off to a stern aunt while her mother experienced a difficult breeding. It had been years since she had thought of that terrifying feeling of isolation.

Emmie climbed up on the chair beside Fiona and folded tiny hands in her lap. Despite that her father was tall, Emmie seemed small for a child of eight. Had Fiona not known her age, she would have guessed the child no more than six.

"How nice of you to join me," Fiona said. "I've been greatly looking forward to making your acquaintance. I would have met you sooner had I not gone and injured myself."

The little girl nodded. "Miss Beckham said you fell down the stairs and broke your leg." Emmie was possessed of the sweetest, cultured voice.

"I did, indeed. One must be careful to always hold the rail when using stairs."

"Does it still hurt?"

"My leg?"

Emmie nodded.

"Yes, actually it does. I do *not* recommend broken bones." Fiona reached for the tray of sweets and held it out the child. "You're to select whatever you want. This is a very special occasion, and you're to eat to your heart's content."

The little girl's eyes rounded, and a smile swept over her somber face as she contemplated the dazzling array. Among the offerings were candied fruits, rolled wafers, toad-in-the hole biscuits, cocoa nuts in sugar, and plum pudding. Before she made her selection, she peered up at her stepmother. "I'm really to have as much as I like?"

Fiona smiled down benevolently and nodded. "One of each, if you like."

Emmie happily proceeded to pile her plate high with a sampling of all the offerings while Fiona filled the child's demitasse cup with tea, to which she added a considerable amount of sugar and cream.

Fiona watched indulgently as Emmie tried to eat with the table manners in which she had so obviously been instructed but which she was too young to have mastered. The result was that, while she kept her mouth sealed as she chewed, smudges of berries and chocolates and dribbles of cream ringed that pleasant little mouth as she chewed. And crumbs and globs found their way to the lap of her pristine white dress. Fiona fought back the desire to laugh.

While nibbling on a square of plum pudding, Fiona watched the child eagerly sampling every item on her plate. "Which do think is your favorite?" Fiona asked.

"The plum pudding." With her tiny hands, she shoved the rest of the pudding into her mouth. When all of the plum pudding had been eaten, Emmie sank back into her seat and sighed.

"Can't finish?"

The little girl shook her head woefully.

Fiona ignored the urge to wipe Emmie's smudged face and hands. She did not want to be perceived as being dictatorial. *Let Miss Beckham play that role.*

Now that Emmie had eaten, they could talk. "Have you any questions you'd like to ask me, Emmie?" Fiona inquired.

Emmie nodded. "What am I to call you? Miss Beckham says you're not going to be my mother."

Did that mean Emmie had hoped for a mother? Poor thing. "I've been thinking about that myself," Fiona admitted. "Most people have always called me 'My Lady.' Do you think you could call me that?"

"If you're a lady, does that make Papa a lord?" Emmie asked.

Fiona laughed. "No. I'm a lady because my papa was a lord."

"Are all ladies pretty like you?"

"I'm flattered that you find me pretty, and I'll tell you a secret."

Emmie's smile spread across her face as she eagerly bent closer to Fiona.

"I think you're the prettiest little girl I've ever seen."

"Really?" Emmie asked.

"Really. And you're very well mannered, too. I shall tell Miss Beckham how impressed I am."

That comment seemed to please the girl.

"Miss Beckham tells me you're especially fond of being outdoors," Fiona said.

A shadow of disappointment fell across Emmie's face. "Nurse used to take me out whenever I wished, but Miss Beckham prefers being indoors."

"Do you miss your nurse? Winnie was her name, as I recall."

Emmie nodded with enthusiasm. "I used to pretend Winnie was my mother because I never had a real mother. When I told Winnie I had no mother, she told me everybody has a real mother."

Fiona stiffened. "Did she—or your father—tell you about your real mother?"

"Papa will not speak of her, but Winnie said she's dead."

The kindly nurse must have been trying to protect Emmie's tender emotions. Better a dead mother than a mother who chose not to be with her own child.

"You're fortunate, then, to have such a fine man for your father."

Tears sprang to Emmie's eyes, and she whirled her face away so Fiona wouldn't see.

"What's the matter, love?" Fiona asked, her voice a melodious whisper. Good Lord, surely Nick had not abused the child in any way! But as quickly as the thought flickered, it died. Fiona knew he was incapable of slighting a loved one in any way.

Emmie shook her little head.

Fiona decided to give the child time to pull herself together, but as the seconds mounted, Emmie could no longer contain her pent-up woes and burst into long, wrenching sobs.

Finally, Fiona could stand it no longer. She settled a gentle hand on Emmie's heaving shoulder and said, "You must tell me why you're so distressed, love."

"I can't."

"I wish you would. Perhaps I can help."

Emmie's head shook frantically. "No, you've already married him."

Fiona's chest tightened. Did Emmie resent that Fiona had married her father? "Tell me, Emmie," Fiona said in a semi-stern voice, "are you afraid that because your father's married me he won't have time for you anymore?"

Her little head nodding, Emmie wailed.

Stroking Emmie's soft curls, Fiona spoke in a gentle voice. "You mustn't worry. Your papa has the biggest heart, and in it there is a special chamber for each of his loved ones."

"But he s-s-said I was his favorite girl, and you're s-s-so pretty—" She stopped to suck in a deep breath. "He won't want to be with me anymore."

"That's nonsense," Fiona said sternly. "You'll always be your papa's favorite girl—just as I'll be his favorite woman." *God willing.*

"But Miss Beckham said it likely you and Papa will have more little girls—"

The very idea unfurled a deep warmth throughout Fiona. "And if we should, you will always be your papa's first little girl—and you'll always be the first in his heart."

Fiona gave Emmie her napkin to dry her tears, then Emmie looked up at her, her eyes red and swollen. She looked utterly forlorn, and it tore at Fiona's heart. "Do you really think so?" Emmie asked.

"Oh, I know so. You see, I'm coming to know your father quite well, and it's perfectly clear to me how important you are to him. No other little girl would ever hold the place in his heart that you occupy."

A tap sounded at the door, and Biddles entered, his gaze darting from Fiona's face to Emmie's tear-stained one. Wretched bad luck, thought Fiona, that he had to enter the room just then. He was apt to think Fiona a wicked stepmother inducing an innocent child to tears.

"Mr. Trevor Simpson to see you, madame," the butler said.

"Show him into the drawing room," Fiona instructed. "I shall join him there in a moment."

Once the door was closed, Fiona turned to Emmie. "Now I wish for you to go clean yourself up because you're going on a special outing today."

"Where?"

"Have you ever been to the zoological gardens?"

Emmie shook her head, her sable curls bouncing. "Is that where they've got a real, live elephant?"

"Indeed it is, and I'm going to instruct Miss Beckham to take you there this very afternoon."

A smile replaced the woeful expression on Emmie's face as she bolted from the room, forgetting Fiona's existence.

Fiona wheeled herself into the drawing room. "And what have you brought me today, dearest Trevor?" she said as she entered the chamber.

"Good news, my lady."

Fiona hiked a brow.

"The blue saloon is finished, and it's quite breathtaking! The game tables you selected are exquisite."

Fiona's lower lip worked into a pout. "Would that I could see it."

Trevor directed a kindly gaze at her. "You've got the rest of your life to spend there." Then he pulled some squares of colored paper from his pocket. "I've found just the right shade of paint for the library."

"We'll *not* change the library, Trev. Nick selected the asparagus color himself, and I believe it will look wonderful with the dark woods in there."

Trevor pulled a face. "Really! What has that man done to so thoroughly manipulate you?" Under his breath, he mumbled, "Besides giving you twenty-five thousand bloody guineas."

"May I remind you, it is his house," Fiona said.

Trevor regarded her through narrowed eyes. "By God, the man must be devilishly good in bed!"

"Trevor! You've most certainly overstepped the bounds of propriety this time. You may be my oldest friend, but I cannot have you speaking of such deeply personal matters."

Laughing heartily, Trevor eyed her. "Because I'm your oldest friend, you can't hide things from me, darling. You're falling in love with the handsome Cit you've married!"

She shrugged. "It most certainly is *not* your business whether I love my husband or not." Of course, she wasn't *in love* with Nick, though she was coming to love him. Being in love was for those whose lives had been intertwined since childhood. Like with her and Warwick. But she would never repeat such a belief to Trevor. She owed it to Nick to convince everyone that she was in love with her husband. After all, he had done so much for her.

Her thoughts flitted to Randy, as they did every hour of the day. Tensing, she said a prayer for Randy's safe return.

"To return to the subject of your husband's library, I agree the green is luscious with the dark woods, but don't you think one room of dark wood's incongruous when all the rest of the rooms are bright and trimmed with gleaming white millwork and cornices?"

"To be an aesthetic purist, you are correct," she said, "but this is not a monument to good taste. It's a home. Nick wants the warmth of a library with dark woods, and I agree with him. All of our acquaintances who have the Palladian homes also manage to keep the traditional libraries."

Trevor gave a haughty harrumph. "And I thought Birmingham House was going to be revolutionary!"

"That was never our intent. We—you and I and Nick—wished it to be beautiful. Nothing more. In fact, I don't think Nick would be comfortable were the house to be too much a departure from the traditional. He's quite stodgy, you know."

"I really know very little about him—though I must say he has fine taste in women. You and Diane Foley are both quite magnificent."

Fiona stiffened. "I beg that you not speak of that woman in this house."

Trevor broke out laughing. "I prove my point. You *are* in love with him."

"Really, Trevor," she said with a stomp of her good foot, "I refuse to have this conversation with you."

At that moment the drawing room door came fully open, and Nick strode into the room. "Can't have what conversation?" he asked, skewering Trevor with a menacing glare.

"Trevor and I don't see eye to eye on the coloration of the library at the new house, dearest."

Tall and exceedingly handsome in charcoal breeches and finely tailored black coat, Nick crossed the room and kissed Fiona's cheek. "How is your leg, my dear?"

"Tolerable," she said with resignation.

His brows furrowed, then he turned to Trevor. "What is the dispute over the library?"

"The dispute, sir, has been settled. Lady Fiona is, as always, correct." Flicking a glance to Fiona, Trevor said, "I must be on my way. I've still to order that royal blue fabric for Birmingham's new bedchamber." He turned and nodded at Nick. "Your servant, Birmingham."

When he was gone, Fiona asked, "Are you quite all right, dearest?"

Nick flicked her an amused gaze. "Yes. Why do you ask?"

"Because it's but half past two in the afternoon. You're never home at this time."

"And you're worried over my welfare?" he said with amusement. "One would think you a concerned wife."

"Were you infirm, I certainly *would* care. I'm your wife, after all."

He smiled and came to sit on the settee closest to her invalid's chair. "As it happens, I was concerned about you. I know you're beastly sick of these surroundings, and when I saw how brilliantly the sun shone today I decided I'd come take you on an excursion. Where, Mrs. Birmingham, would you like to go?"

The prospect of an afternoon outing was as welcome as rain after a drought. "Oh, Nick, I'm so very eager for an outing. Could we go to our new house? Trevor said the blue saloon is complete, and I'm dying to see it."

"Then it's to Piccadilly we go." He summoned a footman to hoist her invalid's chair on top of the carriage, then he swept Fiona up into his arms and carried her to the coach.

On their way to the new house, she said, "I had a nice chat with Emmie today."

Nick tensed, and it was a moment before he spoke. "And how did you find the little scamp?"

"Besides being exceedingly pretty, I found her manners to be all that could be desired."

Though she didn't hear a sound, she could almost have sworn that Nick exhaled with relief. His whole countenance relaxed. Emmie must be very important to him.

"I assure you I was perfectly kind to her, but I must tell you the poor dear broke into tears."

He whirled toward her, his face clouded with worry.

"She confessed that she was afraid that since you've married me you will no longer find her your favorite girl."

Fiona had thought he might chuckle at his daughter's feminine jealousy, but instead he looked as if he had the weight of the world on his shoulders. "Were you able to assuage her fears?"

How had Nick known that is precisely what Fiona tried to do? That she would not look upon the child as her rival, as other stepmothers throughout history certainly had? "I told her she was your favorite girl, and that I am your favorite woman, and that your heart is very large and in it you've chambers for all those you love."

Nick took her hand and brought it to his lips. "Thank you."

"Thank *you* for having a chamber in your heart just for your vexing wife!"

His jet eyes whisked over her. "You're not vexing."

"You must admit this wretched injury has been most vexing, and now you're missing a session of the Exchange because of me."

"Because of you I've an excuse to enjoy this glorious day."

Glorious it was, despite the frigid air. As they pulled up to the new house, she was sorry that she hadn't thought to let Emmie see it. Tomorrow she would instruct Miss Beckham to bring her here, and she would arrange for Trevor to conduct a tour for the sole benefit of the master's daughter.

"What shall you name the house?" Fiona asked.

"We'll name it together. Have you any ideas?"

"Goodness, no. Do you know, Nick, it has never occurred to me that I would ever come into possession of a brand new house."

He nodded. "Because the houses in your family have been there for generations."

"Yes, I suppose so."

He lifted her from the carriage and installed her in the invalid's chair the coachman had taken down, then Nick wheeled her through the entry courtyard, tipped her weight to the back as he rolled her up the steps, and they came to pause in the opulent entry hall that centered the house.

"Trevor commended you on your selection of chandeliers," she said.

His gaze swept over the ceilings. "They are rather sparkling."

She giggled.

They went first to the China red dining room for which she and Trevor had selected a twenty-five-foot-long table and some two dozen matching chairs, all made of rich mahogany. The cabinetmaker had made the suite for the Duke of Richmond's country house, but owing to the delay in the duke's remodeling agreed to allow the Birminghams to have it while he built another for the duke. Fiona's gaze leaped from the table to the scarlet silken draperies, which went well with the heavy strokes of pure gold that brushed the room.

Fiona's glance flicked to Nick, whose eyes shimmered as he surveyed the room. "You, my dear wife, have exceeded my expectations. The room is lovely." He frowned. "And I suppose your little friend is also to be congratulated. I must say he has extraordinary taste." Nick walked to the gleaming table and ran a hand over its polished surface. "This is very fine wood, indeed."

"Trevor found the cabinetmaker. He apprenticed with Sheraton."

"Then I'm indebted to Trevor Simpson."

"We must go see the blue saloon. It's the only other room that's finished now."

Nick was appropriately complimentary over the saloon. Its walls had been covered with an embossed silk damask of a subtle floral pattern, a much lighter shade of blue than the rich royal blue of the silken draperies. The settees were upholstered in rich, royal blue silk that was speckled with brilliant gold stars. He walked straight to the matching pairs of game tables that flanked either side of the fireplace, and he touched the smooth surface of one. "The loveliest game tables I've ever seen."

"That's what Trevor said. I selected them," she added smugly.

He turned to gaze at her with a deep, pensive expression on his rugged face. "Have I told you," he said in a low, mesmerizing voice, "that I'm very happy you picked me out?"

Her heart fluttered in her breast. She thought it almost stopped beating as she bore his penetrating gaze. After several seconds, she gathered her composure and offered a flippant reply. "Must you always remind me that *I* picked you? That's hardly gallant of you."

"I did have the good sense to return to you, drop to one knee, and beg you to marry me," he said with equal flippance.

Chapter 12

The bloody waiting was what William hated most. He had arrived on the third and immediately spoken to the innkeeper, a mustachioed man named Gilberto who spoke heavily accented English. "My name is William . . . Hollingsworth," he had said, "and I believe a letter will be delivered to me here in the next few days." After removing a bag of gold coins from his pocket, he handed it to Gilberto. "I'm willing to pay handsomely for you—or one of your employees—to present my letter to the person who's delivering the letter to me." From his breast pocket, William withdrew his letter and handed it to the man. "There will be another pouch of coins when I have proof that you've followed my directions."

Gilberto's eyes widened, and a smile leaped to his face. "I be happy to see that the letter of yours is delivered into the right hands and will also alert my staff."

That first day, once the letter situation had been handled, William had traveled to Lisbon with four armed postilions, five outriders who were also armed, and three guards sharing the carriage with him. Within a matter of a few hours, William bought up twenty-five thousand pounds worth of French francs, confident the city had been depleted of French currency. After securing the francs beneath the seats of the carriage, they returned to Figueria by nightfall.

On the fifth William received the message from the viscount's captors, with Gilberto attesting to the fact the messenger had indeed been given William's letter. The bandits' message—a demand to meet in the mountains—was negated by William's own instructions.

The eighth was yesterday, and he'd still had no word about the exchange. William began to wonder if the bandits were ignoring the instructions conveyed in his own letter. Would they be waiting up in the mountains for him? If he botched this, Nick would never forgive him.

What if something had happened to the viscount? Surely he hadn't died. If anything happened to Lord Agar, Nick would not be happy. He remembered how adamant Nick was that Lord Agar's safety was his chief concern. Obviously, Nick would do anything to keep that wife of his happy. Whether he knew it or not, his brother had fallen in love with Lady Fiona.

William was getting bloody tired of the inn's tavern and even more tired of the incessant Portuguese, which he did not understand as well as he understood Spanish. As he was swigging a glass of port late in the afternoon of the ninth, Gilberto approached him and spoke in a low voice. "The man you've been waiting for has arrived, Mr. Hollingsworth. Come with me."

William sped after the innkeeper, who led him to a small office behind the reception desk. There stood a rather tall Spaniard dressed in a battered uniform of the Spanish army. The man's black eyes bore into William. "You are Señor Hollingsworth?"

"That is the name I'm using," William said.

The Spaniard glared. "You will instruct your men to lay down their arms now."

"First I must see Lord Agar."

A frown etching his dark face, the Spaniard finally said, "Come with me."

William followed him from the inn, across the plaza where his men guarded the wagon bearing the ransom money, and along the main road out of town. It was almost dusk, and William hoped like hell they could resolve this before night blackened the village.

After two more blocks they came to a wall of mounted men, at least twenty of them. William quickly scanned the group. Amidst all the dark faces there was one fair one: Randolph, Viscount Agar, whose hands were tied behind his back. His blond hair hung ragged, like his soiled Guard's uniform. Unable to shave for several weeks, the viscount had sprouted a red beard.

William nodded, then addressed the man who had accompanied him. "You may come with me back into the city and observe that all my men will disperse and lay down their arms before your men ride into the plaza with Lord Agar."

The Spaniard glared, then nodded.

Once back in the plaza, William walked to its center, drew a breath, and shouted, "I'm calling all my Englishmen to join me at once in the plaza."

Within ninety seconds, all twelve riflers formed a circle around William and the Spaniard, then one by one each man walked to the center of the plaza and laid down his rifle.

"Will you need further proof that my men will not provoke you?" William asked.

The Spaniard's gaze whisked around the plaza and settled on the old church's bell tower. "I will take a look in the church, if you please."

"Go right ahead," William said.

A moment later, the Spaniard rejoined him.

"Satisfied?" William asked.

"Yes."

Then the Spaniard did a peculiar thing. He strolled to the pile of arms and plucked out a rifle. For just a second, William froze with fear. Then the man fired a shot into the sky.

The air swished from William's lungs. He did not like the Spaniard's crude way of delivering a message to his men.

A moment later a great wave of tattered Spanish deserters began to ride into the city, kicking up dust from the unpaved street. Their leader's gaze swung from William to the wagon.

"You're free to inspect the coins," William said, nodding toward the wagon.

Following their leader's instructions, the Spaniards pried off the crate lids. Four wooden boxes bulged with the guineas, the gold shimmering under the waning sun. The men raked their hands through the staggering amount of clanging coins, their swarthy faces lifted in mirth.

"We've kept our part of the bargain," William said. "Now you will release Lord Agar."

His eyes glittering, the Spaniard strode to the viscount's horse and untied the bindings on Randolph's hands. "*Vamos,*" he said.

Randolph winced as he dismounted, then he limped toward William.

In the meantime, the Spaniards had hitched the cart to one of their horses and began to head out of town, leaving behind a small contingent of men to assure the Englishmen did not re-arm themselves.

"I'm Agar, your servant, sir," Randolph said to William.

William effected a bow. "William Birmingham, at your service, my lord."

"I well know the name Birmingham," Randolph

said. "The bankers who are richer than nabobs. You are one of them?"

"I am."

"How, might I ask, was my sister able to enlist your help?"

William did not answer for a moment. Then he drew a breath and said, "By marrying my brother."

Randolph gasped as if he'd been struck by mortar. His eyes shut tightly as a pained expression furrowed his face. "Oh, bloody hell."

Mr. and Mrs. Nicholas Birmingham began moving into their new mansion five days after Nick had carried her through its threshold to inspect the blue saloon. Nick had not favored moving until Fiona's leg was healed, fearing that it would be too taxing for her. She had countered by assuring him it would be much easier for her to oversee the completion of the furnishing were she in residence. Nick gave in. It seemed there was nothing he could deny her.

Over the course of the three days it took to move their household, Fiona positioned herself at the base of the central stairway so that she—with help from Mrs. Pauley—could direct the movers. To appease her husband, she sat in her invalid's chair and propped the wax-plastered leg on another chair to keep down the swelling.

Were he delirious with a raging fever, Trevor could not have stayed away. He happily strutted to and fro, barking orders to her servants. When he saw the scratching and scuffing to the polished marble entry floors, he nearly had apoplexy. "We really must cover this lustrous marble with rugs from the old house while these careless creatures traipse across it." He shot a disdainful look at the offenders. "We can remove the blight when they finish," he said with a shake of his head and shrug of his shoulders. So Turkey rugs from the old house served their purpose for three days.

During those three days the cabinetmaker had delivered the remainder of the newly ordered furnishings, and drapers were scaling tall ladders to install silken window coverings, as other servants hung priceless paintings on the newly painted walls.

On the evening of the third day, Nick came home early. He had been worried about Fiona all day. She was trying to do too much and sleeping too little. He was frightfully afraid she would become ill, and in her delicate state, he feared . . . the worst. This house that he'd once thought his crowning achievement could very well be his curse if it caused him to lose Fiona, who was more dear to him than a hundred palaces.

As the eldest child, Nick was used to being responsible for his siblings, but he'd never before been so consumed with worry over his brothers and sister as he was over this wife of his. Was the perpetual, nagging worry part of being a husband? Perhaps it was the terrifying vision of her tumbling down the stairs that had him fearing for her life every hour of the day.

He paused inside the doorway and watched as his weary wife examined a half-dozen bolts of silk that Trevor was showing her. Her leg was propped on the chair as Nick had instructed, but he could tell by the awkward way she kept shifting it that it must be hurting. To make him even more concerned, her milky white skin seemed even paler, more tinged with blue.

Drawing in a deep breath and striving not to allow her to see how upset he was, he strode to her, removed the silk from her hands, returning it to Trevor. "You, Mrs. Birmingham, have done quite enough for one day," he said sternly, bending to kiss her cheek. "Allow me to wheel you to the drawing room."

He cringed as she slowly set her leg down, and

when they reached the saloon, he swooped her up and deposited her on the sofa. "Stretch out your leg on the sofa, love," he instructed.

Trevor stood just inside the doorway, watching with amusement. "I shall take my leave of Adonis and Artemis. If you two get any cozier, I believe I'll turn blood red."

"What a wicked mind you have," Fiona said, her eyes flashing with mirth—until she met her husband's scowl.

Once Trevor had departed, Nick softened. "You're going to relax and have a large glass of madeira. Doctor Birmingham's orders."

"Yes, master."

He poured two glasses and came to sit beside her. "You look devilishly tired, my dear. I've told you, you're doing too much."

Her cheeks dimpling, she tried to effect a scowl. "How flattering you are! Every lady longs to hear that she looks devilishly tired."

His arm settled across her shoulders. "Oh, you're still quite lovely, but you won't be if you should go into a decline."

She turned to him. "I'm appreciative that you care for my welfare, Nick. Truly. But your worry's misplaced. I've merely broken my leg. I'll be healed and back to new in a few more weeks. My health's excellent."

"Good sleep's vital to good health, and I know you've not been sleeping."

"The perils of sleeping with one's husband," she said dryly. "You know me too well." She flicked a tuft of hair from his stern brow. "Which room shall we sleep in tonight, dearest?"

The vixen! She was deliberately being seductive with him. "Mine," he growled, nibbling on her delectable neck. "My new one. I propose that all the Birmingham babes be conceived on the same bed." Realizing what he had just said, Nick went stiff. He must school himself not to be so transparent. He must not allow Fiona to know how thoroughly besotted he was over her, how he was coming to long for her to grow plump with his babes.

She stiffened too. "Then," she finally said, "perhaps when we name our house we could choose one of my old family names—to bridge the two families."

"I would never have been so presumptuous."

She took a long sip on her wine, then handed her glass to him. "Do you object?"

"Not at all. Have you any ideas?"

"My mother's mother was a Menger. I like the idea of Menger House. It's a solid old name but has no aristocratic bearers who've attached the name to another house."

Nick pursed his lips. "I like the sound of it, too. Menger House. Very solid."

"Like you," she said sweetly.

He could ravage her here on the satin sofa! Good Lord, he'd be happy when her leg was mended and he could thoroughly love her again. Though their bedroom activities had brought immense pleasure to both parties, nothing was as wondrous as feeling himself *inside* her.

Nothing on earth.

He had best change the subject or he'd be babbling declarations of his affection. And he could not allow himself to do that. "Does your brother have any idea that the monies from the estate are gone?" he asked.

"I don't know. When Papa was alive, we knew there had been many financial setbacks, but I doubt if Randy understood the depth of the setbacks. Randy's really not awfully good about money."

"Do you think he'd allow me to assist him?"

She gave him an odd look. "As in a reverse dowry—or do you mean you'll provide financial counseling?"

"A little of both, I suppose."

"I can't let you give him any more money. Twenty-five thousand is quite enough."

"I can't allow my viscount brother to live like a pauper. We Birminghams have a certain image to uphold," he said, a lazy grin softening his face.

She did not say anything for a moment, then finally sucked in a breath and said, "I'm not at all sure my brother would allow you to assist him. He's a terrible snob, you know."

"Yes, I know." He remembered that day at Tattersall's when Randolph had been so reluctant to introduce a Cit to his refined sister.

"I'm somewhat concerned that at first he might even be hostile toward you for marrying me."

"I would expect him to be."

Her brows nudged together. "And still you'd be willing to help him?"

"I'm a very rich man, Fiona."

She cupped his face as delicately as a butterfly's touch. "You're also a very generous man."

He offered her glass to her and she drank, then handed him back the glass. "Dearest?"

"Yes, love?" he answered.

"If we . . . have a son, I would like to name him Jonathan."

He felt like he was in one of those balloons soaring over Hyde Park. Until this moment, he had not allowed himself to hope for a son. Especially a son with Fiona. A son with Agar blood. "Jonathan was my father's name," he said solemnly.

"Yes, I know. I would like our child—if we're blessed in that area—to be named after him."

His lighter-than-air heart was hammering against his chest, and he was almost overwhelmed with a sense of well being. "But you never even knew him."

"But I owe him so much."

Those few words conveyed more than he'd ever

dared to hope for. She understood about his father's careful molding. She was pleased with the final product. "What makes you think I'd entertain such a proposal? Do you even know if I was on good terms with my father?"

She allowed her torso to sink into his lap as she languidly stretched out on the sofa. "Tell me about him, about your relationship."

He had never told anyone about the strange father–son relationship before, but for some reason he began to try to put it into words. "The man who raised me was *not* the same father who raised Adam and William—and especially not the same man who doted on Verity. The others were allowed to be children, allowed to be less than perfect." His face hardened. "But not me. When we were students, if Adam carelessly hurried through his assignments with less than adequate results, our father would be disappointed but never outraged. If I were to botch an assignment, I would be angrily chastised—and often beaten. Were Adam to tie his cravat sloppily, our father would shake his head, but if my cravat wasn't perfect, my father would go into a rage."

"How could your mother have allowed such injustice?"

Nick gave a little laugh. "Because she was as browbeaten as I. Their marriage was never a partnership. My father was completely and thoroughly dictatorial. She was allowed to spend her generous settlement in any way she chose, but in all other matters, my father made the decisions."

"Then . . . you had no affection for your father?" she asked.

"There were times when I thought I loathed him, but not anymore. My biggest regret is that his sudden death prevented me from thanking him for making me the man I am now. I'm sorry that we were never close." His voice was anguished when he said, "I wish to God he'd lived longer so we could have shown affection toward one another."

Fiona's eyes glistened. "How old were you when he died?"

"He died five years ago—when I was seven and twenty."

"He must have been terribly proud of you."

Nick's voice lowered, his fingers combing through her fair locks. "It was the deucest thing. During his last few years, our roles reversed. He became strangely reverent toward me."

"His own creation," she said pensively.

"I," Nick continued in a somber voice, "was to be the embodiment of all his aspirations. I was to become the gentleman he would have been had he been born into more genteel circumstances."

"I wish I could have known him," she said.

"Despite all his money, he neither dressed nor spoke like a gentleman, but he paid dearly to ensure his children would be indistinguishable—at least physically—from those of the upper classes. Of course, your brother and others like him know the difference."

"Once Randy understands that I was completely in favor of this marriage, and once he gets to know you, he'll adore you."

This wife of his was talking like *she* might be learning to care for him. A Cit. Dare he hope?

Chapter 13

Stretching out her legs on the sofa in the blue saloon, Fiona looked up gratefully at Trevor as he handed her a cup of tea. "Tell me, Trev, do you have as beastly a time sleeping as I? Ideas for completing these rooms keep flashing into my head as I'm trying to fall asleep at night."

"Oh, darling, I go to sleep the minute my head hits the pillow," he said, dropping into a chair in front of the tea table. "Then I dream about the rooms. I must say the most scrumptious ideas come to me in dreams." He poured tea into a fragile cup and began to drink.

Fiona wasn't being entirely honest with Trevor. For several nights now the arrangement and decoration of the rooms had kept her awake. But not last night. Last night she'd thought about the boy Nick had been. Her heart went out to the little boy who'd been so cruelly groomed by a fanatic father. She wondered if either his father or mother had ever praised Nick or shown him the affection that should be every child's birthright. Her knowledge of the icy Dolina Birmingham rather convinced her that Nick had been denied such affirmations.

As Fiona had lain in the dark room beside him last night, she'd wanted to smother him with the affection so lacking in his childhood. She had never felt closer to another human being. Not even Warwick, who during the three years of their engagement had shared with her every hope for the future, every disappointment of the past.

Last night she and Nick had kissed passionately and had greedily taken pleasure in each other's bodies, but Nick had refused to cover her body with his. "It won't be long now before you're healed," he had whispered. "I can't do something that would jeopardize your recovery."

After he had fallen asleep, his arm stretching across her, his hand secured at her waist, she felt as if she were drowning in pleasure.

"Tell me, my lady," Trevor began, a devilish glint in his eyes, "that Cit you've married indulges in that middle-class practice of sleeping with one's spouse all night, does he not?"

She scowled at him. "I fail to see what business it is of yours whether my husband and I sleep together."

"Czar Nicholas himself let the cat out of the bag yesterday when he said you weren't sleeping properly. Is he as good a lover as he's purported to be?"

"You can't really expect me to discuss that with you! And I don't like for you to call him Czar Nicholas."

"But the man's so completely dictatorial!"

Perhaps Nick was dictatorial. *Like his father.* It came with being so supremely confident. But unlike his father, Nick had a huge capacity for affection. He had shown it in his dealings with Emmie and his siblings, with his mother, and most of all, with her. He had only been controlling toward her when her welfare was at stake. The very thought wrapped her in a blanket of deep contentment. "And I don't like you dredging up Nick's old lovers!"

Trevor cocked his head to one side and gave her a decidedly mischievous gaze. "I believe you're jealous."

"If you must know, I am. I don't know why I should be jealous over something that occurred before we married, but the fact is I am." Her voice became forlorn. "I can't bear to think of him with those other women. I have no right to expect fidelity. He only married me to help Randolph and to align himself with the Agars."

"Don't be silly! The man obviously cares for you."

"Oh, he does, but he also cares for his child, his brothers, his mother, and his sister."

"What he feels for you is decidedly different, I'll vow. The man seems to be perfectly besotted. You, my dear friend, must be devilishly good in bed!"

"Trevor!"

"Can you deny that the sex has been sublime?"

"I refuse to have this conversation with you." But sublime did seem to describe their lovemaking.

He did not say anything for a moment. "Darling, I believe you've fallen in love with the czar!"

Her shoulders slumped. "Oh, Trevor, I believe you're right." How stunned she was to admit it, but now that she had, she realized she'd spoken the truth. She had indeed fallen in love with her husband.

Now that the move was complete and most of the rooms were finished, Fiona needed to catch up on her correspondence. She stayed in her study this afternoon, her throbbing leg propped up, while she wrote the first letter to Verity, urging her to come stay at Menger House. Knowing her new sister's preference for green rooms, Fiona had seen that Verity's chamber be done up in varying shades of fern green. Her first thought of doing the room in emerald she discarded after reflecting on Verity's subdued taste.

Emerald was too striking. The more natural shades of green would suit Verity much better.

Fiona's next letter was to Miss Peabody, urging that young lady to call at Menger House and explaining that her own broken leg prevented her from making morning calls. As she began to close the letter, she set down her pen. Should she extend the invitation to Miss Peabody's sister, Lady Warwick? Six weeks ago she could not have done so, for the hurt of losing Warwick to the beautiful brunette was too painful. But now Fiona held no animosity toward the countess. Now Fiona understood Warwick had not been the man for her. Nick was her destiny, just as the countess had been Edward's.

She picked up her quill and added,

> *It's been a long time since I've seen Lady Warwick. It would give me great pleasure to show her Menger House.*

She signed it, *Mrs. Fiona Birmingham,* not just to let the countess know she now belonged to another man but because doing so filled her with pride.

As she was sealing the letter, Biddles announced a caller.

"Who is it?" she asked.

"Lord Agar, madame."

Randy! She was seized with a feeling of profound, explosive joy. Her brother was alive—back on English soil! "Please bring him here directly, Biddles."

At the stunned look on the butler's face, she realized he found the impropriety of directing a gentleman to his mistress's private chambers distasteful. "'Tis my brother—back from The Peninsula!" she added.

A sliver of a smile tipped the butler's lips. "Very good, madame. I shall bring him here directly."

When Randolph came limping into the room a

moment later, her heart caught. When she saw the fury in his eyes, the breath caught in her lungs.

He stood just inside the doorway and glared. "So it's true. You've married that pompous bastard."

Her chest tightened. "I'll not have you speak of my husband in such a manner."

"It's obvious that he demanded you as payment for my freedom, damn him."

Randy must have realized the timing of his release corresponded with the timing of his sister's marriage. "He did no such thing. He offered to *give* me the money, Randy, with no strings attached. He was too much the gentleman to profit by my misfortune. It was I who begged him to marry me."

Randolph came into the room and stood before her, glaring. "You're only saying that to ease my mind."

She had once been prepared to feign an attraction to Nick in order to relieve Randy's guilt, but such deception was no longer necessary. She drew in a deep breath. "I'm very sorry you've suffered, but I've come to think your abduction the luckiest thing that ever happened to me, for it brought me Nick."

Her brother winced. "Good Lord! You can't possibly be in love with him. He's the spawn of crude, ignorant parents, and you're the daughter of a viscount."

"I'm not judging Nick on the basis of who his parents were. I've never known a more gentlemanly man than Nick. Can you tell me one thing in his demeanor that points to low origins?"

"Money can buy a lot, Fiona, and it appears that along with his privileged education, it has now bought him an aristocratic wife."

Her hands fisted into tight, moist balls. "I understand your displeasure, but I will not tolerate it. Nick spent a great deal of money and jeopardized his brother's safety to secure your release. I will expect you to be civil to all the Birminghams—and especially to Nick. Whether you approve of him or not, he is now your family."

He sank into the chair across from her. "Dear God, this is worse than being captive."

"It most certainly is not, Randolph Hollingsworth! You've returned to those who love you. Now tell me why you're limping. What did those beasts do to you?"

"'Tis nothing. A superficial wound that will quickly heal."

"I thought you'd be going back to your regiment."

"I thought so, too, but that didactic William Birmingham had other plans." Under his breath he grumbled, "Demmed Birminghams think they rule the world."

"I suppose he wished you to return to England for medical attention."

"That . . . and he had the audacity to suggest I might wish to return to England to attend to my grave financial matters. Tell me, Sis, how much of the twenty-five thousand came from my estate, and how much from Birmingham?"

She swallowed as if she were gulping down bitters. Would that she did not have to tell him. "There was no money in your estate."

He dropped his head into his hands. "I wish they'd killed me in Portugal."

"I'll not allow you to talk like that! You're alive. You've been restored to your loved ones. Nick will help you rebuild your fortune."

He jerked up and glared icily at her. "I'll not take another farthing from him!"

"Don't be so obtuse! If there's one thing the Birminghams know all about, it's money. If you won't accept his charity, at least accept his loan—a loan to help restore your holdings to productivity. Then you can pay him back."

Randolph stood up and began to storm from the

room. "I'll bloody well do that. I'll pay him back the entire twenty-five thousand quid!"

At dinner that night Fiona was unusually quiet. Nick was fairly certain he knew the source of her uneasiness. "Did your brother come to you today?" he asked.

She answered without looking up. "Yes, he did. He's walking with a limp, but he tells me it's a superficial wound that will quickly heal. I didn't dare ask how he received it, for, I assure you, I did not want to know what those beastly men did to him."

She was babbling, trying to divert him from the true source of her worry.

"If it will make you feel any better, William confirmed that Agar's wound is nothing more than a trifle." William had also confirmed that Randolph was seething over his sister's marriage.

"I cannot worry over his wound when I'm so relieved he's been rescued from those vile creatures." She looked up and favored him with a smile. "I do thank you, dearest, for making his release possible."

"There's nothing I wouldn't do for you, Fiona."

Her pulse leaped. "You're such an exceedingly gallant husband."

She would discuss anything but what was uppermost in her thoughts: Her brother thought Nick unworthy of Fiona. Nick had hoped that when Agar saw that Fiona seemed happy, that when he saw she resided at the finest address in London, he would not be displeased over the union.

But he'd thought wrong. Randolph's reemergence only solidified Nick's own doubts. He wasn't good enough for Fiona. She should be married to an earl like Warwick. Damn the man.

"Did you and your brother compare leg injuries?"

"Actually he only stayed a few minutes, and I had

no occasion to stand so he's not aware of my stupid misfortune."

If her brother left quickly that could only mean one thing. They had quarreled over her marriage. "I would have thought you and he would have had much to discuss."

"I daresay he had much that required his attention. He's been away for almost a year."

So she was not going to apprise Nick of her brother's discontent. Was she foolish enough to believe it would go away? "I hope you told him my brothers and I are eager to offer our services for financial advice."

"I did mention it."

"And?"

"I believe he's considering it, but you must know my brother is beastly proud. It won't be easy for him to come to you."

"But we're family now." Though Agar would as lief not admit to it.

After dinner, instead of their usual game of cribbage or chess, Fiona cried off with a headache.

No doubt brought on by that insensitive brother of hers.

Though he seldom drank, Nick ensconced himself in his library and got exceedingly drunk.

Chapter 14

If it wasn't one thing, it was another that conspired to rob Fiona of sleep. She was concerned that her leg was not healing as quickly as she had hoped. It had been a month now, and despite that she had not put her weight on the leg, she was never free from throbbing pain. In addition to the woes of her infirmity, now she was upset by her obtuse brother. His snub of her husband was simply intolerable. As she lay alone in her bed, the crackle of the fire the only noise in the room, she held a dozen imaginary conversations with Randy. He must allow himself to get to know Nick, for to know Nick was to admire him. But what could she do to lubricate the process? She had already admitted her deep affection for Nick, and that had only served to rankle her wretchedly snobbish brother all the more.

Perhaps Randy would soften when he saw how well the *ton* would accept Nick once they began to entertain on the lavish scale she had planned. She was assured the grand ladies and gentlemen who inhabited Mayfair would flock to Menger House, if for no other reason than to see the finest townhouse in all of London.

Miss Peabody's come-out would be sure to draw

any number of peers because Rebecca Peabody was, after all, connected by marriage to Lord Warwick. Warwick's stature—now that he'd become foreign secretary—was such that he moved in the most exalted circles. He was even a confidante of the Prince Regent himself.

Incredibly weary but utterly incapable of sleep, Fiona waited for Nick to come to bed. After several hours her fire went out and, clutching the bed coverings up to her neck, she shivered all the way to her bones. Why had Nick not come? She suddenly realized she'd forgotten that he said they would sleep in his bed. No wonder he hadn't come to her chambers. He must think she had no desire to sleep with him.

She managed to slip from the bed without putting her weight on her broken leg, then she eased herself into the invalid's chair and rolled to the chair where she had tossed her Kashmir shawl earlier in the evening. Still shaking with cold, she directed her chair toward Nick's chambers, deciding to go by way of the hallway rather than through their crowded, carpeted dressing rooms. Wheels, she had learned, glided much more easily over hard surfaces.

Once she was in the hallway, she heard a child's muffled cries. Panic struck her. *Emmie!* What could be wrong with the child? Her heart leaping to her chest, she bolted from the invalid's chair and sped to Emmie's room at the end of the hall, careful to keep most of her weight on the good leg.

Inside the little girl's room there was just enough firelight for Fiona to see the child sitting up in her bed, her little fists jammed into her eye sockets, sobbing. "Pray, love, what's the matter?" Fiona asked, collapsing on the bed.

"I want to go back to my other house," Emmie said in a forlorn little voice.

Poor lass. She was afraid to sleep in the strange new

room. "But this is your new house," Fiona said softly. "You're understandably upset because this is unfamiliar to you, and it's dark and quiet, and you're alone. I promise that once you get used to it, you won't be frightened anymore."

The little girl shook her head, her rumpled tresses scattering. "I want to go back."

"But, love, there's no one left at the old house. You'd be all alone."

"Miss Beckham could come."

"That wouldn't be fair to her, to take her away from all her other friends."

"Please, can't I go back? I don't wish to be here."

Fiona held out her arms, and Emmie flowed into her embrace. All of Fiona's senses awakened to the feel of this child, to her sweet, herbal scent. "Don't you like your lovely new room?"

"I only like it in the daytime," Emmie whimpered. "Not at night."

"Would you feel better if I lit some candles?"

Emmie shook her head emphatically.

Fiona's first instinct was to summon Miss Beckham to sleep in the child's room until Emmie became used to her new surroundings, but she decided that rousing the poor governess from her sleep was too cruel.

"Would you like to come to my room and sleep with me?" Fiona asked, sweeping lazy circles on Emmie's heaving back.

The little girl sucked in a deep, quivering breath and nodded, the last of her tears sliding down her reddened cheek.

"Come along then." Fiona began to limp toward her chambers, Emmie clutching her nightshift. When they reached Fiona's door, she instructed the child to wait for her right there. "I've got to go tell your Papa something. I shall be right back."

To allay Nick's concerns, Fiona sank back into the

invalid's chair for the short trip to his chambers. She had to see him, to speak to him before she could sleep. Nick must not think she hadn't desired to share his bed.

When she entered his room her glance darted to his huge, curtained bed that had belonged to a French prince. It was dressed in royal blue silks that were illuminated by bedside candles. "Nick?" she called softly, but there was no answer. Only an eerie silence. She came closer to the bed and discovered it had not been slept in. Could he have gone out for the evening?

Disappointed, she returned to Emmie, who stood just inside Fiona's doorway. "Come, love, climb up on my nice, big bed," Fiona said.

Having made a miraculous recovery from her hysterics, the child settled her head on the pillow closest to the window. "Winnie used to sleep with me when I was sick," she said wistfully.

Winnie had likely been the only person to ever show the child real affection—except for Nick, but men never concerned themselves with a child's emotional needs.

"She used to tell me stories, too," Emmie said, her mouth puckering into a pout.

Fiona smiled down at the child. "Should you like me to tell you a story?"

"Ever so much." A radiant smile transformed Emmie's solemn face. It was such a delicate face with a dusting of freckles across her nose, a fringe of feathery lashes, and a dimple in one cheek. Just like her father.

"What story should you like to hear?"

"*The Life and Perambulations of a Mouse.*"

That had been a great favorite of Stephen's. "I used to tell that story to my younger brother," Fiona said.

"Is he little like me?"

"Not anymore. He's twenty years old now and at university, but when he was your age, he loved the mouse story. I know it by heart."

"So do I," Emmie said in her wispy little voice.

"Then perhaps you should tell it to me," Fiona teased.

Emmie shook her head. "Please, My Lady, you tell it."

With a smile on her face, Fiona reached to stroke her palm along the child's bouncy curls. "Very well."

As Fiona told Emmie the story, the child's eyelids became heavy, and before she had finished, Emmie was fast asleep. The crying must have worn out the poor child. For a few minutes Fiona peered into the little girl's angelic face, her heart wrenching. Then she lifted the covers up to Emmie's shoulders and bent to press a whispery kiss on her brow.

The sound of the child's breathing was oddly comforting, yet Fiona still could not sleep. She missed Nick dreadfully. Had he stormed from his room after not finding her there? Did he think she had no desire for him? Or, worse still, had he sensed her brother's hostility and thought her guilty of the same bigotry? Her eyes began to mist. How could Nick not realize how much she was coming to love him?

For the next several hours she tormented herself, wondering where Nick could have gone. The very idea that he might have slaked his physical hunger between the thighs of Diane Foley made Fiona ill. She cursed herself for breaking the leg, for driving him away. She vowed to never again retire at night earlier than he. She cautioned herself to never say or do anything that would point to any disparity in their stations. Then she lay in the dark gently weeping until sleep finally released her.

It was the bloody discomfort that woke Nick early the next morning. He had no notion of where he was—

even after he awakened, which was understandable, given that he'd not yet familiarized himself with his new surroundings. As he came fully awake he realized he was folded in a deuced uncomfortable chair in the library of Menger House. He bolted up, every muscle in his body crying out in protest. "Bloody hell!" He had allowed himself to get so bosky he hadn't even made it to bed.

Thank God he'd awakened on his own. He wouldn't have liked for a servant to find him in this condition. He had no sympathy for those who overindulged, and he certainly would not expect his servants to respect a man who carried on in such a manner.

He was grateful, too, that Fiona had not found him like this.

Shoving a hand through his disheveled hair, he cursed, then painfully raised himself from the damned chair. He went first to his bedchamber. Would Fiona be there? Would she be worried? Angry with himself, he suddenly realized Fiona would not have been able to come down the stairs without someone carrying her in the sedan chair. He hoped to God she had gone to sleep before his tardiness caused her to miss him.

Stepping into his bedchamber, he was mildly disappointed not to find her there. The silken bed coverings that Ware had turned down the night before were undisturbed, the bedside candle completely burned down, like the fire in the ashen grate. Had she forgotten he wished them to sleep in his bed? Or had the headache that sent her to bed early caused her absence from his bed?

Good Lord! What if she'd been lying sick in her room all night, awaiting him? He tore off toward her chambers, fairly flying through the connecting dressing rooms and flinging open her chamber door.

She stirred, then came up from her mattress on one elbow to face him. "Nick!" Her eyes trailed over the dark shadow of beard on his face and over his mussed clothes. "You're just coming in?"

He tensed for a moment. He disliked telling her the truth, afraid he would lose her respect. Yet he disliked lying more. What if one of the servants *had* seen him sprawled drunkenly in the library and that information got back to Fiona? "I'm ashamed to admit I spent the night in my library—after drinking too much."

Her brows collapsed. "I thought you abhorred those who overindulge."

He gave a disgusted grunt.

She patted the bed beside her.

Relief flooded him. She was not disgusted by him. He came to drop a kiss on her cheek, then sank onto the mattress beside her, breathing in her lavender scent. Her elegance in a skimpy nightshift never failed to heat his blood. As lovely as she was on their wedding day, she was ten times more beautiful within rumpled sheets, with rumpled hair, her milky flesh as smooth as satin.

"I was so worried about you," she said, "and to think you were here all along!"

Could it be possible she worried over him as he worried over her? "Forgive me for making you worry." As he drank in Fiona's fair loveliness he became aware that she was not alone in the bed. He stiffened, his heart hammering, his suspicious thoughts scrambling.

Then, rubbing her eyes and yawning, Emmie poked up her little head. The air swished from his lungs. "What in the world is the muffin doing here?" he asked.

A smile arching across her little face, Emmie sat up and addressed her father. "I was frightened last night, and my new mother—" She turned to apologize to Fiona. "I mean My Lady said I could sleep with her."

He gave his daughter a mock scowl. "You came to Lady Fiona's room?"

Fiona, her face solemn yet kindly, reached out to

trail her hand along Emmie's sable hair. "No, I heard
her crying and went to her. The poor little lamb was
frightened in her new surroundings."

His heart overflowed with the love he held for
these two females who lazily stretched out before
him within the silken bed coverings. He'd swelled with
pride as he watched Fiona's delicate hands stroke
Emmie's hair, as her voice softened when she spoke
to the child who was so precious to him.

"I want to go back to my other house," Emmie said.

"That's nonsense," Nick said sternly. "This is your
new house, and there's nothing wrong with it."

"Until she gets used to it," Fiona said, "we can ask
that Miss Beckham sleep in her room."

"Why didn't you ask her last night?" Nick
demanded.

"It was after midnight, and I didn't wish to awaken her."

"She's a servant!"

"Now you sound like my wretched brother!" Fiona
said, frowning.

Her brother who thought only one class of people mattered.
Fiona had done well to put Nick in his place. "I take
it you refer to Lord Agar."

"I'm sorry I brought him up."

Her anguished words conveyed so much that re-
mained unspoken. Their minds were beginning to
blend like those who had been married for half a cen-
tury. He reached out to tenderly touch his index
finger along her perfect nose, to touch her full lips.
He wished Emmie weren't here so he could be intimate with his wife. "Is your headache gone?"

She favored him with a smile. "I feel much better
this morning. Would that I could say the same for you.
Methinks you must feel wretched after being so
naughty last night."

A smile crinkled around his eyes and pinched his

cheek. "And how would my wife know about men who overindulge?"

"Your wife has two brothers," she said with a laugh, then stroking Emmie's thin arm, she looked up at her husband. "Why do you not freshen up and take your little muffin riding? Perhaps the fresh air will invigorate you."

His gaze flicked to Emmie, who was giggling. "Go get dressed, muffin."

He and Fiona exchanged amused smiles as the laughing child bolted from the room, then he spoke throatily. "Thank you for your kindness to my daughter."

"How could I be anything else? She's a lovely child."

"I wish to kiss you, madame, but not until I freshen up."

She favored him with a gentle smile.

Chapter 15

The dreaded meeting with Lady Warwick did not go nearly as badly as Fiona had anticipated. For so many months Fiona had been so possessed of a crippling jealousy and animosity toward the countess that she was not sure she could let go of those violent feelings. But as the hour of their reunion came, a peace settled over Fiona, and she wanted nothing so much as to thank the countess for taking Warwick away from her. Theirs would not have been a good marriage. Her fate was with Nick; Edward's with his Countess Maggie.

When Lady Warwick and her sister arrived at Menger House, Fiona swept to the door in her invalid's chair to greet them. "I'm so very glad you could come," she said. "Would you like to see the house?"

"Are you sure you're up to it?" the countess asked, casting a troubled glance at Fiona's invalid chair.

"It would give me great pleasure to show you our new house—but for obvious reasons, our tour will have to be confined to the first floor."

The countess subsequently made the obligatory exclamations over the celestial ceilings, and the soaring Palladian windows, and the gleaming Carrara and Sienna marble of the floors. She had inquired about the cabinetmaker and nearly swooned over the beautiful and abundant silks, the fine Sevres porcelain, and the broadloom carpets that had been specially made for Menger House.

The last room they came to was Nick's library, the darkest room in the house but also the coziest because of the rich walnut wainscoting and the tranquil greens of its decor. That morning the servants had hung Nick's portrait over the mantle. He had not changed since it had been painted two years previously. The painter had done a masterful job of conveying Nick's innate power with dark colors: Nick's deep brown hair, pensive near-black eyes, olive skin that complemented the rich chocolate-colored frock coat he wore. Contrasting with all the varying shades of brown was the stark white of his eyes and teeth. Gazing affectionately at the portrait, Fiona said with pride, "That handsome man is my husband, Nicholas."

The countess's face softened as she looked at the portrait. "You've married well. He's incredibly handsome."

Even Miss Peabody, who seldom noticed those of the opposite sex, pushed her spectacles up the bridge of her nose and stared at Nick's picture. "If he has a brother, I'll take him."

Fiona and Maggie broke out laughing. "As a matter of fact," Fiona said, "he has a brother who looks enough like him to be a twin."

"Then I shall very much look forward to my come-out," Miss Peabody said.

Returning to the blue saloon, Fiona said, "That's the very reason I've asked you here today. Remember, I promised to sponsor you, and I'm greatly looking forward to your come-out. It will be the first grand fete in our new house."

Maggie stiffened. "Are you sure you still wish to do that?"

There would never be a better time than the present to clear the air between her and the countess. "My lady," Fiona began, looking earnestly into the countess's beautiful face, "by coming here today you've taken the first step toward restoring the friendship we once shared, and I'm indebted to you."

Maggie's head inclined, her huge black eyes softening.

"I cannot deny," Fiona continued, "that at one time I was extremely jealous of you, but I assure you that is no longer the case." She sank back in her invalid's chair. "Do you believe in destiny?"

"I do," Maggie whispered.

"I do, too. And I believe you were Edward's fate, not I." She drew a deep breath. "I now believe that Edward's meeting you was the best thing that could ever have happened to me."

A slow smile came over the countess's face. "Because Nicholas Birmingham was your fate?"

Fiona nodded. "Most definitely."

"I cannot tell you how happy I am to learn that," Lady Warwick said.

"I only wish Warwick could understand," Fiona said. "I know he feels beastly guilty about how everything happened."

"I'll try to convey all this to him," Maggie said.

Staring at the beautiful countess, Fiona wondered if Lord and Lady Warwick were as close as she and Nick. It seemed almost inconceivable that anyone else could ever experience the unity she and her husband shared.

As she beheld the countess, Fiona could well understand why Warwick had fallen in love with her. Was there a lovelier creature on the entire earth? The countess was possessed of a head of rich, dark brown hair and huge almond-shaped eyes so dark a brown they looked black. Her milky skin was highlighted with deep pink cheeks and a luscious rose-colored mouth, and her figure was statuesque—with a large bosom. If one looked especially close, one could see the swell of the Warwick's second babe. No woman with child had ever looked lovelier.

Fiona had once observed that every color Maggie wore became peculiarly her own. Today she wore a dress the color of salmon, and once again Fiona could not believe anyone else could be so lovely wearing that shade. The gods had indeed blessed Maggie in every way. And now she had a husband who adored her and a babe of her own, Fiona thought with a stab of jealousy.

It would give Fiona great pleasure if she could bear Nick a son. "How are you and Warwick enjoying being parents?"

The countess instantly turned from gracious beauty to gushing mother. "Oh, we adore him! He looks just like Edward, and he's such a joy."

"Now *that* I'm jealous of," Fiona said with a smile. She eyed Miss Peabody, who pulled a slender volume from her reticule.

Her sister instantly chastised her. "You will not read when you're a guest at someone's house!" Turning to Fiona, she said, "Please forgive my sister's shameful manners."

Her cheeks red, Miss Peabody shoved the book back into her reticule. Fiona thought perhaps Rebecca Peabody was not yet ready for the Marriage Mart. Even her manner of dressing—today in a sprigged muslin, high-necked gown—was more like something a younger girl, not a girl of marriageable age, would wear. "You are nineteen now, Miss Peabody?" Fiona asked.

"I am."

"I suppose it's time you give thought to getting married."

"If I should get married," Miss Peabody responded wistfully, "it would be to get a little boy as delightful as my nephew."

"Becky dotes on Eddie," the countess said.

"How fortunate you all are to have a little one to dote upon. I shall be glad when I'm in your shoes. For now, though, I'm happy that my family is enlarged. At long last, I finally have a sister."

"Birmingham's sister?" the countess asked.

"Yes, her name is Verity, and she's the same age as Miss Peabody. We expect a visit from her in the next few weeks. I'm trying to persuade her to come out with Miss Peabody."

"I should be delighted to have someone with whom to share such a frightening event," Rebecca said.

"Have you decided when you'd like to have the ball?" Maggie asked.

"I thought perhaps in early June."

"Splendid," the countess said.

"But don't let us wait until then to rekindle the friendship I so desire," Fiona said.

"I won't," Maggie said, visibly moved by Fiona's olive branch.

As Nick sat across the ale house's wooden table from Lord Warwick, his last decade of unparalleled power was suddenly stripped away. He was once more the outsider he'd been at Cambridge. Despite his immense wealth and despite that he was one of the few lads at Christ's who had the luxury of his own valet, he had never been accepted by the likes of Warwick and Randolph Hollingsworth and their set. Today he was once again the recipient of Warwick's condescending arrogance.

He detested the man. The earl's presence would have been much easier to accept if he'd been less handsome, if Fiona had not loved him, if Nick was confident Fiona no longer loved the man. But Nick had no such confidence.

"I was surprised, my lord," Nick said, meeting the earl's amber eyes, "that you were familiar with this public house since it's in the financial district and far removed from Whitehall." It was Warwick who, via a note delivered to Nick that morning, had suggested they meet here.

"I'm less well known here," the earl replied. "It's especially important to me that our meeting appears to be of a social nature rather than an official encounter. I do thank you for seeing me today."

If Warwick weren't the foreign secretary, Nick would not have come, but because of the earl's vital work Nick could not refuse him. "You will no doubt be pleased to learn that my brother purchased all the francs in Portugal during his recent visit there," Nick said.

Warwick nodded. "About that visit . . . I've only just learned from Agar about his captivity. Forgive me for not acting upon it in an official capacity. We thought he had been killed."

Nick glared at him. "And you neglected to tell his sister?"

"I wished to wait for confirmation before imparting such sad news to Lady Fiona."

Nick detested hearing his wife's name on Warwick's lips.

"She should have come to me when the bandits made their demands," Warwick said.

"So that she wouldn't have soiled herself by marrying me?"

Anger flashed in Warwick's eyes. "I didn't mean that. It's only that I feel it was the government's responsibility to rescue one of its distinguished officers."

"I daresay Agar wishes you had."

The earl said nothing.

Nick lifted his bumper and took a long drink. "I've decided to help my country." It rankled him to say he would help Warwick. "My brother leaves tomorrow for Prussia, where he'll buy up a hundred thousand guineas' worth of francs."

Warwick's eyes rounded. "I had no idea you were possessed of such a large amount of discretionary funds."

The Birminghams might not have pedigree, but they had staggering wealth, and this once he wished to brag, to show Warwick that Fiona had not married so very badly. "We're the richest family in England."

"Then I'm very happy I selected you for this mission."

Did the pompous bastard wish to take credit for what Nick's father, his brothers, and Nick himself had built? It was all Nick could do not to slam a fist into Warwick's smug face. "You should be happier still that I accepted."

"I'm very grateful." Lord Warwick sipped on his ale. "You do realize the necessity for complete secrecy?"

"I do, and I realize that's why you did not come to my establishment this time."

"In the future, if you would be so kind, our meetings need to take place at night."

Nick nodded. "A wise choice."

"I'll be bloody glad when all this is over with, and you'll be able to reap the credit for all you're doing."

Nick's anger flared. "I'm not doing this for personal recognition."

"Forgive me if I implied otherwise." Warwick's gaze traveled to the fire in the dimly lit room of the low-ceilinged tavern. He had selected well. No one shared this room with them. "I'm told your wife suffered a broken leg."

Hearing Fiona referred to as his wife filled Nick with pride. "It's been beastly rough on her, but we're hoping the surgeon will remove the cast today." He had arranged his schedule so that he could be there to talk with the surgeon.

"Then I hope she has a full recovery."

Nick stood at her bedside, his back to the bank of windows, his handsome face brooding with concern as the surgeon saw Fiona in her bedchamber. First the surgeon removed the leather sheath from her leg, then he peeled off the linen that held the waxed cast in place, and when he began to cut at the cast, Nick's warm hand clasped hers. Surprisingly, she felt no pain whatsoever. She supposed the surgeon had been right to have her wear it two more weeks than the originally proposed six weeks.

Once the leg was free of all the wretched bindings, the surgeon asked her to lift it up and down and from side to side. She was frightfully embarrassed for Nick to see her leg looking so dirty and puckered. Then the surgeon instructed her to put her weight upon it. Nick helped her from the bed and, leaning on him, she began to walk, but her gait was not without a limp. "I vow, it doesn't really hurt," she said, "I don't know why I'm limping."

"That's perfectly normal," the surgeon assured her. "It will take a few weeks before you're back to your old self."

"You're sure it's healed properly?" Nick asked. "Is she really ready to put her weight on it?"

The bespectacled surgeon turned to address Nick. "Your wife is a healthy young woman who's perfectly capable of growing new bone. I'd say she's had an excellent recovery, and you, sir, are to be commended for ensuring that she stayed off the leg during the healing process."

"See, my darling," she said, smiling up at Nick, "your being an ogre was justified."

With the expectation that the cast would come off that afternoon, Fiona had ordered a bathing tub be set up in front of the fireplace in her room. As soon as the doctor departed, she glanced from the tub to Nick. "I cannot tell you how I've longed to sink this body—and this wretched leg—into a nice warm bath. It's been two long months."

His dark eyes sparkled and he murmured. "Allow me to assist you, my lady." He stepped closer and began to unfasten her dress. When he finished she lifted her arms, and he removed the dress, then lifted off her chemise. She turned around to face him. His smoldering gaze dipped to the tops of her breasts that squeezed out of the stays. He stepped closer and began to unlace her until her breasts were uncovered. He drew in a breath as he smoothed the corset over her slender hips and, with those magical hands of his, dragged her drawers down with the corset until she stepped out of them and stood before him completely naked.

She was aware of what great control he exercised when he huskily said, "Hold on to me while you climb into the tub." Her husband always put her needs above his own.

With his help she slithered beneath the warm water. Nothing had ever felt so good. Well, actually, there was one thing . . . and she hoped she'd experience that, too, this afternoon.

After removing his coat and rolling up his shirt sleeves, Nick fell to his knees and began to trickle warm water over her shoulders. "Allow me to massage your leg," he said softly. Moving down to the other end of the tub, he lifted her foot and massaged it, then slowly moved up her calf, the water lapping at the sides of the tub. He moved past her knee to massage her thighs. "Your leg is perfect," he murmured.

When he finished the leg he scooted to the middle

of the metal tub and began to cup handsful of water that he trickled over her breasts. Her breasts felt heavy, like her breathing, and she was embarrassed to see that her nipples had turned into little spears.

"Your nipples are puckering," he said in a low, husky voice.

A deep, burning flush hiked into her cheeks.

"Did I embarrass you?" he asked.

"It's just . . . I've never heard that word used before."

"Nipples?"

Brazenly meeting his heated gaze, she nodded.

"Say the word, Fiona. Tell me how your nipples feel right now."

She drew in a breath. "My nipples, like the rest of me, need you, Nick."

"Tell me how you feel."

Her coyness vanished. This was Nick. Her other half. She was powerless to conceal anything from him. "I never thought a woman could feel such an overwhelming need. I know men are consumed with this need to lie with women, even women they care nothing for . . ." Is that what their lovemaking had been to Nick? Was he greedy to make love to her because he was so pleased with the lovemaking skills he had taught her? Was there not some flicker of something more, something even stronger than his carnal needs?

Those black eyes of his bore into hers. "Tell me what you want me to do to you, Fiona."

She could not look him in the eye when she spoke. "I . . . I want to feel your lips on mine, to feel my tongue mingling with yours. I want to feel your hands gliding over my flesh." Now she allowed herself to gaze into his simmering eyes. "I want . . . I need to feel you inside me."

A smile stole over his dark face, and he stood up. She saw that he was aroused. Taking his hand, she stepped from the tub and he swaddled her in thirsty toweling, then scooped her up and carried her to the bed, easing her down as if she were made of fragile porcelain. Next he went to the casements and drew the draperies shut, one by one.

Her heart thumped when he turned around to face her, his smoldering gaze sweeping seductively over her. As he came to the lavender-scented bed, he began throwing off his own clothing, tossing it behind him in a haphazard trail until he stood beside her, his bronzed body lithe and powerful and totally aroused.

Never removing her gaze from his, she raised up on the bed and placed her hands on each side of his stiff rod as she drew her head closer, as her mouth opened to take him in.

She was strangely aroused by his deep groans, by the masculine scent of him, by the quick thrusts he seemed to have no control over.

After a moment, he pulled away. "I bloody well can't wait another second."

Her breathing now unbelievably labored, she fell back onto the bed, and Nick quickly covered her body with his. He nudged her thighs open wider, then plunged into her.

The little thread of control she had hung onto snapped. She couldn't seem to raise her hips fast enough to meet him thrust for thrust. She was drenched and winded, and spasms kept rocketing through her as she felt his seed seeping into her womb. She had never in her life felt so utterly complete.

A few minutes later, totally spent, Nick collapsed beside her, securing his hand at her waist. "Well worth the wait," he said.

Still panting, she snuggled against his moist, sweaty flesh. "Yes, it was, wasn't it?"

She was vaguely aware of footsteps outside her door and prayed they would not stop. But they paused, and a knock sounded.

"Yes?" she asked, hoping whoever it was would not come in, wondering if Nick had the presence of mind to lock the door.

"Miss Verity Birmingham has arrived, madame."

Chapter 16

Nick cursed when he drove up to his business establishment later that afternoon and saw Randolph's crested coach in front of the building. Not only was he displeased that this visit would prevent him from completing the work he'd left unfinished, but he also disliked the prospect of facing his abrasive brother-in-law. He drew in his breath and cautioned himself not to alienate Randolph with words or actions. Fiona was, after all, excessively fond of her brother.

And Nick would never do anything that would make his well-loved wife unhappy.

Offering the viscount a stiff bow, Nick said, "Your servant, Agar. Won't you come into my office?"

Like his father before him, Nick kept his office as austere as he could get by with. The two men lowered themselves into utilitarian wood chairs. Nick eyed Fiona's brother. Except for their blond hair and blue eyes, the siblings looked nothing alike. The delicacy that defined Fiona was lacking in her well-muscled brother, who was also taller than average. Agar seemed less offensive than he had during their last meeting. "To what do I owe the pleasure of your visit?" Those were the same words Nick had used a few months earlier when Fiona had paid him an unexpected call, the day she had made the proposition that had changed his life. If only today's visit could portend an occurrence half as satisfying.

"After speaking with my solicitor," Randolph said. "I'm here to eat crow."

Nick raised a single brow.

"It would seem I'm not only indebted to you for the sum of twenty-five thousand quid, but if I'm ever to repay you—which I assure you I intend to do—I've got to put my financial affairs in your hands."

"I did suggest that to your sister, and I'm pleased that you've not taken offense. But as to paying me back, that's not necessary. To me, twenty-five thousand's a trifling sum." With a smile hitching across his face, Nick remembered the day before they wed when Fiona had told him that while twenty-five thousand pounds *was* a great deal of money to most people, it wasn't to him. "I was expecting to strike marriage settlements equal to that amount."

"Nevertheless, I wish to repay you."

Agar was too damned proud for his own good. "I hope you don't mind that I've taken the liberty of looking into your finances."

"With my sister's blessings, no doubt."

"Of course." Nick had to tread carefully now. He could not come off as being didactic, for Randolph would storm from the room. "First, I must ask if you're going to sell your colours." That Agar sat there wearing his regimentals did not bode well for Nick's plan.

"It seems I've no choice but to stay in England and try to make something out of the muddle my father left."

"Good. The money you receive from selling your commission should be enough to cover your expenses for a year—provided you practice economy."

Randolph's blond brows squeezed together. "What kind of economy?"

"I know it's difficult for one who's been raised as you have, but until you can rebuild the family fortune, you'll need to make changes in the way you spend money."

"What kind of changes?" Randolph asked suspiciously.

"For starters, I'd recommend letting the London townhouse for the season. A bachelor, after all, doesn't need all that room—or all that staff. Letting Agar House not only would give you funds that are needed elsewhere but would significantly reduce your expenditures. You're welcome, of course, to stay at Menger House. In fact, I'm sure your sister would be delighted to have you."

Randolph shook his head. "I'd prefer to take modest bachelor lodgings."

"As you wish," Nick said. "I would also recommend that you curtail a few activities."

"And which activities would you be referring to?" Randolph asked, a sour look on his face.

"For one, gambling. It's a fact that over a long course no one ever comes out ahead at games of chance." He watched Agar for a reaction, but there was none. "My other suggestion would be to stop maintaining a carriage. The livery fees alone are quite staggering for one in your circumstances."

Randolph glared at him. "So the first steps in recovering the family fortune are to live a life of deprivation?"

"Better deprive yourself while you're a bachelor with no family to care for."

"Good Lord!" Randolph hissed, as if he were angry at himself for having forgotten something of importance. "What of my brother?"

"It's your sister's wish to see to Stephen's needs. In fact, he will come to Menger House on school holidays."

He was lying, not about the holidays but about the financial arrangement with young Stephen Hollingsworth. Never having to be cognizant of financial matters, Fiona had not given a thought to Stephen's financial needs. Fortunately for the youth, Nick had been sending the young man a modest quarterly income.

Randolph nodded. "I intend to relieve my sister of that burden—once I've restored our fortune."

"Then you're willing to make the sacrifices I've suggested?"

"I am."

"As for your sources of income . . . there are but two at present: the lands in Yorkshire and highly devalued stocks. You should be able to reap a goodly sum over the next year off your lands. If I were you, I'd reinvest that—even consider expanding your acreage to reap higher yields the next year."

"You simplify matters."

Nick was too used to dealing with slow tops. His brother-in-law was more shrewd. "Let's just say I have confidence in your ability to enhance your Yorkshire holdings."

Randolph's hostility noticeably lessened.

"Regarding the stocks," Nick said, "your father, in his quest to make money quickly, invested in high-risk areas. With your permission, I should like to reinvest in safer stocks."

"As the 'Fox' of the Exchange, you will, of course, have free rein there," Randolph said.

"Then oblige me by bringing all your documents here in the next week, and I'll begin buying and selling your stocks."

Rising, Randolph nodded. "I'm forced to accept that my sister is married to you, but I cannot like it."

Nick tensed. "I'm aware that no man of my class would ever be good enough for Lady Fiona."

"I'll admit," Randolph said, glaring down at Nick, "that I initially objected to the disparity in your stations, but I believe—with my sister at your side and your gentlemanly tastes and vast wealth—you'll be accepted everywhere."

"Then?" Nick tried to act casual, tried to hide his own pendulous emotions.

With a hopeless shrug of his head, Randolph raked a hand through his blond hair. "My sister's very dear to me. I had wished her to marry a man who would cherish her—not a man who's a noted womanizer, a man who's littered the country with his bastards. Why, even at Cambridge you—"

Nick bolted from his seat, his hands fisted, his voice shaking with fury. "I've not been with another woman since the day your sister honored me by becoming my wife."

Randolph's icy blue eyes raked over Nick. "You'll forgive me if I reserve judgment until the honeymoon's over? Leopard's spots, I've observed, don't change." Then Randolph turned on his heel and left.

Nick sank back into his seat, his pulse thumping with rage. But he could not fault Agar for the shameful way he'd lived—before Fiona.

Once Verity had been shown to her room and had changed from her traveling clothes, she and Fiona partook of tea in the scarlet and gold morning room, which had the benefit of late afternoon sun.

As she sat back on the satin settee and studied her sister, Fiona wondered if she would ever be able to look at Verity and not be struck over her keen resemblance to Nick. Not that Verity was masculine looking in any way. She was possessed of a graceful slimness and a sweet, cultured voice that bespoke elegance.

Sadly, her choice of clothing did nothing to enhance

her attributes. Though there was nothing in her manner that was less than tasteful, she lacked her brother's flare. She was trying too hard to appear staid. The colors she wore—including today's charcoal—were subdued and monotonous, and the necklines of her gowns were unfashionably high. Fiona could not wait to take her to her own dressmaker, Mrs. Spence.

"I cannot tell you how happy I am that you've come to us," Fiona said.

"I cannot tell you how happy I am to finally be able to see Menger House. It's incredibly lovely." Her voice sobered. "I only wish Papa could have lived to see it."

"I'd like to have known your papa."

"He wasn't a gentleman, you know."

"Yes," Fiona said. "Nick told me. Nevertheless, I have a great admiration for him." *Except for his harshness toward the little boy that had been Nick.*

Verity smiled. "You're all that's kind. How did you know that I'm fond of green? My bedchamber's wonderful."

"I copied the color in your room in Nick's old house." Fiona poured the steaming tea and handed Verity a dainty cup and saucer. "I'm so happy you've decided to let us bring you out."

"I've never been more nervous in my life," Verity said. "I'll be so vulnerable."

Vulnerable to snobbery and effrontery. "Miss Peabody, I believe, feels the very same," Fiona said.

"But Miss Peabody is Lord Warwick's sister-in-law. I'm nobody."

"You're Lady Fiona's sister-in-law. My family's older than and as respected as Warwick's." Fiona did not like to boast, but she liked even less for poor Verity to worry. "Your come-out will be *the* event of the Season—if for no other reason than everyone will want to get a glimpse of Menger House."

"But that does not assure that I'll have dancing partners," Verity said.

"With your extraordinary looks—and wealth—I'm persuaded you'll not lack for men to dance with." Fiona put sugar in her own tea. "Nick said you'd always balked at taking dancing lessons for the same reason you'd thought not to come out."

"Because I'm too low for your class and too high for mine?" Verity asked with a little laugh.

Fiona nodded.

The butler stepped into the room and cleared his throat.

"Yes, Biddles?" Fiona asked.

"Mr. Trevor Simpson to see you, madame."

"Please show him in."

Just inside the door, Trevor stood dead still, his head cocked to one side as he stared at Verity. "Well, if she isn't a female version of his czarness," Trevor said.

Verity lifted a quizzing brow.

"This, Miss Birmingham, is my friend Trevor Simpson," Fiona said, scowling at Trevor. "He's taken to calling your brother a czar."

Verity Birmingham then did a most undignified thing. She almost spit out her tea in a fit of laughter. "Then Mr. Simpson must know Nicky well," Verity finally managed. "He is rather dictatorial in his dealings with others."

"I beg to differ," Fiona defended. "Nick has never been anything but perfectly solicitous of me."

"That, my dear lady," Trevor said, squeezing onto the same settee with Fiona and Verity, "is because the man's besotted with you."

If only he were. "He's no such thing," Fiona said. "He's merely a considerate husband."

"I think, Mr. Simpson," Verity said, smiling, "my brother may very well be besotted over Lady Fiona."

"You're not to call me 'lady,'" Fiona scolded. Then

taking Verity's hand, Fiona said, "But just between you and me, I am besotted over your brother." Fiona felt she owed such an explanation to her sister after her heavy silence during their last visit—when Verity had disclosed how happy she was that Nick had married a woman who cared for him.

"Oh, pul-eeeeez," Trevor said, lifting his eyes toward the celestial ceiling, "spare me the mush." Even with his head tilted upward, Trevor's shirt points completely bracketed his slender face, his elaborate cravat comprising yards of freshly starched linen. He leaned forward and directed his attention to Verity. "Lady Fiona tells me you're coming out with Miss Peabody?"

"I may regret it, but I've consented," Verity said.

"Miss Birmingham's afraid no one will ask her to dance," Fiona said.

"I, for one, would be honored to dance with you," Trevor said, "even though I fear you're taller than me." Then gaping some more at her, he said, "Of course you'll have to allow me to dress you."

Clasping her hands over her breasts, Verity sent Trevor a shocked look.

"Not literally," Fiona said, laughing. "I believe Trevor fancies helping you select a new wardrobe."

Verity looked at Trevor as if he'd suddenly sprouted a second head.

"He's awfully clever about fashion," Fiona explained.

"And I can tell you, Miss Birmingham, you're wearing the wrong color." Trevor's gaze lazily perused Verity, then her charcoal dress. "One with your olive complexion and dark features cries out to wear red or snow white. Those are the only two colors I'll permit you to wear," he said with a limp flick of his wrist.

Verity sat stone still, obviously shocked.

"You must humor him," Fiona told Verity. "Please say you'll allow us to take you to Mrs. Spence's tomorrow." Anyone who read the newspapers or ladies' magazines would know Mrs. Spence was the modiste to the *ton*.

Her brows nudging down, Verity said, "I shouldn't like to look too . . . too undignified."

Fiona laughed. "Showing the better part of one's bosom is not undignified, dearest. Everyone does it."

"And even though I suspect your bosom's no more generous than poor Lady Fiona's," Trevor said to Verity, "I truly believe the lower neckline will accentuate your stunning coloring and the elegance of your long neck."

Scarlet tinged Verity's cheeks.

"Don't be embarrassed because Trevor's discussing your bosom," Fiona said. "You just need to think of him as one of the ladies."

Now Trevor scowled. "Perish such a thought."

After she and Nick made love that night, they lay in each other's arms, two damp, bare bodies that had so recently been one. She listened to the crackling sounds of the fire and to the sounds of his heavy breathing and thought she had never known such contentment.

"Trev and I shall take Verity to the modiste tomorrow," Fiona said in a whispery voice, pressing soft kisses into the mat of dark hair on her husband's chest.

He squeezed her shoulder. "Good. She needs a bit of guidance. Her tastes are too . . ."

"Too plain. She'll sparkle with the right clothing."

"I think she will." His hands glided over a smooth, bare hip. "So what did my sister think of Trevor?"

Fiona gave a little laugh. "I think she was actually quite stunned over him."

He chuckled. "I doubt she's ever met his likes before."

"Like Scotch whiskey, Trevor's an acquired taste."

"And like Scotch whiskey, a little bit goes a long way."

"You naughty man."

"Allow me to show you just how naughty." He nuzzled his face into her hair, kissing indiscriminately, his hands touching her intimately. "Did Verity say what made her change her mind about the come-out?" he asked in a husky voice.

"It was William," she answered breathlessly. "When he went to stay with her before he left for Prussia, he urged her to have a Season. He said he didn't like to think of her becoming an old maid, a spinster aunt to her brothers' children." The very idea of Nick and her having a child together had filled Fiona with a frothy sense of well-being. "He told her she would do well to look to the *ton* for a husband worthy of her."

"That's what you'd already told her," Nick said, nibbling on her neck.

She breathed in his scent that was a mixture of sandalwood; exotic cigars; and pure, heated male. "I had played on her desire to marry a well-educated gentleman."

"God, but I hope she does. I pray she'll not be snubbed."

"That's worrying her, too." Fiona laughed. "Trevor promised to dance with her."

"Heaven help her."

"You mustn't worry about her not taking, dearest," Fiona said, stroking his muscled arm. "I truly believe she'll meet someone who values her as we do."

"I pray you're right." He softly kissed her cheeks, her eyelids, her mouth. "Are you sure your leg's not hurting anymore?"

"I'm fine. Even my limp is less pronounced than it was earlier today."

"Then perhaps you can get on top this time," he growled, hauling her on top of him.

Chapter 17

"You've got to have a scarlet velvet riding habit," Trevor told Verity as he and the two ladies examined drapes of fabrics at Mrs. Spence's. "You do ride?"

"You can be assured," Fiona said, "that Jonathan Birmingham's children had the best instructors in all endeavors—including riding."

"All except dancing masters," Trevor quipped.

For a very good reason. Jonathan Birmingham knew his children would not be welcomed in aristocratic ballrooms, but Fiona had no wish to remind Verity of that fact now. Now that she would make her debut in one of those ballrooms. "I've decided you shall teach Miss Birmingham to dance," Fiona told Trevor.

His green eyes brightened. "I can think of no one better than I to school the lady." His eyes traveled over Verity. "Pity she's not shorter."

Fiona did not like his references to Verity's height. The poor girl was nervous enough without him making her feel an Amazon no man would wish to dance with. "Fortunately, most of the gentlemen who will dance with her will be possessed of more height than you, dear Trevor."

"There must somewhere be a beguiling dwarf awaiting my kiss," he said in a martyred voice.

"Not a dwarf, dearest. Just a person of no great stature," Fiona said, a smile eking from her pursed lips.

They had already selected an elegant ball gown in snow white crepe for Verity to wear to her come-out, and Fiona and Trevor had encouraged her to order all new dresses. "Though your clothes are beautifully made," Fiona had said, "they're not quite the mode for London."

They commissioned muslin and merino morning dresses, worsted and velvet pelisses, and the scarlet riding habit.

Verity lamented her old wardrobe. "It seems such a pity to waste perfectly good clothing."

"It won't be wasted," Fiona said. "I assure you my maid will be only too happy give them to the less fortunate."

"But," Miss Birmingham countered, "it seems such a waste to spend so much money on me. It's not as if I have a lot of friends with whom to socialize."

Fiona patted her arm. "But you will shortly. You've such a sweet, nonthreatening nature I'm certain all of my friends will adore you."

The look on Verity's face was not at all reassuring.

"And really, Verity," Fiona added, "you don't need to be so thrifty! It's not as if you aren't disgustingly rich!"

"I'm afraid I'm less like Nick and more like Papa when it comes to spending money," Verity said. "Papa did not amass so great a fortune by spending foolishly."

When they left Mrs. Spence's, they went to the milliner's on Conduit Street and tried to remember the colors of all the new dresses in order to match them with new bonnets. It was at the milliner's that Fiona eyed a child's muff in ermine. "I must purchase that for Emmie," she said, fishing in her reticule for a handful of shillings with which to pay for it.

Once they got back in the carriage, Trevor said, "Pray, is Emmie the bastard?"

Verity's stiffening did not escape Fiona's notice. "You are not to *ever* call her that!" Fiona scolded. "She's a perfectly lovely child. I can't have you blame her because her parents were wicked. But, of course, Nick's no longer wicked." At least she hoped with all her heart he was no longer cavorting with ladies of dubious reputation.

"Thank you for championing my niece," Verity said to Fiona.

Some champion I am! The poor little girl desperately needed a mother, but as fond as Fiona was of the child, she could not bring herself to call Emmie her daughter. "She's a dear." Changing to less uncomfortable conversation, Fiona asked, "Do you think she'll like the muff?"

"She'll love it."

Nick felt beastly that he'd been so damned busy he'd scarcely had time for his sister during her first two weeks in London. But tonight he would finally be a good host. He surveyed the dinner table before him. The first course had been laid, and footmen dressed in the Birmingham livery of blue and yellow stood by ready to assist. His wife faced him at the foot of the table, her lovely face bathed in candlelight from the gleaming chandeliers overhead.

Dressed the dandy, Trevor Simpson sat next to Verity, and Adam across from them. At Nick's left sat the Duchess of Glastonbury, one of Fiona's oldest friends. Not accompanied by her elderly husband, the duchess was exceedingly pretty with flame-colored hair. And she was exceedingly *available.* The few times Nick had met her, she had let Nick know just how available she was.

Fiona had also invited Randolph, but he had made an appallingly insincere excuse for not coming. She had not seen Randolph since that first day he returned to England, and Nick felt responsible for the rift. Could he give her the moon and stars he would gladly do so. A pity he could not command Agar to be a dutiful brother. God knows Fiona deserved Randolph's allegiance. She had, after all, made great sacrifices for her brother, though Nick loathed to admit it since her greatest sacrifice had been to pledge herself to a man unworthy of her.

Nick might not be worthy of her, but no man could love her more. Not a day passed that he did not thank God for the Spanish bandits who'd brought him Fiona.

"More wine?" he asked the duchess.

"Yes, please," she said.

He replenished Verity's glass next, then replaced the stopper on the decanter. "Tomorrow night we'll go to the theatre."

"To Miss Foley's new play?" Adam asked.

His wife's laughing face went suddenly white, her posture rigid. Surely, he thought, she doesn't know that Diane Foley had been his lover. "Yes," Nick answered. "It's supposed to be a great comedy."

"Then I shall look forward to seeing it," Verity said.

His glance whisked over Verity. She looked truly lovely in a peach-colored dress that draped off her shoulders—and that displayed the tops of her breasts. He'd never before noticed his sister was possessed of such an attractive bosom. "You look . . . actually beautiful, Verity. Elegance becomes you." Then his gaze flicked to Fiona. "I perceive you've had a hand in my sister's lovely transformation."

Still looking a bit shaken, Fiona shrugged. "I can't take credit for her own dazzling beauty."

"Yes," Adam said, staring at his sister, "you really are beautiful, Verity."

"The woman's a goddess," Trevor proclaimed. "That bosom was made to be displayed."

Her face turning scarlet, Verity threw her arms up around her chest to conceal her soft, feminine curves. "I daresay," she said in a shy voice, "you make me feel like a horse being auctioned at Tattersall's."

"If you were a horse," Trevor said, "you'd fetch a hefty price."

"Trevor," Fiona chided, "you must know women are embarrassed to have their brothers looking at their bosom." She sent Nick an amused glance that said husbands looking at their wives' breasts was an altogether different matter. It was just one of the little looks they had begun to share with each other, one of the little ways they were growing close.

The memory of Fiona's breasts, their feel, their taste, had him instantly aroused. No woman had ever aroused him as she did. When he was away from her and she would cross his mind, he became suddenly erect.

After dinner the ladies went to the saloon to play the pianoforte and sing, but the men would not join them until they had drunk their port and smoked their cigars. When the ladies got up to leave the lavish dining room, Nick froze for a moment. He was not sure which gender Trevor would align himself with. Even though Trevor surely had more in common with the women, he stayed behind.

"So, brother of mine," Adam said, "I had my doubts about this marriage of yours, but it looks as if you and the lady were made for one another."

Physically, yes. He and Fiona were decidedly compatible. If only she wasn't in love with that damned Warwick. "I can't speak for Fiona, but I certainly have no complaints. She's all a man could want in a wife."

"Well, I can answer for her," Trevor said with a flick of his wrist. "She's completely besotted."

Nick did not believe it for a moment, but he was

grateful for Fiona's feigned devotion. She had certainly fulfilled the vow she'd made to him the day he'd dropped to his knee to beg her hand. "I'll make you a good wife," she had said. And she had in every way.

If only Warwick had not long ago won her heart.

"Nick's always had a devastating effect upon women," Adam said to Trevor. "I perceive that the Duchess of Glastonbury is no exception."

"You naughty man!" Trevor said. "I wasn't going to mention the sizzling looks she gave your brother, though I daresay Lady Fiona could not help but to notice." He turned to Nick. "Did your wife not seem ill at ease?"

She did, but Nick attributed that to Diane Foley. He supposed a lady—even a lady who was in love with a man who was *not* her husband—would hardly tolerate her husband offering his protection to a vulgar actress.

There was little entertainment available to one who was economizing, Randolph, Lord Agar, had discovered. Since he was not staying out late—devilishly difficult to drink and game when one had no money to spare—he had taken to rising early, walking round to the livery stable for his mount, and taking a good romp through Hyde Park each morning.

A good ride always seemed to release the tension in his body. There had been a great deal of tension since he had returned from Portugal. He missed his sister and knew his own stubborn arrogance had estranged them, but he could not bring himself to come face to face with her knowing she had sold herself to an arrogant Cit. For him.

Never mind that Birmingham was wealthier than a nabob or that women of every age and every background made fools of themselves over him. He was still a social-climbing Cit who was using Randolph's sister as rungs in his social ladder.

Randolph dug in his heels and sprinted forward. The fog was beginning to lift, and for as far as he could see, he was alone. He was not in the mood to be civil to another human. He was too devilishly angry with that blasted Birmingham. The pity of it was Fiona had actually tried to convince Randolph that she had fallen in love with the Cit!

It wasn't just Birmingham's inferior social standing that roused Randolph's fury—though he certainly could not overlook that, where his sister was concerned. It was the man's reputation with lewd women. And everyone knew about his bastard—or bastards, possibly! Such a pity that Fiona would be saddled with such an ill-begotten child. Fiona, who had been an innocent virgin. Before Birmingham.

Randolph snapped his riding crop angrily and forged ahead. But he was no longer alone. Some fifty feet away a lone rider, a woman, was cantering toward him. As she drew closer he was able to make out her features. Lovely features they were, too. Rich, dark brown hair swept into a stylish hat that was bright red, like the red riding habit she wore. He saw that her eyes were as dark as her hair, her cheekbones high, her face beautiful. But what impressed him even more than her abundant beauty was the way she sat her horse. He'd never seen a woman ride more fluidly.

There was no doubt she was a gentlewoman. Her horse was unquestionably expensive, as were her clothes. And only a person who'd had the finest riding masters could sit a horse like that. But Randolph could not understand why she had no groom with her, even if she were a married lady—which he distinctly hoped she was not.

As she passed him, he tipped his hat and nodded.

She tipped her head, a smile lifting the corners of her lovely mouth, and rode on.

The rest of the day Randolph was unable to dispel the lovely brunette from his mind and from his thoughts. There was something in her dark beauty that was vaguely familiar. Perhaps it was the coloring she shared with Countess Warwick, whom Randolph had worshiped. Of course, the countess was much more voluptuous than the elegantly slender lone rider he'd seen that morning.

He found himself eagerly awaiting his next ride through the park.

The following day he saw her again. As she drew near, his heart drummed when his eyes met hers and he tipped his hat. Once again, she almost indiscernibly nodded to him and rode on.

Every day for three weeks he rode in the park, and every day he crossed the path of the woman in red and silently tipped his hat to her. His morning rides became the highlight of his days, the woman in red the substance of his nightly dreams.

He was becoming obsessed with her. Visions of her dark beauty were with him wherever he went. On every street he looked for her. In every theatre or rout or assembly he scanned the women in the hopes of finding her. His thirst to know her identity was so great he even considered following her from the park, but such an ungentlemanly action would only serve to alienate the beauty were she to discover him.

Surely their paths were fated to cross outside of Hyde Park. After all, they must belong to the same set, for he had no doubts as to her gentility. His only doubts concerned her marital state.

He hoped to God she wasn't married.

Chapter 18

As Fiona and Maggie huddled over the escritoire drawing up guest lists for their sisters' ball, the young honorees were on their way to becoming fast friends.

"My sister tells me you were as reluctant as I to have a come-out," Verity said to Miss Peabody.

Rebecca Peabody shrugged. Verity thought she bore a remarkable resemblance to the beautiful countess who was her sister—except for the spectacles, which had a habit of slipping down her nose, and except for her absence of a bosom. "I confess that I'm much more enamored of books than I am of men. Of course if real live men were as noble as Mr. Darcy in *Pride and Prejudice*, that would be a horse of a different color."

A smile tweaked at Verity's mouth. "Indeed."

"What persuaded you?"

"To agree to come out?" Verity asked.

"Yes."

She thought about her answer for a moment before articulating it. "Two things, I think. First, my youngest brother said if I did not allow myself to be presented I would end up being a spinster aunt to my brothers' children." This she said with her voice lifting in laughter.

"I declare, you're describing me!" Miss Peabody said with a morose laugh. "Pray, what was the other reason?"

"If I did not come out I'd never have the opportunity to meet a man who could be my soul mate." It was the oddest thing, really, about soul mates. A month ago the very idea would have been alien to her, but for the past three weeks Verity had been haunted with the feeling the handsome blond man she saw riding in the park every morning was her soul mate. It wasn't at all like her to be so silly over a man. For all she knew, the blond Adonis could be a happily married man. "You see, my chances of meeting an eligible man at our home in the country are nonexistent. My mother's the most unsocial creature imaginable, so the only men I ever see are footmen and grooms."

Miss Peabody was staring at her as if Verity was delusional. "Define for me, if you will, what precisely is a soul mate?"

When Verity had come to London, her wish was to meet a man who was her intellectual equal, but now she wanted so much more from that man. It took her a moment to analyze those feelings so she could impart them to Miss Peabody. "A man who enjoys the same things I enjoy, who wishes to spend his life with me because of all the women on earth I'm the one most suited for him, a man who's my destiny." She remembered Fiona telling her Nick was her destiny. "I believe Lady Fiona feels that my brother is her destiny—despite their divergent backgrounds."

Miss Peabody sighed. "I cannot tell you how happy I am to learn that, for I've been most distraught over my sister's shabby treatment of Lady Fiona last year."

This was news to Verity. "I cannot believe Lady Warwick could ever have treated Fiona shabbily."

"Then you don't know?"

"Know what?"

"My sister stole Lord Warwick away from Lady Fiona."

Verity's heart thudded. Fiona had loved Warwick?
Did that mean Fiona had grabbed Nick on the rebound? The knowledge disturbed her, especially
since Nick was so completely in love with his wife.
"They were engaged?"

Miss Peabody pursed her lips. "Unofficially."

"I suppose things happen for the best," Verity said
with resignation. "I'm sure Lord and Lady Warwick
are most happy with each other—just as Fiona and
Nicky are."

"I think your brother's more handsome than Warwick, though I've only seen his portrait." Miss
Peabody's demeanor brightened. "I'm told you have
another brother who could be his twin."

Verity gave an amused laugh. "It's hard for me to
think of my brothers as handsome, but I must say girls
have always adored Nicky; later, women did."

"And the other brother?"

"Adam? He's quite different from Nicky—though
they do look a great deal alike." Sensing that Miss
Peabody was mildly interested in Adam, she added,
"I shall introduce you to him at our come-out. I'm sure
he would be delighted to stand up with you."

"I don't think I'm ready to marry," Rebecca said a
moment later. "Being void of any need for a soul
mate, I shall probably end up a doting spinster aunt."

"You're much too pretty," Verity said. A pity Miss
Peabody always had to wear those spectacles.

"Yes, she is," Fiona agreed, walking up and sitting
beside Verity. "I have fears of men coming to fisticuffs
over the both of you at the come-out."

"I do, too," Maggie said as she sank onto the settee
across from them.

"They might even come to fisticuffs tonight at
Almack's," Fiona said.

"You've received vouchers?" the countess asked.

Fiona nodded. "Yes, the Duchess of Glastonbury,

one of my oldest friends, insisted on procuring them for us even though I told her the Countess Cowper and I are on the best of terms."

"I still shake in my slippers each time I see Lady Cowper," Maggie said with a laugh.

Fiona's gaze swung to Verity. "Don't be frightened by Lady Warwick's fears. Lady Cowper is all that's amiable, and I'm sure she'll adore you." Then smiling at Maggie, Fiona added, "I daresay your colonial background has rendered you a bit wary of English stiltedness."

Verity was no colonial, but she most assuredly was wary of English stiltedness.

The door to the saloon slammed open and Emmie flew into the room. Her warm brown hair trailed down the back of her butter yellow dress, and her hands were stuffed into the ermine muff. "My Lady! Miss Beckham says I can wear my new muff to the park today. I wanted to show you."

The governess being mentioned scurried into the chamber, an embarrassed look upon her face. "Miss Birmingham!" she shouted, "You're not ever to disturb your stepmother when she's entertaining callers." She flicked an apologetic glance to Fiona. "Please forgive me."

"There's nothing to forgive. This is, after all, Miss Emmie's house, too," Fiona said. Directing her attention to the little girl, she said, "Come closer, love, and show us how lovely you look." Fiona proceeded to introduce Emmie to the countess and Miss Peabody. "This is Nick's daughter, Emmie, my lady, Miss Peabody. Is she not a pretty little thing?"

The ladies exclaimed over her—and her beautiful muff.

Before she left, Emmie curtsied, then came to kiss her aunt and stepmother.

* * *

It had been an age since Fiona had been at Almack's. She was so utterly looking forward to strutting around the assembly rooms on the arm of her handsome husband. This would be her first opportunity to introduce him to many of her old friends.

She was seated at her dressing table watching her maid fasten small diamonds in her hair when Nick tapped at their adjoining door and stepped in, his gaze seductively whisking over her.

"Thank you, Prudence," Fiona said. "That will be all."

Once her maid departed the room, Fiona watched Nick through her looking glass as he moved to her, then bent to nibble at her neck. "You look good enough to eat," he murmured, one hand possessively cupping her breast. "I'm partial to that dress. It matches your incredible eyes."

She gazed into the mirror. She did not recall having worn the pale blue gown in front of him before.

He reached into his pocket and withdrew a velvet case. "You wore this gown at the theatre that night you sat in the box across from mine, before we were married."

She was touched that he remembered the dress, even more touched that he had noticed her. "You remembered me that night?"

"A man doesn't forget the most beautiful woman he's ever met."

Her gladness flowed to every cell in her body. Nick had praised her beauty before but never with such superlatives. "So you really did notice me that night at the theatre?"

"How could I not?" he asked with a devilish glint in his eyes. "You stared at me throughout the entire play!"

"You odious, conceited, arrogant man!"

"Can you deny it?"

She effected a pout. "No." Though it had been just three months since that night, that night belonged to a different world, a different person. It seemed like three years ago rather than three months.

He opened the velvet case and took out a stunning sapphire necklace, which he placed around her slender throat. "I've bought you sapphires, to match your eyes," he said, fastening the necklace.

Though the jewels were extravagantly expensive, it was the thoughtfulness of the gesture that touched her most deeply. Nick had taken time from his busy days to select it for her. "It's beautiful!" she exclaimed. "Quite the loveliest piece of jewelry I've ever owned."

He bent to kiss her neck. "Such a lovely neck demands lovely jewels. Of course," he said in a husky voice, "I prefer you wearing nothing at all."

"I beg that you don't speak of such, for I shall want to climb into bed with you, and we'd never make it to Almack's."

He straightened up, a frown on his pensive face.

"What's the matter, dearest?" she asked.

"I'm sorry to say I won't be able to accompany you to Almack's tonight."

She whirled around to face him, her brows lowered. "Why?"

"Business."

Her heart pounded. "But the Exchange isn't open at night! What kind of business claims your nights?" She was possessed of the most horrid feeling that he was lying to her. Could it be he feared rejection tonight at the hands of her aristocratic friends?

"A very important man whose financial affairs I see to has asked that I meet with him tonight. He'll only be in London for one day, and this is the only time we can meet."

Anger, disappointment, and the most dreadful feeling that he was lying collided within her. Why had he not named the important man? Her shoulders sagged. In her dressing table mirror she saw him standing behind her, watching her with sultry eyes. "I cannot tell you how very disappointed I am," she said. "If you aren't going to Almack's, then I'm not either."

He scowled. "I'm honored that you seek my company, but I beg that you go to the assembly rooms. For Verity's sake."

Of course she was being exceedingly selfish. It would not be fair to Verity to miss Almack's because Fiona was in a pout.

"I give you my word I'll go to Almack's next week," he said. "I daresay there will be many more opportunities for me to be scrutinized by your friends."

She looked up at him. "You cannot deny that you lack enthusiasm for the social event I was so looking forward to."

He shrugged. "While my enthusiasm is not as great as yours, you can be assured that for the sake of my wife and sister I'm willing to be paraded about on your arm. Just not tonight."

Turning a cold shoulder to her husband, Fiona went to the assembly rooms with Verity. Her friend, the Duchess of Glastonbury, had been the first to rush up to her. A luscious redhead dressed in a sparkling rust gown, the duchess had come out the same year as Fiona and like Fiona had attracted a throng of well-connected suitors. Unlike Fiona, Hortense was happy to marry an elderly peer for the sake of an exalted title.

"Where is that husband of yours?" the duchess asked. "I was so looking forward to seeing him."

Fiona stiffened. "You will have to wait until next week. He had an out-of-town visitor tonight."

It wasn't until midway through the evening that a chilling thought slammed into her like a tidal wave. *Nick's with Diane Foley!* That would explain why he was so vague about the "important" client, why his "meeting" had to take place tonight.

Fiona began to tremble, and she felt so hot she was

afraid she would faint. She could not even make conversation with Trevor, who was dancing with her.

"What's wrong?" Trevor asked, backing away from her in order to gaze into her suddenly blanched face. "Are you ill?"

She was too upset to formulate a thought. Blurring accusations and wrenching grief whirled through her. Her eyes filled with tears. She could not even see Trevor.

"My lady! What is it? Can I get you a drink?"

All she could do was nod.

He led her to a chair where other peeresses sat and commanded her to sit. Trembling, she dropped onto the chair. The pain she had felt when Warwick married another was a mere trifle compared to this paralyzing agony, her love for Warwick barely a trickle of that which she now lavished on her husband.

"Lady Fiona," said Lady Jersey, who was seated at her left, "I was so hoping to meet your husband tonight."

"You will meet him next week," Fiona said, willing herself not to dissolve into tears. A lifetime of gentility prevailed. Her tears did not fall. "You have met Miss Birmingham?" Fiona asked the patroness.

Lady Jersey fanned herself. "A lovely girl."

"Thank you." Fiona felt wretchedly hot. Drawing in a breath, she said, "All the Birminghams are blessed with good looks." *Especially Nick.*

"So I've heard."

His short legs scurrying like a frightened mouse, Trevor came up, put a glass of lemonade into Fiona's trembling hand, and like a doting parent, watched her drink. Then he sank onto the chair beside her. "You must let me take you home." Under his breath he cursed Nick for not being at his wife's side when she had taken ill.

"I daresay it's the heat," Lady Jersey said, shooting

Fiona a concerned glance and fanning herself even more vigorously. "Beastly hot in here tonight."

"Lady Fiona's never been so affected by hot rooms before." Trevor scowled at Lady Jersey. "The lady's obviously sick, and I'm taking her home."

"Pray, not yet." Fiona's blurry gaze drifted to the dance floor. Verity had not sat out a single dance. Elegant looking in a simple white gown, she executed her dance steps flawlessly. "I shouldn't wish to deprive Miss Birmingham's dancing partners."

Trevor watched his pupil. "One would never know Miss Birmingham hadn't spent the last year in ballrooms."

"Because she had such a fine dancing master," Fiona said, her voice a monotone. If only she could keep talking. Perhaps it would rid her mind of painful thoughts of Nick with Diane Foley. Was he lying beside her at this very moment? Would he put his mouth on Miss Foley's breasts? The thought was like a saber to Fiona's heart. She squeezed back the new tears that threatened.

"I don't care what you say," Trevor said. "I'm taking you home as soon as this set is over. It won't hurt Miss Birmingham to leave. She'll have many more assemblies and balls."

Dabbing at her eye with her gloved hand, Fiona nodded.

Even after he met with Warwick that night, Nick was not convinced the meeting had been necessary. After all, he had not even heard from William yet. Nick suspected Warwick's insistence on meeting tonight was to keep from having to go to Almack's. Deadly dull gatherings, he'd been told.

One thing about their meeting—besides its devilish location an hour's drive from London—disturbed

Nick. Warwick had repeatedly brought up Fiona. *How did Lady Fiona find Menger House? You, Birmingham, are a most fortunate man to have wed Lady Fiona.* When they discussed the come-out for Miss Peabody and Miss Birmingham, Warwick had said, "I'll never forget Lady Fiona's come-out. I thought her the most beautiful woman I'd ever seen." Was Warwick now sorry he'd wed another? Was he still in love with Fiona? With a sickening thud in his chest, Nick wondered if Fiona was still in love with Warwick. Nick was well aware of the lack of fidelity in *ton* marriages. Was Warwick hoping to have an affair with his wife?

When Nick had agreed to marry Fiona he had not bargained on the remarkable highs and incredible lows his love for her would bring him. No pain could ever be greater than finding his wife in another man's bed. Warwick was entirely too virile looking. Damn but Nick hated the earl!

Later, as he approached Menger House, he was filled with the usual sense of well-being that mushroomed inside him at the prospect of seeing his wife. Then, remembering how out of charity she had been with him earlier in the evening, he had no right to expect her to come to his bed tonight.

His mood morose, he trudged up the stairs with only a single taper to light the way. Three months of very satisfying matrimony had given Nick a dislike for sleeping alone. Even if he did not have the pleasure of making love to Fiona, having her beside him was enough to fill him with joy. But, of course, not tonight. Her sulkiness would no doubt keep her in her own chamber.

When he eased open the door to his bedchamber he was astonished to see Fiona lying in his bed.

Fiona had told herself that a man recently sated by lovemaking had little desire to repeat the action with another woman the very same night. But she was powerless to stay away from Nick. Where he was concerned, she was rapidly losing her pride. Even if he didn't want her, she needed to lie beside him.

He met her gaze. "Still mad?"

"I wasn't mad," she said, sitting up. She had worn a soft blue nightshift because Nick liked her in blue. "I was disappointed."

He came to sit on the bed beside her, his hand molding to her cheeks. "I'll make it up to you," he murmured.

Her voice purred like a contented cat. "Now?"

His head dipped to hers. "Nothing would give me greater pleasure."

Their lips met, gently at first, but the tenderness quickly ignited into a searing passion that swept them up into its roaring tide. She was stunned by his own rapid breathlessness, by his eagerness that matched her own. He quickly tore off his clothing and just as quickly yanked off her nightshift.

It was as if their need was so desperate neither of them could spare a second for gentle foreplay or tender words. He rolled with her across his wide bed until she was flat on her back and he was poised over her, spreading her thighs and murmuring heated exclamations. Then he plunged into her and rode her faster and harder than he'd ever done before.

Explosions rippled within her as he trembled, called out her name, then stilled. Her arms were a vice across his rock-hard back as she lifted her hips to meet him, pulsing with the most extraordinary pleasure she had ever experienced.

In his most heated moment, Nick cried out, "Oh, my love, my Fiona."

Long afterward, they lay in each other's arms, completely spent and totally sated. And long afterward she remembered his words. *Oh, my love, my Fiona.*

Chapter 19

Fiona missed Randolph dreadfully. She kept telling herself she should be used to his absence since he'd spent the last year in The Peninsula, but it was the knowing that he was in London and refused to see her that hurt so keenly. That they had always been exceptionally close made the estrangement even more difficult to bear.

From Randy's frank talks with her, she had learned much about men and their desires. Now, more than ever before, she wished to pick his brain in order to better understand the enigmatic man she had married. But now, more than any time in their lives, her brother was completely inaccessible.

More than once she had stopped herself from initiating a meeting with Randolph. Though she wished to alleviate her fears over his recovery from the injuries he'd sustained in captivity, she was too out of charity with him to make the first move. Going to him would condone his shabby treatment of Nick.

Such blatant hostility toward her husband could never be accepted.

She was plagued with worries that Randy and she would never reconcile. As painful as that prospect was, it was a separation she could live with were so forced to do so. A separation from Nick, though, was unthinkable. Unbearable. She did not know how she could continue to draw breath if she ever lost her husband—or lost his affection.

She wondered if she would have agreed to marry him had she known she would fall so madly in love with him that every separation from him would torment her. This marriage was so different from what she had prepared herself for. She had expected to be mildly infatuated with him, to be content to spend his money and bear his children, but she'd never anticipated such a crushing, choking, debilitating love to consume her.

Last night's agony of worry that he was in Diane Foley's arms was as great as the deepest grief she'd ever known.

Just when she was in the depths of despair, Nick had come and swept her up into the heavens in his arms. She tingled inside and grew breathless every time she recalled his words. *Oh, my love, my Fiona.*

She had gone through the morning cloaked in a fuzzy warmth induced by recalling the mesmerizing touch of his hands on her bare body, the sound of his husky voice, the feel of his powerful body stretched out over hers. Surely he could not have wanted her with such hunger had he just come from Diane Foley's bed, could not have spoken so tenderly.

Could he?

That was one of the things she would liked to have asked Randy. That, and if words uttered during passion were truthful or merely an accouterment to overwhelming physical pleasure. For only in his bed did Nick's guarded reserve drop. Only in his bed did he treat her like a flesh-and-blood woman and not an untouchable peeress.

Later that afternoon Trevor came to take her for

a ride in Hyde Park. The Misses Peabody and Birmingham were walking there, but owing to Fiona's still-mending leg, she chose to ride instead. It was a lovely day, brisk and blazingly sunny, and a variety of colorful spring flowers relieved the long stretches of green. Because the weather was so fine, they had to wait with a long procession of conveyances before they could enter the park gates.

Not long after entering the park in Trevor's phaeton, Fiona cleared her throat. "I don't suppose you've ever made love to a woman?" Being a married woman had made her brazen. Three months ago she would have been unable to speak of so intimate a subject with a member of the opposite sex.

Trevor's grip on the ribbons tightened. Looking straight at the barouche in front of them, he said, "Had to try it. Once. When I was at Cambridge. There was a most exceedingly willing little wench who lifted her skirts any number of times on any given night."

"I don't suppose men—under such circumstances—would be obliged to utter any passionate declarations of a romantic nature?"

"The only thing a man would be obliged to do—under those circumstances—would be to open his purses," Trevor said with a wicked laugh.

"Would you think that . . . if a man makes romantic declarations during passion, his words are colored by 'the moment'?"

He nodded to a lone horseman passing by. "If it's Birmingham you're asking about, the man is besotted over you."

"I wish I had your confidence of his regard," she said. "Do you know if . . . if he's still seeing Miss Foley?" Her heart almost stopped beating.

"A man don't need a mistress when his wife sees to his sexual needs."

Her cheeks burned. How did Trevor know that she'd become adept at seeing to her husband's sexual needs? "You didn't answer my question."

He pulled on the ribbons, coming almost to a stop, then turned to face her, his face earnest. "To my knowledge his czarness no longer 'sees' Miss Foley."

She could have clapped her hands with glee. It was a glorious day! She seemed suddenly aware of the scent of roses and freshly mowed grass. "I suspect you wouldn't tell me if he were."

"No, I wouldn't. You're far too smitten with him for your own good." He flicked the ribbons. "But I am being honest with you."

After they circled the Serpentine, nodding to acquaintances and pausing to speak with old friends, she asked, "What do you know of Randy?"

"He's become a hermit. No Almack's. No Boodle's. No gaming. I even heard he's let Agar House and sold off the old carriage. Haven't seen him even once. He's become utterly unsocial."

Her heart drummed. "Do you think his injury . . . ?"

He shook his head. "Harry Lyle told me your brother's had a complete recovery."

"Thank goodness," she said, every muscle in her body relaxing.

"I know the fellow's been beastly ill-mannered to you, but I've heard he's somewhat patched things up with your husband."

She whirled toward Trevor. "How so?"

"He laid his finances at Birmingham's feet."

"I don't understand why he'll speak to Nick and not to me."

Trevor shrugged. "No doubt your obtuse brother feels guilty that you've had to 'sacrifice' yourself for him."

She gave a bitter laugh.

* * *

Cognizant that since she was not born to gentility she would be unduly scrutinized, Miss Verity Birmingham had spent a lifetime carefully grooming herself to be unobtrusive. Never initiating a conversation, she spoke only when spoken to. She had eschewed social situations and dressed with modest dignity befitting someone of twice her years. She had liked nothing better than blending into the pale walls.

Until the day she donned her red riding habit. And began crossing the path of the most ruggedly handsome man she'd ever seen. For five weeks now she had not missed a single morning ride.

Nor had he. He of the broad chest, long legs, and whitish blond hair. He who sat magnificently on his equally magnificent chestnut. His customary nod to her had extended to a smiling "Good morning," but the acceleration of their acquaintance was entirely too slow to satisfy her.

She must have a bit of her father in her. "Don't wait for yer ship to come in," Jonathan Birmingham had always said. "Swim out to meet it."

Today she would swim out to meet Him.

She had roused her maid early that morning to arrange her hair in a most becoming fashion, and after she donned the elegant scarlet riding habit, she had sprinkled perfume at her wrists and beneath her ear.

She planned to canter in the southern portion of the park where she usually saw Him, then she would jump a low hedge. Though she was an excellent horsewoman, this morning she would "fall" from her horse.

Arriving at the park a little earlier than usual, she cantered in a circle until she caught a glimpse of him in the distance. She watched him as he came closer, her heartbeat hammering. Then she dug in her heels, hunkered down, and raced toward the hedge. She had practiced the move in her mind a hundred times, especially the night before when her excitement had kept her from sleep. As the horse began to sail into an arc, she slid from its back and with an unrehearsed scream, she landed on her backside.

Even though her "accident" had been carefully staged, tears gathered in her eyes, and her heart pounded so loudly she hadn't heard him ride up and leap from his mount.

From the corner of her eye she saw him streak toward her. "Are you hurt?" he asked in a panicked voice.

Her face lifted to his, but when she went to respond, she had no voice.

He dropped to his knees in front of her, the features of his handsome face crushing with concern. "Can you move?"

"I don't know," she finally managed.

"Allow me to help." He settled an arm around her, then came to his feet, tugging her with him.

She was ever so glad to see that at her full height, she did not come past his formidable shoulders. Thank God he was tall. She was ever so glad, too, that she had thought to apply the perfume. He was definitely close enough to smell its light floral scent. In fact, this was the closest she had ever been to a man who was not her brother.

And she decided being so close to this man was quite agreeable.

"Try to walk," he urged.

Putting her arm around his waist, she took a wobbly step. Then another. Thankfully, she had not broken any bones or suffered any serious injury. Though this man would have been worth harming herself for. Her gaze locked on his shiny black Hessians. She could not believe she was actually beside Him, so close she could smell his leathery scent. They were actually touching each other!

"Are you in pain?"

"My dear sir, one does not fall from a horse without experiencing pain." My, but she was not being her complacent self. This man had a most singular effect on her. And on her tongue.

"Allow me to rephrase. Does walking hurt?"

"I don't think so."

"Then you have been most fortunate."

She was pleased that he kept his arm around her. "I expect my pride's as bruised as anything. I'm not usually such a poor rider." Good Lord, she had even taken to boasting—which was something she had *never* done before.

"I must say I was surprised when you fell, for I've often admired your superior riding skills."

That was a start. Now if he only admired other things about her. "I've had the occasion to admire your riding, too, sir, which makes me exceedingly embarrassed that I've made such an idiot of myself in front of you."

He reached to gently sweep a lock of dark hair from her brow. "You could never look like an idiot."

"Perhaps *inelegant* is a better word than *idiot*," she suggested.

His eyes were the exact shade of blue as Lady Fiona's. And there was concern in them. "I don't believe you could ever be inelegant, either."

She laughed. "Oh, I'm quite sure I was inelegant when I sprawled out on my derriere."

He laughed, too. "Allow me to walk with you until I'm assured of your recovery."

"Perhaps you should secure our mounts first."

She felt bereft when he let go of her to tie his obedient mount to a skinny tree. It took longer for him to find hers and secure it. Something touched her soul as she watched his bent head as he secured her mount, her gaze whisking from the tip of his blond head, down his chocolate-colored coat to his fawn breeches. Everything about him bespoke power. She could see him commanding hundreds of men.

When he returned to her, he offered his arm, and they began to walk along a path. "A well-born young lady like yourself should not be out without her groom, you know. Your . . . husband should ensure his wife is better taken care of."

This was good. He was obviously interested in learning if she was married. "I have no husband."

"I'm happy to learn that."

Her pulse stampeded. "Does that mean that you are unmarried?" She held her breath.

"Yes, I'm a bachelor."

She could have swooned with relief.

They walked along in silence, her senses never before so alive to the chirping of birds and the wind slapping at the petals of spring flowers.

A moment later he said, "Surely you've come out?"

"In a little over a month, actually."

He muttered something under his breath. If she wasn't mistaken, he was blasting the men who would fall at her feet. *If only he knew.* She still believed she would be a dreadful wallflower, her brothers and Trevor Simpson her only dancing partners. She fleetingly wished herself brazen enough to invite this stranger to her ball, but she was mindful of her need for propriety. It was vital that to this man she be indistinguishable from the upper born.

"You live near the park?" he asked, smiling down at her.

"For the Season. I'm staying with my brother and his new wife."

"And the rest of the year? You live where?"

"In Kent."

"Is that where you learned to ride?" His blond hair ruffled in the wind.

"Actually I learned to ride right here in Hyde Park.

As a child I lived in The City. After my father died, my mother was granted her wish to live year-round in the country." Verity hated to see that the fog was beginning to lift, for that would mean He would be going.

"So that explains why you haven't been snatched up."

For the first time in her life, Verity Birmingham acted the coquet. "Pray, sir, whatever do you mean 'snatched up'?"

"I mean that as soon as you're presented you'll be besieged with offers of marriage." His brows plunged and he sounded quite grumpy.

Which was wonderful.

"You're much too kind."

"It's not kindness," he snapped. "You're entirely too lovely."

On the spot, Verity decided this was the most wonderful day of her life. Her dark lashes lowered and she whispered, "Thank you."

They had come back to where their horses were tied, and he turned to her and spoke with disappointment. "I regret that I must go now or I will be late for a meeting with my brother-in-law—a man one does not keep waiting. Would I be too ill mannered if I asked permission to ride with you tomorrow morning?"

Would she be too ill mannered if she agreed to? After all, genteel young ladies did not meet with men—especially strange men—unchaperoned. Her desire to be with him was stronger than her desire to preserve respectability. "Only if you promise to tell me about yourself tomorrow," she said. "You asked all the questions today."

He bowed and took her hand, settling soft lips on her gloved fingers.

That was when she saw the signet ring.

She recoiled as if she'd been struck by a viper. She

only vaguely heard his words: "Be assured that I shall look forward to furthering my acquaintance with you."

Her heart thundering, she nodded as she allowed him to help her mount.

"Are you certain you're unhurt?" he asked with concern.

"Yes, quite," she snapped, digging in her heels and letting the pounding horse whisk her away from Him. Her blond Adonis was a peer! Why, out of all the men in London, did she have to fall in love with an aristocrat? Once he found out who she was, he would no doubt treat her as one would a leper.

Her knuckles white from her harsh grip on the reins, she realized there would be no more morning rides. She could not meet him tomorrow—or ever again.

"How are you liking Almack's, dearest?" Fiona asked Nick.

He looked down into his wife's face. "Waltzing with the most beautiful woman here is most enjoyable. Everything else is as dull as I'd been told."

She pouted. "But you must admit Verity has taken quite well."

"For that I'm grateful. Do you find that she's attracted to any of her suitors?"

"While she's all that's amiable, I don't think any man has captured her heart."

When that set was finished he went to procure lemonade for his wife and sister, but upon his return Lord Warwick was leading Fiona onto the dance floor. Another bloody waltz!

As painful as it was to watch his wife with the man she had been in love with, Nick was unable to tear away his gaze. They made such a stunning couple, Fiona delicate and fair, Warwick dark and powerful.

Warwick was smiling down at Fiona, and they gave the appearance of enjoying each other's company excessively. Damn Warwick.

"They make a lovely couple, do they not?" asked the Duchess of Glastonbury, who had come to stand beside him and followed his gaze.

He glared down his nose at the beautiful redhead. "To whom are you referring?"

"To your wife and Warwick, of course. Even as a young girl Lady Fiona was mad for him, and I think he was mad for her, but since he had no hope of inheriting a fortune and title—at that time—he merely worshiped her from a distance. I always thought they would spend their lives together."

As did everyone else in the ton. Nick tensed. "Then it's my good fortune that Warwick has found love and fatherhood with another woman."

"I thought he had," she said, still staring at the couple swirling across the dance floor, "until I saw him with Fiona again tonight."

Nick's thoughts exactly. He had often wondered how Warwick could ever have preferred another over Fiona. "Surely you realize they have been lifelong friends," he said. "It's not like *my wife* to turn her back on old friends."

"Of course you're right," said the duchess, placing a hand on his sleeve. "Lady Fiona is one of the dearest people I know." She lowered her long lashes, "Forgive my boldness, Mr. Birmingham, but I should love to waltz with you. I adore waltzing with tall men. You know my Glastonbury is exceedingly short."

And absent. Nick could not bloody well refuse this brazen woman.

"I've never seen you more radiant," Lord Warwick said to Fiona as he smiled down at her, their hands clasped, his other hand at her waist as they executed the steps to the waltz.

"That's because I've never been happier."

"I wished to thank you for telling my wife your observations about 'fate.' You've greatly relieved my conscience."

She gave a little laugh. "I knew the minute I saw you with your countess that she—not I—was your fate. I'll admit that at the time it was painful for me. But now I can truthfully tell you I've never been happier. Nick may not be high born, but out of all the men on earth, there's not one better suited for me."

Warwick nodded. "He's a good man. You've done well for yourself, Fiona."

"It's not just the money, you know."

"I do know."

As she watched Nick sailing across the dance floor with the Duchess of Glastonbury, she stiffened. They were smiling and laughing with one another. Fiona did not at all like to see her husband with her old friend. Hortense was not only a noted flirt, but she also was known to bestow her sexual favors indiscriminately.

And if Fiona wasn't mistaken, Hortense had set her cap for Nick.

Chapter 20

The morning mist had lifted, the sun rose higher in the gray skies, and still she had not come. This was the second morning Randolph had waited for her, the second day she had not come. As each new rider entered the park, he would look up hopefully, anxious to see her scarlet riding habit, but each time nothing but disappointment greeted him.

At first he worried that something had happened to her. After all, in five weeks she had not missed a single morning ride. Until now. Had she taken ill? Then, remembering the topple from her mount, his gut clenched. He feared she had suffered injuries during the fall from her horse. He cursed himself for not more closely examining her after she had taken the spill.

Then his mind would race on and he would wonder if she might have lied to him. Perhaps she really was married. Perhaps her husband found out about their meeting and intervened. But why, he asked himself, had she concocted the story about her come-out if she was married? Cursing himself for doubting her honesty, he knew she was an innocent. She had told him the truth. She was a maiden up from the country for her come-out.

He racked his brain, trying to determine if he had said something that might have repulsed her. He'd said nothing that was not utterly complimentary. Perhaps that was it. Perhaps she did not like to be praised by a strange man.

His ardent interest in her obviously was not returned. Was her absence her way of rebuking his overtures?

Looking back on their meeting two mornings ago, he wished he had done everything differently. Why had he not asked her name? Why had he not discovered where she lived? He felt like a man who'd come away empty handed from a gold mine.

No woman had ever affected him so profoundly as the elegant woman in red. Not even the countess. There was something about the dark beauty that had dazzled him, something besides her stunning beauty. She was so utterly elegant, her movements on the horse so fluid. He had never before gazed into eyes as dark or as mesmerizing as hers. When they had finally met, she was all he could ever want and more. Her voice was lovely and cultured. Her graceful figure smoothly rounded in the right places. She possessed a sense of humor.

With an acceleration in his breath, he recalled how intoxicated he felt when she had slipped her arm around his waist and had taken those first few steps after her fall. He had never before been so flooded with a sense of protectiveness, never been so close to a more desirable woman.

And now he was left with nothing.

Even though he knew how fruitless it was to wait for her, he could not stop coming here each morning. He would come every day with the hope that she would come again.

* * *

Fiona was seated at the gilded French writing desk in her study when Biddles knocked on the door. "You have a caller, madame."

No doubt it was another young man bearing posies for Verity. With her beauty and fortune, Verity Birmingham had not lacked for suitors. A pity none of the men appealed to her. "Who, Biddles?" Fiona asked, setting down her plume.

"The Duchess of Glastonbury."

"Show her to the saloon. I shall be right down." Truth be told, Fiona was out of charity with Hortense. The woman—who was far too pretty—had positively thrown herself at Nick last night at Almack's.

But when Fiona strolled into the saloon a few minutes later, she concealed her displeasure. "How nice of you to call," she told the duchess as she came to sit on a silken settee, her gaze taking in the duchess's lovely peach gown. And generous bosom.

"Where is Mr. Birmingham today?" the duchess demanded.

She could at least have had the decency to wait before acknowledging her true reason for coming today! "My husband," Fiona said with emphasis, "never misses a session at the Exchange."

"I had quite forgotten. He's known as The Fox of the 'Change, is he not?"

Nodding, Fiona beamed with pride. "He's terribly clever about money and such."

Hortense's gaze whisked over the tiny grid on the specially loomed emerald and gold carpet and along the freshly painted white columns that soared to the trompe l'oeil ceiling that gave the illusion of being a dome. "He certainly knows how to spend his money, too. Menger House is positively stunning."

Biddles appeared with a tea tray.

"Tea?" Fiona asked.

"Yes, please."

Fiona poured the tea into two delicate porcelain cups and handed one to the duchess.

"You must tell me how you met your husband," Hortense said.

The woman's an open book! "Actually, my brother introduced me to him some time ago. They were at Cambridge together, you know."

"I didn't know Birmingham and Agar were friends."

"Oh, they're not." Fiona took a sip, not deigning to elaborate.

"Then however did you manage to snare the handsome Mr. Birmingham?"

He is handsome. And he's mine. "Our paths crossed again in December, and a . . . spark ignited." Which was something close to the truth.

A devilish look on her face, the duchess said, "He could light my spark any time."

Bristling, Fiona shot her old friend a brazenly chilly glance. "The only spark I should like him to light is mine." She felt like a cat marking her territory.

The duchess shrugged. "I would imagine he's wonderful in the bedchamber."

Fiona met her gaze boldly. "He is, but we must cease this conversation at once. Miss Birmingham's expected to step into the room at any moment, and we need to be cognizant of her maidenly sensibilities."

Before Hortense could answer, Verity joined them and came to sit beside Fiona.

"You look a great deal like your brother," Hortense told Verity.

Verity rolled her eyes. "Exactly what a lady does *not* wish to hear."

"But your brother is extraordinarily handsome," Hortense said. "And you share his best features: his leanness, his high cheekbones, his piercing eyes, and the olive complexion."

Hortense took entirely too thorough notice of Nick. "I'm

told I look a great deal like my elder brother, too,"
Fiona said, "which I find exceedingly offensive, given
that he's quite a large, muscular fellow."

The duchess directed her attention to Verity. "I
daresay the only thing Lady Fiona has in common with
her brother is their coloring—the blue eyes and
blond hair. Have you met Lord Agar?"

"I haven't had that pleasure," Verity said.

Fiona shrugged. "Randy's become the hermit since
his return from The Peninsula."

"Yes, I've heard he's even let Agar House."

"I thought that was quite clever of him, considering
how large it is for just one inhabitant," Fiona said.

"I wonder what he's doing with himself. He's not
even been to Almack's," the duchess said. "He will be
at Miss Birmingham's and Miss Peabody's come-out
ball, won't he?"

Fiona stiffened. How would it look if Randy stayed
away? His absence would underscore his disapproval of
Nick. For Nick's sake, Randy *must* come. "Yes, I suppose
he will." She was not about to acknowledge the rift between Randy and her to the biggest gossip in London.

The door to the saloon burst open, and Emmie, her
long hair flowing behind her, rushed in, an exas-
perated Miss Beckham on her heels. "My Lady!"
Emmie shrieked. "I fell down, and my lovely white
muff got all dirty."

"Come here and let me see," Fiona said, hooking
an arm around the little girl's shoulders as she examined it. "Don't worry, pet, it'll wash off," Fiona said.
"Remember the fur used to be on an animal, and
they're always frolicking in the mud, but the rains
come and bathe them, making them clean again."

"I'm ever so glad," Emmie said with a sigh, restuffing
her little hands into the muff.

"Come along, Miss Emmie," Miss Beckham said
sternly. "Your stepmother has important visitors."

After Emmie left, Hortense scowled at Fiona. "Stepmother? Surely . . . surely you don't allow that bastard to live here with you?"

Fiona's eyes narrowed. "That 'bastard' is my daughter, and I shall ask that you not malign her with such a description."

Verity's brown eyes sparkled as she flicked a smile at Fiona, then faced the duchess. "And that child is my niece. A lovely little girl, don't you think?"

Hortense looked stunned as she nodded.

Later that day Fiona paid a visit to Lord Warwick's offices in Whitehall. She was pleased that after more than a year of estrangement they could now resume their old friendship, comfortable that the relationship was just that: friendship. Nothing more.

Smiling, Warwick got up from his desk and greeted Fiona. "To what do I owe the pleasure?"

She held out her hand while he brushed his lips over it. "I was hoping you could tell me Randy's direction." If anyone knew where Randy was staying, it would be Warwick. They were lifelong friends.

"He's got lodgings on Marylebone." Warwick picked up his pen and wrote down the number, than handed it to her. "He's certainly a changed man since his return from The Peninsula."

She nodded. "I'm hoping he won't be so much the hermit that he misses Miss Peabody's and Miss Birmingham's come-out next month."

He scowled. "He needs to be there. For your husband's sake."

Warwick understands. She nodded. "I must apologize for keeping you from your important work." She waved the slip of paper. "This was all I needed from you."

"I'm never too busy for an old friend." He offered his arm. "Allow me to walk you to your carriage. It's devilishly difficult to find one's way back to the entrance in this maze of corridors."

The Birmingham couriers delivered a communication from William as Nick was leaving his offices that day. He was hungry to get home, to see Fiona. All day long he had tortured himself by picturing how she had looked waltzing in Warwick's arms at Almack's the night before. Nick needed to feel her in his own arms, needed to hear the little whimper in her throat his kisses always elicited, needed to assure himself she wanted him as fiercely as he wanted her.

He tucked William's letter into his pocket to read during the coach ride back to Menger House.

In the carriage he quickly deciphered the code the letter was written in. William had been making the rounds of the major German cities, buying up francs, and was now on his way to Naples. He asked that Nick arrange a transfer of money to him from their man of business in Naples in order for him to deplete the Neapolitan coffers of francs.

Nick would see to that first thing in the morning. Tucking the letter back into his pocket, he settled back against the squabs of his luxurious carriage and leisurely looked out the window. Then his spine went rigid, his eyes narrowing. If he was not mistaken, his wife's carriage was parked just a few yards away. What could she possibly be doing here in the Whitehall area?

Then he saw her. Her arm tucked into Warwick's, she smiled and laughed up into the earl's face.

Suddenly everything became so clear to Nick. Warwick *did* regret that he had not married Fiona.

And now Nick's wife was to be Warwick's lover.

Chapter 21

Nick would have to meet with Warwick that night to apprise him of his brother's success in Germany, but after seeing the earl with Fiona that afternoon, Nick was not sure he could even be civil to the man. The only thing Nick was sure of right now was his desire to run his sword through the foreign secretary.

For the sake of king and crown, though, Nick would set aside his personal dislikes.

After discreetly sending a note around to Warwick, Nick informed his wife he would not be taking dinner with her.

He tried not be affected by the forlorn look that crossed her face. "Why?" she asked, wide solemn blue eyes gazing up at him.

"Something's come up. Business."

He braced himself not to be affected by the hurt look on her face. If she could stealthily meet with Warwick, she did not deserve his sympathy.

"But . . . Adam will be here. And Trevor, too. Could you not have told me earlier?"

He gave her an icy glare. "As a matter of fact, I could not. The important matter that calls me away has only just come up."

She started to say something, then clamped shut her mouth.

That she had wanted to question him, he did not doubt. Fortunately, she was an obedient wife, complying with his request that they never discuss his business.

A pity she could not be so obliging in other matters. A pity Warwick had snared her heart before Nick ever got the opportunity to. Were it not for Warwick, Nick was certain he and Fiona would have suited very well.

Would have? His hands fisted, he cursed under his breath. He and Fiona *did* suit. Dammit! She was the most passionate lover he'd ever known. She was good to Emmie and to Verity, and solicitous of Nick's every need. So why could Nick not be grateful for all she had given him?

Because, he admitted ruefully to himself, he would never be content until he possessed her completely, body and soul.

Her brows lowered as she scanned his hardened face. "What's the matter, dearest? You're not yourself. You're angry."

How could she call him *dearest* when she had just come from her lover? "It's nothing," he snapped, storming from the house.

He had asked Warwick to meet him at a public house in out-of-the-way Hampstead, where Nick waited for some time, sipping his ale in the dark, firelit room before the foreign secretary finally arrived.

"It's rather difficult to extricate oneself from one's prying wife," Warwick explained as he came to sit beside Nick, "when the secretive nature of our business cannot be revealed. But I suppose you know all about that—being a married man yourself."

"A married man who values honesty and fidelity in a marriage," Nick said, scowling.

Warwick gave him a puzzled glance. "Another

matter on which we are in agreement, then." Warwick relaxed. "I take it you've had some communication from your brother?"

"I have," Nick said in an icy voice. "He's depleted the major German cities of francs."

"I thought he must have." Warwick nodded. "My contacts in Paris tell me the French minister of finance is becoming nervous."

Nick gave a sly grin. "And this is only the beginning. In two months—if our plan succeeds—they will be frantic." He paused, giving Warwick a quizzing look. "Do you think they suspect your hand in this?"

"All they know is that the Birmingham family is trying to manipulate the French currency. To my knowledge, they've made no connection between you and the English government." Warwick frowned. "I would advise you and your brothers to exercise caution. There's the possibility French assassins may wish to put a stop to your 'activities.'"

Nick raised a brow. "My brother William is well guarded at all times." That he or Adam would be in danger had not crossed Nick's mind until now, but he quickly realized Warwick was right to warn him. Adam, too, needed to be apprised of the danger.

"Yes," Warwick said, "I suppose he would have to be well guarded—carrying around such vast amounts of money."

A moment later the foreign secretary said, "I feel obligated to ensure your family's safety. Perhaps I should assign Horse Guards to protect you, your brother, and your wife. They will, of course, *not* be in uniform."

Fiona! Surely no one would try to harm her! Nick would kill with his bare hands anyone who ever threatened his wife. He stiffened, his hands fisting as he eyed Warwick. "Birminghams take care of their own."

"But no one's better trained than the Guards."

"Be that as it may, can you vouch for their complete integrity?" Nick's simmering gaze locked with Warwick's. "A careless word from one of them could jeopardize my wife's safety."

Warwick's face blanched, which did not surprise Nick. Of course he would worry about Fiona. He was in love with her. "We're speaking of his majesty's finest soldiers," Warwick protested.

"I don't care who we're speaking of !" Nick snapped. "The fewer people who know of my involvement with you, the better."

Warwick watched him with narrowed eyes. "I must insist that Lady Fiona be guarded at all times."

"She will be, dammit! I'm perfectly capable of seeing to my wife's every need." A pity their most well-trained men were on the continent. Nevertheless, before he returned home tonight, he would detail a pair of trusted employees to guard Fiona day and night.

The next few minutes were tense. Both men feigned a high degree of interest in the flames dancing in the room's fireplace.

"Where does your brother go now?" Lord Warwick finally asked.

"To Naples."

"A brave man," Warwick said, "given the fact that city's a French stronghold."

Nick's gaze flicked to Warwick, silently cursing the man's exceptionally broad chest. "I'm hoping my brother's friendship with Napoleon's brother there will provide him immunity from danger."

"Since Bonaparte rules the city, your faith is likely not misplaced."

Nick's dark eyes sparkled. "Plus, my brother is adept at greasing the right palms."

"Bribery's good," Warwick said, grinning.

"Ale?" Nick asked.

"I believe I will."

After a bumper of ale was placed on the well-worn table in front of Warwick, Nick drew in his breath. "As I was driving down The Strand today, I saw you with my wife." Nick's eyes narrowed. "Do you care to explain?"

Stiffening, Warwick did not answer for a moment. Then he said, "I suggest you ask Lady Fiona."

With a mumbled curse, Nick slammed his bumper onto the table and stalked from the establishment.

His fury with Fiona did not keep him from driving to James Hutchinson's establishment in Cheapside. Even if the man was asleep, Nick would have no compunction about waking him. The sixty-year-old Hutchinson owed his comfortable circumstances to the Birmingham coffers. It was Nick's father who had hired the former dragoon, who was as skilled with weaponry as he was with pugilism.

That a light shone at Hutchinson's upstairs window pleased Nick. He would not have to awaken him. Dismounting, Nick's gaze flicked over the establishment's bay window and up to the suspended placard that read, "Hutchinson's School of Fencing." Paying students, of course, were never accepted. The school was a training ground for the Birmingham's private army of skilled guards, men who were paid generously enough to ensure their allegiance to the Birminghams, men who passed Hutchinson's rigorous tests.

"Mr. Birmingham! To what do I owe the pleasure?" asked Hutchinson as he swept open the rough timber door.

Nick would not answer until he was satisfied that no one could overhear them. Once he had divested himself of his coat, climbed steep wooden stairs to Hutchinson's living quarters, and sat in a comfortable chair facing Hutchinson's hearth, he answered. "I have urgent need for your men—our men—to guard Mrs. Birmingham at all times."

From the grave look on Hutchinson's face, it was obvious to Nick that the man thought Nick distrusted his bride. "A man in my position makes many enemies," Nick explained. "I should not like an enemy of mine to seek retribution on my innocent wife." As angry as he was with her, the very idea of anyone injuring Fiona was unbearable to contemplate.

Hutchinson's bushy gray brows lowered. "Have there been any threats against Mrs. Birmingham?"

"No, but a good defense can unhinge the most aggressive offensive. Hasn't that always been our belief?"

Hutchinson's florid face brightened. "Indeed it has. On that, my dear sir, we are in perfect agreement."

"Is anyone available?"

"As it so happens I've a pair of talented young men who've just completed their training. They're shrewd, good with their fists, and skilled with pistols and swords."

Nick stood up. "I should like to see that they guard my wife day and night."

It had been a wretched night. Fiona had been so obviously upset at dinner that Adam and Trevor departed as soon as the plates had been removed. Even Verity—who was the most amiable of creatures—had sensed Fiona's distress and leaped at the first opportunity to excuse herself from her sister's company. "If you should need someone to listen," Verity had said in a grave voice, "I stand at the ready."

Fiona's heart softened even more toward her sister. In her wisdom, Verity had not asked if Fiona were ill, nor had she intruded on Fiona's privacy by demanding to know the source of her misery. Intrinsically, she had connected Nick's absence to Fiona's sulkiness.

Fiona had thanked her, then went to her own bedchamber, weighed down by the almost unbearable grief of Nick's absence and the hostility of their parting.

Had he gone to Miss Foley or to the Duchess of Glastonbury? Dismissing her maid, Fiona collapsed on her bed. As hard as she had tried to be a loving, dutiful wife, she had failed. She could not even hold Nick's affection long enough to get her with child.

Before her own marriage, she had complacently accepted the fact that married men of the *ton* had their lady birds. Her own father had several over the course of his marriage, and her mother had known the identity of most of them. Even her mother had taken the occasional lover while maintaining a perfectly harmonious, affectionate relationship with her husband.

But Fiona was obviously not cut from the same cloth as her parents. Under no circumstances could she ever accept her husband taking a lover. The very thought was like a vise crushing and twisting her bleeding heart.

She wished to be angry with Nick, but how could she when love had never been part of their marriage? He had neither promised to love her nor asked for her love. He had fulfilled his part of the agreement by supplying the twenty-five thousand pounds for Randy's release and by giving Fiona his name and access to his vast wealth. In return, the house of Birmingham was uniting in every way with the prestigious Agar family. She sobbed. Was siring a child with Agar blood the only reason Nick had bed her?

Had he not shared that all-consuming hunger that had devoured her? A pity she lacked bedroom experience. How was she to know if his desire to make love to her was genuine? He had certainly given every indication that his hunger for her matched hers for him.

From her desk she took the slender volume that

Nick had given her on Christmas morning. She clutched it to her breast for a moment before turning to the page featuring "The Garden of Love," a morose poem she knew by heart, and with tears gathering in her eyes she read.

I went to the Garden of Love,
And saw what I never had seen:
A Chapel was built in the midst,
Where I used to play on the green.

And the gates of this Chapel were shut,
And Thou shalt not writ over the door;
So I turn'd to the Garden of Love,
That so many sweet flowers bore.

And I saw it was filled with graves,
And tomb-stones where flowers should be;
And Priests in black gowns, were walking their rounds,
And binding with briars, my joys and desires.

Now weeping, she extinguished all the candles and climbed upon her lonely bed. As she lay in the darkness of her bedchamber she wondered if her husband was lying beside Miss Foley or Hortense at this very moment. Would he remark on their beauty as he had on hers? Would his hands skim over their heated flesh while he proclaimed his affection? Would his lips taste the other woman's lips and neck; would his mouth close over her nipple in the same way he had tasted Fiona? The very memory of it made her throb deep and low.

She rued the day she had allowed herself to become his wife. Marriage to Nick had profoundly changed her life. And not for the better. Because she had married him, she had lost so much. She had lost her brother's affection; lost her own pride; and most of all, lost her heart, completely and irrevocably.

Yet had she to do it all over again, she would still marry him, still give him her body and her heart. Despite the near-debilitating pain that now consumed her, she had never been more alive.

She would not go to his room tonight. Even though he had said he wished to sleep with her every night, he must not have meant it. He'd been so utterly short tempered with her earlier tonight she was convinced any shred of affection he might have had for her had now been destroyed.

But why? Why had he been so angry with her? She had done nothing to deserve his wrath. And what had happened to his big heart—that she'd once told Emmie was big enough to embrace all those people he cared about?

Ever since Hortense had begun to throw herself at Nick, he no longer seemed to hold Fiona in affection.

She lay there on her bed, listening to but not really hearing the sounds of the fire crackling, of the wind howling beyond her windows. She tortured herself by imagining her husband languidly making love to Hortense. Would they make love all through the night like he had done with Fiona in the early days of their marriage?

As she lay there she thought she heard his footfall on the corridor outside her door, and she jerked up, the counterpane slipping from her bare shoulders. She held her breath as she listened. It couldn't be Nick for—at just past eleven o'clock—it was far too early. She crept from her bed and quietly went to their adjoining dressing rooms to assure herself that the sound she had heard was Nick. As much as she wished to rush to him and feel his lips on hers, feel his arms closing around her, she wished to maintain some semblance of control over her racing emotions, to maintain some semblance of pride.

When the door to his dressing room eased open, though, she found herself staring into her husband's flashing black eyes.

"Have you come to sleep with me, my dear?" he asked in a brittle voice that was at odds with the genial man she knew him to be. He had just shed his coat and was still holding it as he faced her.

Her glance skimmed over the lean planes of his distinctly male body. "I . . . I don't believe so. I was merely assuring myself that you've made it home safely."

He snorted. "Forgive me if I doubt your concern."

She stiffened. "Suit yourself." She went to turn around, to return to her bedchamber, when she felt his hand banding around the flesh of her upper arm as he whirled her to face him.

"Come, my dear," he said in an icy voice, "have a glass of brandy with me. I have not had the opportunity to ask you about your day."

Pain seared through her arm. "There's nothing to tell, Nick."

His hands relaxed. "Humor me."

She saw that he had brought a decanter with him. "As you wish." She came to sit in one of a pair of chairs near the fire.

"I hope you don't object to sharing my glass," he said.

"We share everything else," she said with a shrug, taking the snifter he handed her and sipping from it.

"So what did you do today?" he asked, sinking into the chair beside her.

Nick's voice was so altered she wondered if he might be drunk. She recalled Randy telling her there were good drunkards and bad drunkards. Nick, she admitted ruefully, was obviously a bad drunkard. She glared at him. This harsh man wasn't the man she had fallen in love with. "My day was decidedly dull," she began. "I wrote letters this morning, then the Duchess of Glastonbury came and stayed for quite a while. After she left, it was time for me to begin dressing for dinner."

"You did not go anywhere all day?" he asked, a single brow raised.

She could not tell him she had gone to find Randy, for she did not want Nick to know she missed her brother. An intelligent man like Nick was sure to realize he was the cause of the estrangement between the brother and sister, and this straining marriage could not sustain any more blows. Besides, she had not found Randy at home that afternoon. "No."

He downed the rest of the glass of brandy and stood up.

A chill ran down her spine as she watched him, his back to the fire, an altogether different fire lighting his angry eyes. "Will you come to my bed?" he asked.

"I think not," she said in a grave voice.

Having convinced herself any marriage would be better than spending the rest of her life buried at Great Acres, Verity Birmingham had come to London with high hopes. As much as she loved her mother, she could not say being with Dolina Birmingham day in and day out was not taxing. Sad to say, her mother had more in common with her servants than she had with her own daughter. In everything from reading material to the fabric for a new dress, Dolina Birmingham's taste was bourgeois. Her grammar was deplorable, and her temperament harsh.

In London Verity had thought to find a man whose interests mirrored her own, a man she could happily spend the rest of her life with. But after coming in contact with her blond Adonis at Hyde Park, she knew she would no longer be satisfied with a comfortable relationship when every cell in her body cried out for a grand passion.

And only one man could spur her to such an alliance: the blond lord she could never again meet.

Even though she had yet to officially come out, Verity was stunned over her own popularity. Or the popularity of her generous dowry. Fiona had, of course, been right. Women with large dowries were well sought after by gentlemen of the *ton*.

One gentleman in particular had determined he must secure her hand: Sir Reginald Balfour, who now sat across from her and Fiona in the blue saloon.

She knew him to be Nick's age because he had been at Cambridge when Nick was there. She knew, too, that Nick was not particularly fond of the baronet—most likely because he was a blatant fortune hunter. It was no secret Miss Glenda MacTavish—heiress to her father's immense beer fortune—had spurned him last month.

As Fiona engaged him in conversation, Verity studied him. He was of medium height, which gave him almost no advantage—more's the pity. His complexion was so fair she was convinced his brown hair had likely been blond when he was a youth. He dressed with excellent taste, influenced by his friendship with Brummel, a connection he never failed to mention.

Since the first time he had danced with her at Almack's, Sir Reginald had made no secret of his desire to secure her hand—and her fortune. He scowled at and disparaged any other man who deigned to seek her for a dancing partner. His excessive flattery of her extended to writing exceedingly bad poetry in her honor, and he persisted in boasting of his lofty connections, both familial and social.

She told herself she should be flattered over Sir

Reginald's interest in her. After all, many young ladies at Almack's had been attracted by his fair good looks.

But not Verity. It was not just Nick's pronouncement that Sir Reginald did not have a feather to fly with that made her skeptical of his devotion. Try as she might, she could not like the man. Even if she had not lost her heart to her mysterious peer, she could never have been comfortable with the pompous Sir Reginald.

She wistfully thought of her single meeting with the man who owned her heart. She had never been so comfortable, so relaxed with a man before.

"I'm getting together a party of twenty or so to go to Vauxhall Gardens next Thursday night," Sir Reginald told Fiona. "Nothing would give me greater pleasure than having you and Mr. Birmingham—" He turned to smile at Verity. "And Miss Birmingham among my party."

Fiona's brows lowered. "My husband is not fond of Vauxhall."

He shrugged. "I admit it has an unsavory reputation, but I give you my word as a gentleman that we shall keep to the well-lighted paths."

If she heard him declare himself *a gentleman* one more time, Verity would gag.

Before she could comment about Vauxhall, Biddles showed in a pair of young men who were no older than Verity, one of whom brought her flowers.

After introducing the men to Sir Reginald, Verity lifted her newly received nosegay to her nose for a deep whiff. "How very kind of you," she told Mr. Merriweather, who had given it to her.

Sir Reginald looked down his aristocratic nose at the younger men. "Thoughtful lads, aren't they? I'm sure that when I was that young I couldn't think past the next race at Newmarket." Then he flicked his gaze to Verity. "Now all I seem able to think about is settling down at Stoneleigh and starting a family."

She did not believe him for a moment. From everything she had heard about him, the races at Newmarket still held vast appeal.

Thank goodness she had Fiona to masterfully direct the conversation and miraculously keep the three visitors from drawing daggers on one another.

Meanwhile, Verity's thoughts drifted to her handsome soul mate. She could not deny there had been something special between them. She would vow he had known it, too.

A pity she could never see him again.

Chapter 22

This was the night of his sister's come-out, the night his wife had been laboring toward for weeks, the night he would be hung on display like a new portrait at the National Gallery. Drawing in his breath, Nick stepped up to Fiona's dressing room door and tapped it with his knuckle.

"Nick?" she asked.

He still had not become immune to the possessive rush he felt at the intimacy of his Christian name on her lips. "Yes." He opened the door and strolled into her bedchamber, his careless arrogance belying the tumult within him. This was his first visit to his wife's chambers in several weeks.

She flicked a quizzing glance at him, then quickly dismissed her maid. "You can finish buttoning me," she said to Nick once Prudence was gone.

As he came closer, his pulse accelerated. His wife had never looked lovelier than she did tonight in the blue gown that was shot with silver threads throughout and with ermine inserts around the bodice, a bodice he found indecently low. He did not like other men to see any part of those delectable breasts, breasts no man had ever touched before him. Thinking of Lord

Warwick's hands on Fiona's bare flesh brought him almost unbearable pain.

His heated gaze skimmed over her. No monarch could have looked more regal, no woman more graceful.

And it had been far too long since he had allowed himself the luxury of holding her in his arms.

She twirled around to present her back to him, and with trembling hands he began to fasten the remaining buttons, cursing himself for buttoning her when all he really wanted was to unbutton her, to bare her milky flesh and feel his lips upon it, to feel himself sinking into her luxurious warmth.

When he finished, she turned to face him, her gaze dropping to his bulging crotch, a casualty of her devastating effect upon him. "I'm so glad you've come," she whispered huskily, moving closer to him.

To preserve the distance between them, he edged backward and cocked a dark brow. "And why would that be, my dear?"

She stopped, a hurt look sweeping across her pale face. "Because this is a very important night, not only for Verity but also for us, dearest. It's our first grand entertainment at Menger House, the first time many of my old friends will meet the man I've married. I . . . " Her eyes watered as she struggled for words. "I wish for them to think us happily married."

He gave a bitter laugh. "I shall be happy to oblige. I can play the part of an attentive husband most convincingly."

Her chest heaving, she did not remove her gaze from his. "When my leg was broken, was your concern merely an act?"

"Of course not, my darling. Your welfare is always uppermost in my mind. In fact," he said, reaching into his pocket, "I've brought you another bauble."

This time it was a diamond necklace with bracelet

and earrings to match, and it had cost him a king's ransom. He hadn't known why he wished to purchase it for her since she had betrayed him, but he found himself strangely beholden to her for presenting his sister, for acting the attentive wife, for not being ashamed of him.

"Oh, Nick! They're beautiful! What could I ever have done to deserve such an offering?"

"You've worked very hard on tonight's fete. I thought you needed a reward."

"Your attentiveness is all I could ever want." She stood on her toes to kiss him.

When their lips met, all his resolve vanished. He pulled her into his arms, into his crushing embrace and kissed her, unleashing his pent-up hunger for her. He nearly dissolved when he felt her cool tongue slide into his mouth, when he heard her hungry little whimpers. *It was just like before. Before she betrayed him with Warwick.*

His own breath harsh and labored, his hands molded to her breasts, his thumb stroking the hardened nub of her nipple. She flowed into him, and when her slender arms tightened around him, it was all he could do not to lift her skirts and take her standing up.

Instead, the vision of his wife beneath Warwick's pounding body obliterated his own blinding need.

He pushed her away.

"Oh, dearest," she said, those soulful eyes of hers scanning his hardened face, "can you not make love to me once more? We've plenty of time before the first guests arrive."

How could she appear so hungry for him when she loved another man? For the briefest moment he allowed himself to believe it was he whom she loved, then the torturing vision of her in Whitehall with Lord Warwick destroyed his fragment of hope. Despite that every cell in his body throbbed with need of her, he put distance between them. "I shouldn't like to mess your lovely hair." Then, with his face inscrutable, he offered his crooked arm. "Shall we go downstairs, love?"

She could not cry. Her heart was being ripped to shreds, but she could not allow herself to cry. Not on this night. She owed it to Verity to play the unruffled hostess, and she owed Nick so very much more. It was not his fault he did not love her. Indeed, he'd never sought her love, never promised his. He had given her much and asked for little. All she had to offer him—now that he no longer wanted her body—was her exalted standing in society. So tonight she would stand proudly at his side, a testament to his worthiness.

For Nick's sake, she would not cry.

But she was bleeding inside. She had been since the humiliating moment when her husband had refused to make love to her. The pity of it was that when she had first kissed him, he *had* responded with the same old searing hunger that had made their nights so wondrous before . . . before the Duchess of Glastonbury had swept into their lives—and stolen Nick's affection.

Later, as they stood with Miss Peabody and Verity in the receiving line, Fiona could not help but be struck over how different tonight was from what she had planned during those many weeks of heightened anticipation. How she had looked forward to standing proudly at her husband's side, her possessive hand on his sleeve as she glowed with her own incredible good fortune in landing so handsome, so worthy a man.

Now she ached from his rejection.

"How good of you to come," she said to the Countess Lieven, who could not remove her gaze from

Nick. Fiona could not remember an assemblage where more peers were in attendance.

"I'm delighted to be here," the countess said, her glance sweeping up the magnificent marble stairway. "I've been dying to see Menger House."

Any doubts Fiona had once secretly harbored over Nick's acceptance by the *ton* were quickly dispelled. Men stood in awe of the scion who had built this magnificent house, the scion who had captured Lady Fiona Hollingsworth for his bride. Women openly adored the sinfully handsome man of wealth.

The mammoth third-floor ballroom that Fiona had feared would look bare was crowded with ladies and gentlemen in their silken finery. Thousands of candles ringed a dozen huge chandeliers that illuminated the room as brightly as sunlight. When the orchestra began to play, Nick led Verity out for her first dance; Lord Warwick stood up with Miss Peabody. This was the first time Fiona had seen Miss Peabody without her spectacles. She was quite as lovely as her sister—except for the absence of a bosom.

Fiona joined the Countess Warwick, and they proudly watched their respective charges flawlessly execute their dance steps. Neither young lady had ever looked lovelier. Trevor scurried up to Fiona and the countess Warwick. "Is Miss Birmingham not breathtaking in her white gown?" he asked, his gaze sweeping across the wooden dance floor.

Thank God for Trevor! Fiona had been on the verge of tears when he had come up. She turned twinkling eyes on him. "And her gown is most stunning. I must commend the person who suggested she wear snow white."

"'Pon my word," Trevor said, gleaming, "that would be *moi*!"

"And look at Miss Peabody," Fiona said. "Is she not exceptionally pretty tonight?" Miss Peabody, who had no interest in fashion, had obviously not selected the elegant cream-colored creation she wore.

Trevor cast a glance at the lady in question. "I declare, she looks positively stunning. I've never really taken notice of her before." He leaned closer to Fiona to whisper, "She's about as sociable as a doorknob."

Fiona swatted him with her fan.

After that first set Nick sought Fiona to waltz with him. She shivered as he pulled her into his arms. Then, brushing aside her own gloom, she looked up at him, forcing a smile. "I can't think of a single person who declined to come tonight, dearest." *Except Randy.* "You—and your magnificent house—are a great success."

"Our house," he corrected.

Her heart wrenched. "I can't take credit for it when you were its driving force, you the one with the remarkable vision that created all of this."

He gave a bitter laugh. "You and I both know my so-called vision would not have been able to fill this room with the beau monde. No, my dear," he said with a shake of his head, "it's my selection of you for my bride that has made tonight's fete such a complete success."

She stiffened. "If you'll recall, you did not precisely 'select' me."

"Oh, but I did," he growled, pulling her closer. "I'm not so great a gentleman that I would not have spurned you had I not decided that marriage to you would be in my best interest."

If only he had decided that marriage to her—that bedding her—was what he wanted above everything! "Honestly, Nick, could you not say something a bit more flowery? I know love was never expected, but could you not pretend that I caught your fancy?" She strived for a light tone though her heart was breaking.

He chuckled. "No pretending needed. I *am* the most fortunate of men to have secured the hand of the beautiful Lady Fiona Hollingsworth. Have I not told you many times before how lovely I find you?"

Never with such brittle detachment before. He used to speak to her with warmth.

Before Hortense.

As they danced she saw the Duchess of Glastonbury watching them, a look of displeasure on her pretty face. It was, Fiona knew, the same look that would be on her own face were she watching her husband dance with Hortense.

She also saw Lord and Lady Warwick glide across the dance floor and thought she had never seen two people so much in love. A pang of jealousy stabbed at her. *If only Nick loved me as Warwick loves his Maggie.*

"Does Verity not look lovely?" she asked.

"Never lovelier."

"Are you satisfied with how well she's taken?"

He held Fiona at some distance and peered into her eyes. "The only thing that will satisfy me is her finding a man who will return her love. I don't care about the man's pedigree, and I distinctly dislike Sir Reginald Balfour."

At least she and Nick were in agreement on the ineligibility of Sir Reginald. "I don't recall Verity ever mentioning love."

His lips were a grim line. "Everyone longs for love."

Dear God! Nick was in love with Hortense! "You've . . . you've never told me you felt that way before."

"You obviously weren't looking for love when you expressed your desire to marry me."

If only she had known then what she knew now, known how passionately she would come to love this man she married. If only they could go back and start over again. If only they could make this a real marriage.

Later that night Warwick asked her to stand up with him. No sooner had they reached the dance floor than Nick asked the Duchess of Glastonbury to be his dance partner. As Fiona watched Nick's smiling face bent to Hortense's, tears gathered in her eyes.

"Fiona, are you unwell?" Warwick demanded, his brows lowered, his hand softly stroking her pale cheek.

"If you must know," she said, "I'm distressed over Randy's absence." A lie was better than the bitter truth of her marriage's failure.

"You've spoken to him?"

"No. He wasn't home the day I went to see him. I left an invitation for Miss Peabody's and Miss Birmingham's ball, but he obviously chose to ignore it."

Warwick squeezed her hand, smiling tenderly at her. "Reserve judgment until you talk with him."

"I don't think Randy wishes to talk with me."

"You're wrong," Warwick said as the dance came to an end and he restored her to her glum husband.

Anyone here would think tonight's ball a great success, but Fiona had never felt so low. She had hoped that when Randy received the invitation, he would come because of tender feelings for his only sister. Obviously she did not elicit tender feelings. In anyone. Her brother did not want her companionship and her husband did not want her body. She was an utter failure.

Verity had never danced so much, never been in so crowded a ballroom, never been so hot. She looked around to make sure no one was watching her, then she slipped away from the ballroom and down a flight of stairs to a pair of French doors that gave onto a second-floor balcony overlooking Piccadilly.

She eased open the door and slid onto the balcony, closing the door behind her. The cool night air felt so good on her scorching flesh. As her hands coiled over the top of the balustrade, she drew in a breath and thought about her come-out. Never would she have believed that she would be so wildly sought after. Even though she knew it was her late father's fortune that had assured her success, she was stunned that she never sat out a single set, never lacked for morning callers a single day since attending her first assembly. There were at least a dozen gentlemen here tonight who would think themselves blessed were she to bestow her affections upon them.

A pity He was not one of them. Even though she knew how fruitless it was to pine over a love that could never be, she had allowed herself to hope that her lone horseman would come tonight. She had kept her eye peeled to the door throughout the evening, watching for him, even though she had known he wouldn't come.

She found herself wondering if he had wanted to find her, wanted to learn her identity.

Then she would chastise herself. He was a nobleman. And noblemen did not waste their eligibility upon unstylish daughters of Cits!

The doorknob turned behind her, and the door cracked open. Startled, she spun around. And faced Sir Reginald Balfour.

"My poor Miss Birmingham," he said, a look of concern on his face. "Wretchedly hot in the ballroom, is it not?"

"Yes, it is!"

He moved closer. Far too close to her way of thinking. "I must confess," he said in a husky voice, "I was devilishly glad to have the opportunity to be alone with you."

Uh-oh. She smiled brightly at him. They were nose

to nose. "Actually, I was just leaving. It wouldn't do for the honoree not to be present at her own ball." She lurched for the door.

His arm shot out to block her.

Scowling, she tried to shove through.

Then, with bruising strength, he pulled her to him. His face was only an inch away from hers, so close she could smell the liquor on his breath. "You, my dearest Verity, must know how I feel about you. I shan't be able to sleep until I know you'll be mine."

She jerked away. "If you're asking me to marry you, sir, I must decline. Now, please let go of me," she said through gritted teeth.

His hands dug into the flesh at the top of her arms, and his mouth swooped down to claim hers.

She twisted and groaned but could not break free from his crushing mouth. Then she remembered Nick's advice on thwarting unwelcome advances.

And she kneed him in the groin.

He doubled over, cursing her with the most vile language she had ever heard as she rushed back to the crowded ballroom.

His house was greatly admired. His sister was a great success. His wife was the most beautiful woman in attendance. He himself seemed to have gained approval from the *ton*. What should have been one of the proudest nights of Nick's life, however, had turned into one of his darkest moments when he watched his wife in Warwick's arms. How could the man have looked down at Fiona with such devotion shining on his face in front of his own countess? How could he be possessed of such gall that he would tenderly stroke the lovely face of another man's wife in front of some two hundred people?

It was difficult for Nick to behave the gentleman

when he so desperately wanted to call Warwick out. It was even more difficult to flick aside his own bruised pride and happily escort his wife into supper later that evening. How could he act as if nothing had changed, as if he were proud of Fiona when he contemplated strangling her?

But Nick was a gentleman. He refused to hold either himself or his wife up to public ridicule. He would have to deal with the matter of her infidelity privately.

After he assisted his wife to a seat at the foot of the supper table, he took his own place at the head of the table. To his right sat the Duchess of Glastonbury, the highest ranking person in attendance. Since marrying Fiona he had learned that attendees at a dinner party entered the dining room and sat at the table in accordance with their rank, an elitist practice Nick must accept even though he did not approve of it.

Another practice of the *ton* he did not approve of was the preponderance of—and acceptance of—extramarital affairs. His gaze flicked to the duchess, resplendent in a shimmering copper-colored gown that complemented her fiery hair. Despite her rank, wealth, and beauty, he pitied the young woman, who was the same age as Fiona. Her hunger for rank and wealth had stripped her of the most important thing in life: love. Now, married to an octogenarian duke, the duchess so longed for a younger man to warm her bed that she had lost all sense of pride, had brazenly offered herself to Nick that night while they were waltzing.

"I detect a cooling in your marriage," the duchess had murmured while they danced.

"You detect wrong," he said in a stern voice.

"A pity," she exclaimed. "However, my dearest Mr. Birmingham, should you ever feel the need for a romantic tryst, I would be a most willing participant."

"I doubt that your husband would approve."

"My husband knows of my . . . indiscretions. Were he

capable of seeing to my needs—which I assure you he's not—I would not have to seek pleasure elsewhere."

"Oh come now, your grace, not ever?" he said, his voice hitched with humor, his eyes sparkling devilishly.

Smiling, she swatted him with her fan. "You naughty man!"

A few minutes after sitting at the supper table, the duchess turned to Nick and spoke in a low voice. "I've been watching Lady Warwick and Lady Fiona, and I do believe Fiona the loveliest. I can't imagine why Warwick would have preferred the darker lady when he could have had the fair Fiona." She gazed at Nick from beneath lowered lashes. "I daresay Warwick regrets his decision."

So the duchess must have seen Warwick's intimacy with Nick's wife, too. Then, with a lurch in his gut, he wondered if Fiona had confided in her old friend. "But you must realize," he said, "you more than anyone, that physical appearances aren't the most important factor in selecting a mate."

She flicked her fan against his sleeve. "I believe physical appearances must have figured strongly in your—and Mrs. Birmingham's—decision to marry."

"I do find my wife the loveliest of women. And I do think Warwick a fool." *Except now Warwick realizes what he lost.* Nick scanned the table to see where Warwick sat, pleased that he was nowhere near Fiona—and pleased that he was giving a great deal of attention to his countess.

"Perhaps not as foolish as you think. I can't help but to wonder . . . The countess captured any number of men's hearts before . . . before she caught Warwick. One wonders if the earl was forced into the marriage."

"A man is not obligated to offer marriage merely because a woman has been 'obliging.' Surely I'm proof of that."

The duchess stiffened. "I think Lady Fiona most

obliging indeed to allow your little 'mistake' to live under her roof."

Nick glared at her. "My wife is not so insensitive as to call an innocent child a mistake." Tossing down his napkin, Nick rose, nodding at the duchess on his right and the marquis who sat at his left, then left the table.

Later that evening—or morning—he and Fiona said farewell to the last of their gushing guests. "You must be very tired," he said to his wife, offering his arm as they mounted the stairs to their bedchambers.

She shrugged. "It's been rather exhilarating."

With each step that brought them closer to his bedchamber, he remembered Fiona's invitation earlier that night. How he wanted to take her up on the offer.

When they reached her door she paused and looked up at him.

"Good night, my dear," he said curtly, brushing his lips against her temple. "Sleep well." He darted toward his own room without allowing himself a glimpse of her lovely face.

As much as he wanted to make love to her, he could not dispel the horrifying vision of her lying beneath Warwick. As much as he wanted her, he could not share her body with another man.

Chapter 23

Perhaps it was his guilty conscience that kept Randolph from sleep. Fiona, his sweet sister who had given up so much for him, had asked so little. She merely wanted his presence at the first ball in her new home. And he had let her down. He'd told himself he could not go to the ball because he had to rise early the next morning for his journey to Yorkshire to oversee his properties, but he could have postponed the trip for another day.

The most likely reason for his staying away was that he could not bear to see her with Birmingham, could not accept that his sister had married a Cit. Because of him. Not only had she wed Birmingham, but she had married into his vulgar family. Randolph's lovely sister was presenting the undoubtedly brash offspring of the uncouth Jonathan Birmingham. Because of him.

He shuddered to think of Fiona gracing the same ballroom as Miss Birmingham. He tried to console himself that Nicholas Birmingham conducted himself as a gentleman. Except, of course, for the fact the man never missed a session at the 'Change. No races at Newmarket for him. No afternoon rides in Hyde

Park. No outings to the Egyptian Hall. He toiled by day as steadily as an ironmonger.

Miss Birmingham was no doubt some social-climbing hoyden who was not fit to be Fiona's sister.

Another reason Randolph could not sleep was the ruckus in the corridor outside his rented chambers. What was that damned Sir Reginald up to now? Sir Reginald's and another man's voices were raised in anger.

"I beg that you give me a few more weeks to repay you," Sir Reginald said.

"That's what you asked last month, and still you've not come up with the money."

"But now I have the opportunity to marry a great heiress—if you'll but give me a few more weeks."

"Why would an heiress wish to marry you?" the other man asked with a snort.

"The lady will have no choice in the matter, once she is compromised. She's to be among my party at Vauxhall tomorrow night, and I assure you that once the night's over, the lady's fortune will be mine."

"One week. And that's all," the other man barked.

Randolph heard the door to Sir Reginald's chambers close, heard the other man's steps descend the stairway. Randolph had never liked Sir Reginald, but his dislike was now intense. The contemptible man was planning to rape a maiden.

Throwing off his blankets, Randolph leaped from his bed and, with a great deal of agitation, lit a candle. He had a good mind to rush to Sir Reginald's chambers and give the man a good thrashing. Randolph jammed his bare legs into limp pantaloons and began to pace his wooden floor, seized with an unwavering urge to protect the heiress. But how could he warn her when he did not know who she was?

Any number of ideas sprang to Randolph's mind as he paced the floor. He thought of threatening the pompous baronet. He considered coming right out and asking the man who his heiress was. He even foolishly considered nailing shut Sir Reginald's door tomorrow night so he would not be able to meet the lady at Vauxhall Gardens. But any such action would only postpone the dirty deed. What was needed was for the lady to be informed of Sir Reginald's evil intentions. But how could Randolph do that when he did not know her identity?

As dawn filled his chambers with murky sunlight, Randolph came to a decision. He would postpone his trip to Yorkshire.

And he would go to Vauxhall Gardens that night.

Nick should have talked to Fiona last night, but he did not want anything to detract from the success of her ball.

Tonight, though, he would speak with her before they left for Vauxhall. Warwick would be among their party tonight, and Nick would not endure another night of humiliation.

Once Ware had finished with his cravat, Nick stormed into his wife's bedchamber, not bothering to knock. She stood before her looking glass, a peach-colored gown molding to the soft curves of her body. Her hair was dressed in the Grecian mode with a jeweled band circling her soft whitish curls. The sight of her loveliness and the depth of his love for her sent a gaping ache hammering through his body.

She faced him, a brow lifted in query. He remembered the pleasure that had softened her face the previous night when he had surprised her while she was dressing. He thought of her husky offer to make love to him. He had swelled with pride and other profound emotions when she had called him "dearest."

No such offers, no such endearments, would come tonight. She looked frightened. Even angry.

Which was fine with him. This conversation called for sternness.

She watched him warily as he came to sit in an armchair near the fire. "Do you recall, Mrs. Birmingham," he said in an icy voice, lifting his cold gaze to her, "the day I went down on my knee in the drawing room of Agar House?"

Her eyes wide, she nodded.

"Do you remember when I told you I should not like to marry you if you were still in love with Lord Warwick?"

She nodded.

"You told me that you no longer loved the earl."

"That's true."

His heart raced. "Can you still make such assurances?" He did not wish to hear her declare her love for Warwick. No pain could be greater.

Her eyes flashed with anger. "Of course! Lord Warwick's a happily married man, and I have no romantic feelings whatsoever toward him."

She's lying. With his own eyes, Nick had seen them together. His face a dark mask, Nick said, "I realize love was not something either of us wished from this marriage, but I want to stress that I will never tolerate infidelity from my wife."

"I'm very glad that you value fidelity, sir," she said with a defiant lift of her chin, "for I do, too. I should not like it if you were to carry on with another woman."

Her words were as unexpected as a slap in the face. "I assure you I'm not only too busy to have time for another woman, but I have no respect for men who are unfaithful to their wives."

A knock sounded at her door, and Verity hurried into the room. "Think you that I will need a wrap tonight?" she asked Fiona.

Fiona dismissed her husband with a glare. "I'm taking a shawl."

Sir Reginald could not have ordered a finer night for his excursion to Vauxhall Gardens, Verity thought. The night was warm, with only a slight breeze coming off the Thames. She had to school herself not to act the country oaf in her exclamations over the delights of Vauxhall. The colored lights strung through the lush tree branches, the orchestra, the dazzling fireworks all vied to make this a most enjoyable evening.

A pity Sir Reginald was so utterly attentive to her. One would think kneeing the man in his groin would have alienated him toward her, but no such alienation had occurred. Indeed, the man was more steadfast than ever in his attentions.

"I beg that you will allow me to stroll with you through the lighted paths," he said to her once they had eaten.

She lowered her voice. "Only if you give me your word you will not try to take liberties with me."

"My dear Miss Birmingham, you have my word. I'm most repentant over my actions with you on the balcony last night, but you must understand that your loveliness overwhelms me."

Not my loveliness, but my fortune. She did not believe him for a moment. She knew without a doubt he would try to kiss her, but she was confident in her ability to protect herself. Thank goodness her brothers had taught her to use her knees. "Very well," she said, giving him her hand.

Randolph was in no position to meet with his sister tonight. After seeing her disembark from her carriage, he hurried off down one of the dark paths of Vauxhall Gardens. Fiona's presence meant he would have to alter his plans. He had intended to stay near the dancing pavilion, keeping his eye on Sir Reginald.

Now, though, he would have to wait down one of the garden paths.

He felt rather conspicuous standing alone as couple after couple wandered down the meandering paths, eyeing him suspiciously. On several occasions he nodded and muttered greetings to acquaintances. In the event Fiona were to come strolling toward him, he planned to duck into the bushes to avoid being seen by her.

The atmosphere was festive with gay orchestra music and voices lifted in laughter. And the night could not have been finer. As he stood there beneath colorful Oriental lanterns where the main path intersected a trio of secondary paths, he heard Sir Reginald's voice and ducked behind a tree.

As Sir Reginald came closer, Randolph drew back to watch to see which fork the sinister baronet would take so that he could follow him, could save the maiden from Sir Reginald's vile clutches.

Then he heard her voice.

His lovely woman in the scarlet riding habit! His heart pounding erratically, Randolph wondered if *she* could be the heiress. By God, he'd kill Sir Reginald with his bare hands!

He stole a glance.

When he saw that the woman accompanying his neighbor was indeed his lady of mystery, his pulse thundered. Instead of wearing her red, tonight she wore a snow white gown that draped off her smooth shoulders and skimmed over the slope of her breasts. He drew in his breath. She was even more beautiful, more elegant than he remembered. His heart thundered. He longed to rush to her, longed to allow his gaze to linger over her graceful beauty, but he had to squelch his desire in order to defend her from Sir Reginald, whom he suddenly wished to murder.

He would attack the baronet. He would lash into

him with untamable anger. But he must be patient. It was imperative that he wait until Sir Reginald revealed his evil intentions to the lady, allow her to know how truly vile Sir Reginald was. Then, Randolph would rescue her.

Then he would avenge her. God help him if he killed the man.

The pair turned onto the southern path, and Randolph followed silently at a discreet distance, not about to let them stray far from him. He must stay close. He must be ready to save the woman he loved. Like a cat on soft paws, he followed them, careful to stay in the darkness, his stomach churning with apprehension for his cherished lady.

They chatted amiably for another hundred yards when Sir Reginald slowed down and faced a dark pocket.

"You gave me your word," she told Sir Reginald, "that you would behave the gentleman." His response was to pull her against her will into the darkness.

Once the couple edged into the dark pocket Randolph could no longer see them, but he heard her voice. "I beg that you not get so close to me, Sir Reginald!"

Rage shot through Randolph as he heard her muffled scream, heard the sounds of their struggle. He bolted toward them, lunging into the clearing. "Get your dirty hands off the lady!" he yelled.

Even though it was dark, there was enough moonlight for him to see two struggling forms, see the baronet drawing away from her as he whirled toward Randolph. "What in the hell are you doing here?" Sir Reginald demanded.

"I've come to save the lady. Last night I heard you reveal your vile scheme to compromise her."

The lady shrieked.

"How dare you!" Sir Reginald bleated as he lunged toward Randolph.

Randolph hurled his fist into the baronet's face. The blow sent him sprawling backward, cursing his assailant as he fell.

"I'll kill you if you ever lay a hand on the lady again," Randolph shouted as Sir Reginald staggered back to his feet, putting up his fists.

Another swift blow from Randolph knocked him down again. Randolph stomped his shoe onto Sir Reginald's chest, then lowered himself to straddle the struggling man. Randolph's fury was so great, he could not stop hitting the baronet, even after he had knocked him senseless. His bloody fists relentlessly pounded into Sir Reginald's face.

It wasn't until he heard her voice that he stopped. "You'll kill him!" she said, trying to pull Randolph off the smaller man.

Hearing her voice brought Randolph to his senses. He got to his feet and tenderly looked down at her crumpled face. "Are you unhurt?" he asked in a tender voice, setting gentle hands on her shoulders.

Her brows lowered, she nodded and lifted one of his bloody hands to her lips to kiss it. "You're bleeding," she said in a voice husky with emotion.

Feeling the brush of her lips on his hand was his undoing. He hauled her into his arms and claimed her lips as his arms tightened around her slender back. To his profound relief, she did not push him away, did not clamp her soft lips shut against the invasion of his tongue. Her body arched against him. Her arms came around him. Her tongue mingled with his as she kissed him with breathless abandon. And when one of his hands began to stroke her breasts, she did not recoil.

But when he realized he was behaving no more gentlemanly than Sir Reginald, he recoiled. "Forgive me," he said in a breathless voice, drawing away from her. "I would never wish to harm you or your reputation in any way. You're too important to me." He eased her into his embrace and sighed. "Why did you never return to me? Have you any idea how strongly I wished to be with you? How keenly I care for you? Why did you stay away?"

She kept her cheek flattened against his chest, her arms linking around him as she sighed. "I . . . saw your signet ring. You're a peer. I'm a nobody."

He drew her even closer. "Don't ever say that. You're lovely and elegant and cultured—and you're everything I could ever hope for. I don't care who you are. I know that I've fallen in love with you."

"But your family . . . Aristocrats marry other aristocrats. They would never countenance a marriage between you and the daughter of a Cit, and as strongly as I care for you, I could never countenance a love affair that did not terminate in marriage."

He was flooded with profound joy. *She cares for me!* "I would never ask you to compromise your reputation. You're a lady. I've known it since the first time I saw you." He stroked her face tenderly. "No one tells me what I can and cannot do. I'm one and thirty years of age and my own master." But he was not in a position to offer for her right now. Even if he did love her. "You're the only one who can ever send me away."

"You say you love me now, but were you to marry beneath you, you would soon regret such a decision." She sighed. "I shouldn't like to destroy what is between us."

"You could never destroy it. No one can."

Her voice was sorrowful when she replied. "But I would. I'd never be part of your world. You'd become ashamed of me."

"Never!"

She twisted away from him. "I beg that you not torment me. Let me go back to my world." She began to walk away.

His heart sank. He could not allow her to get away

from him again. He sputtered toward her. "Please! You must tell me your name."

She shook her head. "It's better this way. We must forget one another."

"'Twould be easier to quit breathing."

"Please, my lord, don't make this so difficult for me," she said in a choking voice.

"I can't let you get away this time."

She clapped her hands to her ears. "No more!" Giving him one last, long, sorrowful look, she said, "If you care for me, I beg that you let me go and don't follow me."

Were he in a position to offer for her, he would never let her go. But he had nothing to offer a wife at this time. He swallowed hard. "I'll find you."

He heard her sweet voice hitch as she ran back to the lighted path.

Chapter 24

Owing to the weather turning cooler, Fiona and Verity had begun to wear heavy wool capes over their pelisses as they rode through Hyde Park, mounds of autumn's leaves crunching beneath their phaeton's wheels. "I vow," Fiona said, eying the nearly empty byways of London's largest park, "there's hardly a soul left in London."

"I beg to disagree," Verity said with a teasing smile. "There are thousands left in the city—just not the beau monde."

"Oh dear, you make me feel the complete snob."

"Never that! In fact, I'm happy to say you're not at all snobbish—as I'd expected peers to be."

"Are you sure I'm not arrogant?" There had to be some reason for Nick's coolness toward her, surely something besides his attraction to the duchess.

"Quite."

Fiona sighed. "I was hoping there was something in my personality that was correctable. I'm willing to do anything to get back in my husband's good graces."

Verity stiffened and went dead silent for a moment. "I'll own my brother has not been as affectionate toward you as he was when I arrived in London," she finally said, "but I truly believe he's in love with you."

After that night in his arms when he'd said, "Oh, my love, my Fiona," Fiona had allowed herself to hope that Nick *did* love her, but his subsequent coolness only reinforced her belief that his achingly welcome words were merely the result of his passion that moment. For weeks now the memory of those words sustained her. Not a day passed that she did not torture herself remembering them. Not a day passed that she did not regret that she had withheld her own declaration that night. Perhaps if she had let him know how much she loved him, the rift between them might have been avoided.

"He cares for you as he's never cared for another woman," Verity continued.

Nick never professed to be in love with her, a fact Fiona would not divulge to the sister she had grown so close to. So she must change the topic of conversation. "Have you noticed the man on the horse behind us?"

When Verity went to whirl around, Fiona grabbed her arm. "I beg that you not be so conspicuous! Allow me to turn onto the next path, then steal a glance."

Fiona steered her phaeton onto the next intersecting path, and Verity moved her head ever so slightly. "The man's following us," she finally declared.

"Indeed he is. And this isn't the first time. For the past several weeks I've noticed him following me."

"Now that you mention it, I realize he does look familiar—not that I've noticed him before, but I have a remarkably observant eye for horses, and I've seen that chestnut many times."

"I'll vow you have!"

"When did you first become aware of him?"

"I noticed him in front of Albany—you know Lady Melbourne's former house that's just down a few doors from our house. I thought nothing of it the first time, except for thinking he dressed too drably to reside at Albany. When I noticed him the next day I became even more puzzled. Just by chance a few days later I discovered that he rode behind Trevor and I when we went to pay a call on the Duchess of Glastonbury. Ever since then I've been watchful."

Verity's brows lowered. "And he follows you everywhere?"

"Everywhere."

"It must be Nicky!"

"What must be Nicky?"

"Nicky's hired men to guard you."

"Why would my husband wish to have me guarded?"

Verity shrugged. "Perhaps he fears cutthroats will harm you for your jewels."

"In broad daylight?" Though, Fiona owned silently, calling today's murky gray skies daylight stretched credibility.

"It's not inconceivable."

"But I never leave Mayfair!"

"Mayfair, my dear sister, is where the best jewels can be found."

Fiona shrugged. "I suppose that's why Nick frowns on me going off without a groom."

"Papa had me guarded once," Verity said. "Enemies from his business dealings made threats, and dear Papa feared for my safety. I'll vow that's why Nicky's having guards watch you."

Fiona wished she could be that important to Nick. More likely, he'd be happy to be rid of her. But, of course, she could not express such doubts to dear Verity. "Perhaps I'll ask Nick—if I ever get alone with him," she said lightly. Though he accompanied her most evenings, they were always with other people. Never alone. It had been almost four months now since they had shared a bed, four months since she had felt the stroke of his hand on her bare flesh.

Verity cleared her throat. "I need to return to Great Acres."

Fiona's hand holding the ribbons went still. Verity was right to wish to return to her widowed mother, but Fiona was loathe to lose her. She would miss Verity horribly, as horribly as she missed Randy. And Verity's leaving London without having made a match would solidify Fiona's many failures: her failure to find Verity a husband, her failure to mend the rift with Randy, and her failure to gain her own husband's affection. "I feel so wretched. I lured you to London with promises of matching you with a compatible husband, and now you'll return to the tediousness of Great Acres, still a spinster."

"It's no more your fault that I failed to make a match than it's your fault Miss Peabody came away from the Marriage Mart empty handed."

"But Miss Peabody deliberately sabotaged her chances of attracting a husband."

Verity peered at Fiona. "How did you know that?"

"Because she persisted in wearing those spectacles."

"The poor lady cannot see without them!"

Fiona lifted her chin. "She did not wear them to the come-out ball."

"Because the countess made her, but Miss Peabody confessed to me that she was unable to clearly see the faces of any man she danced with."

"Oh dear, then I suppose she really must wear them. One must know what her future husband looks like."

"My friend is disinterested in love."

"Perhaps next year she will be."

"Perhaps," Verity said with a shrug. "I'm grateful to you for doing everything in your power to link me to a man who'd be a good match. I daresay a dozen of the men I've met would have—" She stopped abruptly.

Fiona, her mouth gaping open, whirled to Verity. "There is someone! You *have* fallen in love, have you not?"

Verity did not respond for a moment. Then she nodded.

"I've been so stupid!" Fiona said. "Now I realize why you would never encourage so many worthy men. Did you know your lover before you came to us?"

"No," Verity said with a shake of her head. "I came to London to find a husband. And I lost my heart to an unsuitable man."

"But either Miss Peabody or I have been with you whenever you've gone out. How, pray tell, could you have had the opportunity to fall in love with an unsuitable man?"

"During my morning rides," Verity admitted in a somber voice. "I've hardly spoken to him, yet no other man will ever do."

They might have spoken very little, but for Verity to have so strong an attraction, Fiona was certain Verity and her lover had exchanged something more than a few words. "Has he kissed you?"

Tears came to Verity's eyes, and she nodded.

"If you feel that way about him he cannot be unsuitable. Your judgment is too good for you to be attracted to an unworthy man."

Verity harrumphed. "Oh, he's a most suitable man. Just not for me."

Fiona reined in the horse. The phaeton came to a stop, and she turned to Verity. "Why not for you?"

"Because he's a peer."

Anger flashed in Fiona's water blue eyes. "That's the most ridiculous thing I've ever heard you say! Of course you can marry a peer! You were without a doubt the best prize of this year's Marriage Mart."

"I cannot marry a peer. Besides, I care too much for him to allow him to ruin his life for his fleeting attraction to me."

Fiona's brows lowered. "Then he's declared himself to you?"

"He . . ." Verity dabbed at her eyes with her handkerchief. "He told me he loved me."

"If he loves you, why hasn't he come to ask Nick for your hand?"

"He doesn't know who I am. And . . . I don't know who he is."

"Forgive me if I sound befuddled, but how can you know he's a peer if you don't know his identity?"

"I saw his signet ring."

"You obstinate goose! That's why you discontinued your morning rides! I perceive that as soon as you realized he was a peer, you quit going to Hyde Park at dawn."

Verity nodded. "I thought in time I would forget him."

"So the poor man's likely been waiting for you every morning for the past few months."

"Not anymore. And especially not since that night at Vauxhall."

Now Fiona was truly perplexed. "I was at Vauxhall with you, and I have no memory of any peer beside Warwick being in our party."

"He wasn't. He did, however, save me from ruination at the hands of that detestable Sir Reginald."

"How romantic!"

Verity burst into tears. "It was u-u-u-tterly romantic! He begged to know my name, begged to call on me." Between more sobs, she managed, "He kissed me most intimately and told me he loved me."

"And you sent him away?"

A deep sob rose up from Verity's chest to become

a wrenching cry. "I begged him if . . . " Sniff. Sniff. "If he cared for me, he not follow me."

Fiona folded her arms across her chest and glared at her sister. "That is the most stupid thing you've ever done!"

"I . . . I also told him I was the daughter of a Cit. Now that he knows how ineligible I am, he'll forget me."

"I'm living proof that he will not," Fiona said in a morose voice.

He had thought that when the balls and routs and musicales wound down at the close of the Season he would get more sleep, would be more alert at the 'Change, but even though he'd gone to bed early the past two nights, he still had not slept. How could he, knowing Fiona lay in bed in the next room? He knew that if he came to her she would do her wifely duty. But that wasn't enough for Nick. He wanted her to want him with as searing a need as he wanted her.

And he wanted her love.

As long as Warwick drew breath, Nick could never have that.

Perhaps he was getting used to the lack of sleep. A pity he could not become inured to the perpetual pain.

Even now as he tried to concentrate on his ledgers he heard her lovely voice raised in song as she and Verity played the pianoforte in the drawing room. How he longed to watch her, to drink in her perfection. Instead, he gazed at the closed door to his library and at the neglected ledgers in front of him. He was like a man lured by opium. Only Fiona was his opium.

The singing stopped, and a minute later the door to his library opened. His wife stood silhouetted against the door frame, elegant in a graceful ivory gown that barely covered the smooth mounds of her breasts. That solemn look that seemed to have become part of her these days was on her face as she shut the door and moved to his desk.

He closed the ledgers and met her somber gaze.

"Why are you having me followed?" she asked, sinking into a chair across from him.

Whatever he had expected her to say, it wasn't that. He watched her with hardened eyes, then spoke icily. "Perhaps I wish all the lurid details of your meetings with your lover."

"Then I daresay you've been vastly disappointed," she said.

He hadn't the stomach to ask her guards if she had been meeting with Warwick. Could it be she hadn't? His thoughts flitted to that day when he had told her he would not tolerate her taking a lover. Had she adhered to his wishes? "Forgive me, then," he said. "Actually, I've made enemies, enemies I fear would do you harm to hurt me."

She began to laugh. A laugh without glee.

His brows nudged down. "Why are you laughing?"

"I daresay you'd reward the man who took me off your hands."

Anger flared within him. "You think I wish something to happen you?"

"Perhaps you don't wish me harm," she said coolly. "You just wish you'd never married me."

Now he laughed. How much pain he could have been spared had he not married her. A thousand times he'd wished she had never come to him with her bizarre proposal, never tempted him with her compelling offer, never captured his heart with her compliant body. But the past could not be undone. "I don't recall ever having lamented that I married you."

"You don't have to tell me, Nick. Your coolness speaks louder than any words. I pledged to be an affectionate wife, but you want no part of my affections."

"There, my dear, you're wrong. My desire for you gives me a great deal of pain."

She left her chair and moved to him, her gaze fixing on his bulging crotch. Then she did a startling thing. She placed her hand on his throbbing erection and whispered, "Let me give you release, Nick."

A torrent of powerful emotions swamped him. He hauled her onto his lap and crushed his lips into hers. His hands raked over her body as their kiss caught him up in a swirl of molten heat. He had never been more hungry for her, never before so exalted in the feel of her, the smell of her. From her hungry response he knew she wanted him with the same scorching need that consumed him. His greedy hands raked over her heated flesh, too flooded with his own need for gentleness. She was so utterly soft, so achingly desirable he was powerless not to take what she offered. Yanking at the skimpy bodice of her dress, he bared her breasts and bent to take one into his mouth, glorying in the shudders that vibrated throughout her body.

When her hand coiled around his shaft, every thought was obliterated, save one: He would make love to her here in the library. And she would allow it. With his inner wrist he began to press against the lowest bone in her torso. She rocked against the movement of his hand, making those little whimpering sounds he had so longed to once again hear. Dear God, he couldn't last another moment without spilling his seed. "I can't wait," he groaned, flicking her hand away.

"Take me here," she whispered in a breathless voice as she cradled his face into her breasts.

He lifted his head away from her soft bosom and watched her smoldering eyes. She had never been more beautiful. "Are you sure this is what you want?" he asked throatily.

Searing hunger flashed in her eyes when she nodded.

Just as his hand dipped beneath her skirts, there was a knock on his library door. He groaned as a sigh swished from his lungs at the same instant Fiona sighed. Then he growled, "What is it?"

"An urgent message from your couriers," Biddles said.

Nick jerked up. *Something's happened to William!* His hands groped at Fiona's breasts as he tugged on the dress bodice to cover them. Then he stood, taking her with him, before he plopped her back in the chair. Still standing behind the desk, he said, "You may come in."

But it wasn't Biddles who entered the room. It was one of the couriers wearing the blue and yellow Birmingham livery. Nick's heart, so recently violently pumping, skidded. The man's glance flicked to Fiona before he handed Nick the sealed letter.

Nick tore open the seal and with his pulse pounding began to read. The letter was written by William's highest ranking guard.

> *My dear Mr. Nicholas Birmingham, It greeves me to inform you that your brother William has been placed under arrest. Joseph Bonaparte, the King of Naples, allows no one to visit or speak to Mr. William Birmingham, and he is forbidden even the courtesy to write letters to his family. Fortunately, our men have been able to protect the carriage bearing the francs at a point northeast of Naples where the French have no power.*
>
> *I shall await your forthcoming instructions. Our couriers know where to find me.*

Cursing, Nick fisted the letter in his hands and hurled it into the fire, then dismissed the courier.

Thank God William was still alive. He must act with haste to ensure he stayed alive.

"What is it, dearest?" Fiona asked, rushing to him.

He turned to face her, his face grave. "Something urgent's come up. I must leave at once."

It tore at his heart to see the wounded look on her lovely face. "It cannot wait?" she asked in a thin voice.

Settling his hands on her slender shoulders, he spoke softly. "It cannot."

She stiffened, "If you leave now, I'll know you've made a decision about our marriage."

"This urgent matter has nothing to do with our marriage," he snapped. He went to take her hand, but she twisted away.

"All your *private* matters are more important to you than me."

"No one is more important to me than you."

"If you mean that, you'll stay."

"Fiona," he said, stepping toward her.

"Don't touch me! I have no power against your touch, and well you know it."

At any other time her words would have been an aphrodisiac. But not now. His brother was in grave danger. "I have to go," he said solemnly.

"Then your decision's made," she said, her voice hitching with emotion as she fled the room.

Chapter 25

With a shaking hand Nick scribbled the note to Warwick, twice crossing out the wrong word. His inability to concentrate was understandable. Every cell in his body wrenched from the painful parting with Fiona. Every shred of his willpower had been put to the test when he did not allow himself to go after her. A wasted moment—even to assuage the doubts of the person who mattered most to him—could cost his brother's life.

He vowed he would make it up to Fiona once this crisis was settled—if it could be settled.

After he sealed the letter he stormed from Menger House and walked around to the mews for his horse.

A block away from Warwick's house on Curzon Street Nick paid a street urchin a crown to deliver his note to the earl. Even though the need for haste was great, Nick could not risk being seen at Warwick House. William's life would be snuffed if anyone learned of the Birmingham connection to the British foreign secretary.

From Curzon Street Nick went directly to the public house in Soho where he had directed Warwick to meet him. There was no time to travel to an out-of-the way location tonight. Nick's blood ran cold just thinking of the fate that had fallen other Bonaparte enemies. He couldn't endanger his younger brother more than he already had. Damn Warwick. Damn Napoleon. Damn this never-ending war.

Nick had selected the Bear & Boar because, unlike other taverns in Soho, this one was large enough to afford a scattering of tables and chairs. He settled at a table in the establishment's darkest corner and awaited Warwick. Another reason the Bear & Boar was an excellent choice for a clandestine meeting was that no one could possibly hear their private conversation over the steady drone of men's voices that filled the room.

As the minutes ticked away and Warwick did not come, Nick grew nervous. What if Warwick was away from home and unable to receive the note? It could be early in the morning before the note fell into his hands, and by then the public house would be closed. While Nick was pondering this glitch, Lord Warwick sped into the pub, divesting himself of his greatcoat as his glance circled the dark room. His eyes brightened with recognition when he saw Nick, then he came to sit beside him. "What's so damn urgent?" he asked.

"My brother's in grave danger."

Warwick hiked a brow.

"Joseph Bonaparte's had him arrested."

The earl sat there staring at him. Nick watched the candlelight's reflection in Warwick's dark eyes and wondered if something had rendered the foreign secretary deaf. Had he not heard him? Finally, the earl said, "I'm very disappointed to hear that."

"I don't give a damn about your disappointment. I want your help. I'll not have the damned French murder my brother."

"I would do anything humanly possible to avert such misfortune, but I'm powerless to help you in this.

We have no contacts in Naples. None whatsoever. Your brother should never have gone there. Were he in, say, Seville, I could detail a unit to rescue him."

Nick's eyes narrowed, his voice turned menacing. "You bloody well knew he was going to Naples!"

"I told you it was risky, but you assured me your brother was skilled at crossing the right palms with silver."

"A practice he's an expert at. The only thing that would negate his 'generosity' would be an accusation that he was helping *you*. You swore to me no one knew of this operation except for you and my brothers and me." Anger flashing in his eyes, Nick leaned toward the earl and spoke with contempt. "Who else have you told?"

Warwick's mouth thinned with displeasure. "I've told no one. I've learned the costly lesson that even one's most trusted colleagues can betray confidences. This mission was too important. Besides . . . I could never jeopardize Lady Fiona's safety. If the French ever got wind that you and your brothers were aiding me, they could use her as leverage to recapture the vanished francs."

God but Nick hated the foreign secretary! Warwick didn't even try to disguise his love for Nick's wife. But because of Warwick's love for Fiona, Nick believed him. He had not told another soul. "I'm sorry I ever let you talk me into this scheme," Nick spat out.

Warwick's gaze flicked to the nearby table where a trio of loud, ill-dressed men had just sat down, then he lowered his voice. "I didn't talk you into it, Birmingham. Your own patriotism forced you to use your vast resources for crown and country."

"Those resources, by God, better restore my brother to me," Nick snapped, getting to his feet. He could see he would get no help from the Foreign Office.

Now it was up to Nick to save William.

He stalked from the tavern.

Adam's eyes came open, and he glared at the candle Nick had slammed onto his bedside table. "What in the hell are you doing here? What time is it?"

"Get up!" Nick ordered. "It's not yet midnight. We have a crisis to discuss."

Adam jerked up. "Something's happened to William!"

"He's being held in a Naples prison," Nick said in a grave voice before plopping down in a chair near his brother's fire.

"Good God! How did you learn this?" Adam asked.

Nick related the events of the evening and concluded by asking, "Have you ever mentioned our brother's mission to anyone?"

"Of course not!" Adam glared at him. "You think I wish Will dead?"

Nick frowned. "I thought as much. It's just that I can't understand the Frenchies arresting him. I know he's bribed all the proper authorities. The only reason I can see for them to arrest him is that they found out he was aiding the Foreign Office."

"Are you certain Warwick hasn't told anyone?"

"Amazingly, I am."

"Then the French can't possibly know anything. More likely, they wish to secure a hefty ransom from us."

"I don't think so," Nick said with a perplexed frown. "One of us would have heard something by now."

"I need to go to Naples," Adam said, moving from the tousled bed.

"Why not me?"

"Because your business would be ruined if you left

the Exchange for several weeks. I, on the other hand, employ competent managers who can run our bank when I'm not there."

"Point well taken. But how can you be assured your bribes are any better than those already offered by Will?"

"Will wasn't bribing jailers. I will."

"You mean to take him from the prison?"

"Can you think of anything else?"

"I can think of a hundred ways you'd be foiled, and I don't wish to have *two* dead brothers."

Adam effected a look of mock outrage. "How would I be foiled?"

"For one thing, William's possessed of coloring markedly different from the Italians. Unlike you with your dark complexion, Will could never pass as an Italian when fleeing from the Naples prison."

"Hadn't thought of that." Adam came to sit in another chair near the fire, then he settled his chin into his hands, eyes narrowed, while he continued to think of a way to save his brother. "Pity he's not married to a French chit."

Nick bolted up and began to pace the creaking wood floor. "You're brilliant!"

"I am?"

"Indeed." Nick pivoted on his boot heel and faced his brother. "Now if you can just direct me to someone who can forge documents."

Adam looked offended. "I'm an upstanding businessman."

"I know that! Actually, I was thinking of Will. Doesn't he have a chap who forges papers for his continental jaunts?"

"By Jove, he does! Fellow in Hackney. And we're in luck. The fellow's French!" His brows dipped with suspicion as he peered at Nick. "But what good would false documents do?"

"Yvonne."

"What, pray tell, do documents have to do with your former mistress?"

"Yvonne is most indebted to me. Through my generosity she's been able to establish herself in Parisian society. The Bonapartes, Murat, and even Tallyrand are among her admirers."

Adam's eyes glittered. "I begin to see. You're going to ask her to say she married Will."

"Exactly."

"Allow me to say you are brilliant."

"If I were brilliant, I'd not have allowed my brother to risk his life in such a manner."

"Don't blame yourself. Remember how excited Will was about the challenge before he left?"

"Will's a callow youth! I'm two and thirty. I should have known better."

"Were you a Benthamite, you'd be willing to risk Will 'for the greater good.'"

"Damn good thing I'm not a bloody Benthamite!"

Adam squinted up at his brother. "How do you know Yvonne will comply?"

"She will."

"I don't doubt that she would were she to see you face to face. Women seem unable to deny you anything. But how can you persuade her when you can't go to Paris?"

Nick turned sharply. "Why can't I go to Paris?"

"In case you haven't noticed, there's a war on. Englishmen are prohibited from stepping on French soil."

"Not Englishmen with very deep pockets, Englishmen who speak French like a native."

But, bloody hell, how would he explain his absence to Fiona?

* * *

For a few precious moments that night the heavy curtain of gloom had been lifted from her heart. Nick had told her he desired her. He'd even said no one was more important to him than she. And most blissful of all, he had kissed her with more passion than he ever had before. He *did* want her.

Until that wretched note was delivered. At first she had thought the letter must be from his lover, but after reflecting on it, she realized it was delivered by a servant wearing the Birmingham livery, one of Nick's own couriers. The urgent matter that had stolen him from her must relate to his business. No matter what he'd told her, his business *did* come before her. It seemed that everything was more important to Nick than saving their marriage.

She had fled to her room, and there she had paced the floor, torturing herself by remembering every word he had said. *No one is more important than you.* If only it were true. She would close her eyes and imagine his urgent hands stroking her, vividly remember the blistering kisses they had shared. He had wanted her.

Was there enough left of his former affection to resurrect their floundering marriage? Dare she cast aside her own pride and forget her demand that he choose between her and his urgent business? Was she willing to forgive his abandonment in order to keep alive the flame that had burned through him that night?

She rang for Prudence to dress her for bed in a fine lawn nightshift, and when her maid was finished, Fiona sat before her dressing table mirror while Prudence combed out her hair. With only the dim candlelight to illuminate the looking glass, Fiona peered at her own reflection. To Nick's eyes, would she be as pretty as Hortense? Hortense's mouth was more full than Fiona's, but Fiona's blue eyes were wider than the duchess's green ones. Were Fiona an impartial observer—which she realized was impossible—their faces were equally pretty.

Then her gaze dipped to the two modest humps beneath her nightshift. The duchess certainly had the advantage over Fiona there. Fiona wondered if Nick would have been more well pleased with her if she were buxom. The memory of his hands touching her breasts, kneading them, his mouth suckling at them, made her breasts feel heavy, made liquid heat gush to her core.

After Prudence left, Fiona scattered drops of light perfume at her wrists and neck. She would cast aside her pride and beg him to forgive her shrewish ultimatum. She would tell him she understood that he would not have left were the matter which drew him away not important. She would vow to not be a meddling wife.

Once her decision was made, she went to Nick's bedchamber and waited for him in a satin-covered chair before the fire, the warmth of being in his room after so long an absence seeping to her very soul.

Dozens of times over the next few hours she practiced what she would say to him. With every recitation she became more acutely aware that no matter what she said or how she said it, nothing could disguise the fact that she was trading her pride for a chance of securing his love.

The prospect of feeling herself in his arms again was worth the risk of fleeting humiliation.

She did not know when she had fallen asleep. Sometime after two, she was sure. When she awoke, it was seven. Her glance flicked to the huge silk-draped bed where she had known such splendor. The bed had not been slept in.

Nick had spent the night with his lover. Fiona was almost overcome by her own despair. Tears filling her eyes, she got up to return to her room. While half of her was thankful she had been spared humiliation, the other half of her cried out for his touch.

As she neared the adjoining dressing room she heard muffled voices. No doubt Nick's valet was helping him out of his evening clothes. She could not face the humiliation of him finding her now in his private chambers. She turned away from the dressing room door with the intention of quietly returning to her own chambers through the main hallway.

But Nick must have heard the soft muffle of her slippers for he threw open the door. "Fiona!"

She whirled away from him and, her vision blurred by tears, stumbled toward the door.

Nick quickly dismissed his valet and raced after her, grabbing her by the shoulders and yanking her around to face him. "What's the matter? You're crying!"

"Leave me alone!" She lifted her chin with defiance and spoke icily. "If you please, allow me to return to my chambers."

"I damn well *don't* please." His eyes softened as he studied her anguished face. Good Lord, had he done this to her? If it took the rest of his life, he would make it up to her for causing her such grief. "Forgive me. I perceive that I had the misfortune of not being here when you had the courage to take that first step toward forgiveness."

She stiffened. "Don't flatter yourself! I merely wished to satisfy my curiosity."

"And you obviously weren't satisfied." He thumbed away a tear from her cheek.

"What woman would be satisfied that her husband prefers being in another woman's bed?"

He gripped both her shoulders. "You really believe there's another woman?"

She drew a deep breath to stem a sob. "What business dealings could keep you away all night?"

"How little you know of my business," he said bitterly. "I give you my word I was not with another woman last night." If his absence hadn't wounded her so thoroughly, he would have rejoiced that she cared enough about him to be jealous. But he could take no pleasure in her pain.

If only he had come home when he left Adam's house last night. He might have been able to reignite what he had started with his wife earlier in the evening. Instead, he had chosen to go to Hackney, to awaken the French forger and wait all night while the man forged the documents.

Now it would tear Nick's heart to leave his wife like this.

But he had no choice.

"Then . . ." Her anger wavered. "Where did you go?"

"I told you. It was business."

"And I'm never to discuss your precious business," she snapped, trying to jerk away from him.

"Fiona, please believe me." God, but he didn't want to tell her he was leaving. "A grave problem has arisen, and I'm the only one who can address it. In fact . . ." his pulse pounded, "I will have to go away for a few days."

Those woeful blue eyes of hers widened. "When?"

"I leave within the hour."

"Where to?"

He did not want to lie, but he could not tell her— or anyone save Adam—the truth. "I'm the leading stockholder of a factory in Essex." That much was true. "I must go there to resolve an urgent labor dispute."

"I see," she said coolly. "Have a good journey."

This time he let her walk away.

The memory of her anguished face crushed him with inextinguishable sorrow.

Chapter 26

The first few weeks he was at Windmere Abbey, Randolph was smugly satisfied with himself. Since he was already paying for the upkeep and the many loyal servants at Windmere Abbey, he thought it a most practical decision to return there. Leaving his lodgings in London had saved him a modest sum, too. And by being at Windmere Abbey he could more closely examine the expenses with an eye to trimming waste.

He had quickly put a stop to the practice of keeping fires in the drawing room. Not planning on having callers, he could conduct all his business from the library and never have to use the drawing room.

Another economy was his decision to sell off his sister's horse. No doubt her rich husband had by now presented her with a much finer beast. Birmingham was noted for his grand stables, though Randolph could not understand when the Cit ever found the time to visit them. Nor could Randolph understand why Birmingham even bothered keeping a country estate when he seldom left London and The Exchange where he'd amassed his bulging fortune.

Randolph fleetingly regretted his decision not to

accept his brother-in-law's financial help. Had he accepted it, he could have offered for his lovely woman in the red riding habit. But Randolph was obsessed with the idea of single-handedly rescuing the family fortunes.

The pity of it was that it would take years.

And by then *she* would have married another. For all he knew she could be betrothed to someone else by now. She was far too pretty not to attract a throng of admirers. His pulse sped up when he remembered that she was also an heiress. More's the pity. With her beauty *and* a fortune, her days as an unmarried woman were dwindling.

On this night as he sat in his library, soothed by the smell and warmth of a rich peat fire, Randolph realized Christmas was just a few weeks away. Stephen had accepted Fiona's invitation to spend Christmas with her at Camden Hall. Which left Randolph bereft of family.

Which left him exceedingly morose.

Like layers from an onion, his contentment began to peel away. How could he have had the audacity to be so smug when his own foolish pride had cost him so dearly? Why had he not embraced Birmingham when it was so painfully obvious that Fiona truly cared for her husband?

Because of his damned pride, Randolph had lost his only sister.

And if he hadn't been so bullish proud, he would have offered for his mystery woman instead of allowing her to get away. But he'd been hell-bent on waiting until he had something to offer her beside a pile of debts. Even knowing she was an heiress had not swayed him. If anything, he became more determined *not* to touch her money.

Because of his damned pride, she would now likely marry another.

He gave a bitter, mirthless laugh. What exactly had his pride gotten him? He had lost those he loved best.

If anyone deserved a lonely, joyless Christmas, it was he.

Nick watched the rows of lighted windows on Yvonne's Avenue Foch house. He would wait until the last guest was gone, the last light extinguished before he dared to knock at the door. It would not do for him to be recognized by a French official—especially since he was traveling under forged French documents.

While he stood across the street in the shadows of a darkened doorway, his thoughts—as they perpetually did—turned to Fiona. He feared for her safety, even though he had extracted a promise from Hutchinson before he left to double his wife's guard and to be ever alert to anything that might threaten her. He had also made Adam vow to stand at the ready to assist her during his absence.

Nick watched the silhouettes of men and women against the second-floor windows of Yvonne's townhouse. And thought some more of Fiona. Nothing had ever affected him more profoundly than her potent need for him that last night he had spent in London. He was certain now that, even if she did love Warwick, she was no longer stealing away to meet him. Did that mean she wished to be a real wife to Nick? Her actions that last night were the actions of a real wife. His heart accelerated when he recalled that she'd actually acted jealous. Could he even allow himself to hope?

As he stood watching an elegantly dressed couple leave Yvonne's and get in a fine coach and four, he vowed to make it up to his wife for leaving her, even if he had to get down on his knees and beg her to forgive him, beg her to give him a chance to win her love.

After that first couple left, one after another of Yvonne's guests began to leave. He waited until all the lights were extinguished before he knocked on her door.

When he opened her door, the butler's face crinkled into a broad grin. "Monsieur Birmingham!"

"Good evening, Pierre. Is *mademoiselle* in?"

There was no need for Pierre to call her. She was already hurrying down the stairs. "Nickee!"

He gazed up at her as she gracefully moved toward him, her blue eyes shimmering with warmth. She was as beautiful as ever. Though her blond hair and blue eyes matched Fiona's coloring, the resemblance between the two women ended there. Yvonne was much larger than Fiona. And much more voluptuous. Unlike Fiona's delicate, subdued beauty, Yvonne's striking beauty and her flair for bold clothes—like tonight's red lace—demanded attention. His lazy gaze traveled the length of her. "You're as beautiful as ever, Yvonne."

Her eyes narrowed and her luscious red lips effected a pout. "And you're even more handsome, *mon cheri.*" She came to link her arm through his. "But I must get you away from the door. Do you not know how dangerous it is for you to be here? You might be recognized."

"That's why I waited until dark—and until your guests left."

She took him to the drawing room, where Pierre had lighted a brace of candles, poured Nick cognac and came to sit on the arm of his chair. "What is the matter, Nickee?" She casually draped her arm around his shoulders.

That was one of the things he'd liked about Yvonne. Her perceptiveness. She could read him as if he were transparent. "My brother, William, is in grave danger, and I need your help."

"I would do anything for you, Nickee. Tell me what you need."

He drew in his breath. "It's a lot to ask, and I'm willing to pay handsomely."

"I do not wish your money."

"But you haven't heard what I'm asking for yet."

The heavy scent of gardenias clung to her. "Then tell me."

He first told her about William being held by King Bonaparte of Naples.

"I know Joseph well. He would not hold your brother unless he thought William was a danger to the empire."

Nick pursed his lips. "There is one small problem in that area."

Her perfectly arched brows hiked.

"My brother's been buying up francs all over Europe." Nick shrugged. "I suppose he's betting on the French to win the war."

She nodded. "Joseph would not like that. The Bonapartes, they want to control everything. If you would like, I shall travel to Naples at once and plead William's case."

"I'd like something even more."

Her eyes narrowed.

"I wish you to say you're secretly married to Will. As the wife of a French citizen—a French citizen who has friends in high-level government positions— he would be protected from cruel punishment."

"And when," she asked skeptically, "did I supposedly marry your baby brother? When I was in England and he was, what sixteen?"

Nick chuckled. "My dear Yvonne, William's almost the same age as you. If you'll recall, you were but seventeen when you came to me from the Duke of Glenweil—even if you did lie and say you were one and twenty."

"Ah, *cheri*, you weren't much older," she said in a faraway voice. "The years they have been kind to you."

He pulled a document from his pocket. "I have a marriage license—forged, of course—that says you and William wed in Seven Oaks six years ago. I know this a lot to ask of you. It will brand you as a married woman. It will prohibit you from marrying anyone else—as long as you choose to live in France. Were you to leave Paris, however, we could own the truth because you would be free from reprisals."

She shook her head. "I cannot leave again. I do not like Napoleon, but I must fly with the wind."

He took her hand. "Will you help me?"

"I will do anything for you, but this is much to ask."

"I'll give you fifty-thousand francs."

"I shall want pounds."

He smiled. "So you're not betting on Napoleon."

"I bet on no one except Yvonne de Cuir. Besides, if the Birminghams are going to control the francs, I'd rather have pounds."

"As you wish, mademoiselle—or should I say madame?" he said, the corner of his mouth lifting into a grin.

She stood and looked down at him. "I shall travel to Naples in the morning." Her voice softened. "Have you a bed to sleep in, or would you like to share mine?"

He brushed his lips across her hand. "I'll begin my journey back to England now. It's best that I travel by night."

She gave him a full-fledged pout. "You greatly offend me, Nickee. I do not appeal to you, no?"

He got to his feet and placed firm hands on her shoulders as he peered into her sparkling blue eyes. "I have a wife."

She stared at him. "Ah, Nickee, I believe you are in love with this wife of yours, no?"

"I am indeed in love with my wife." That was the first time Nick had ever admitted his love for Fiona to another person.

After Biddles announced Trevor, Fiona put down the tiny cape she was sewing for Emmie's doll as a Christmas present. Trevor burst into the room, went directly to the fire, removed his gloves, and made sweeping circles with his bare hands inches from the flames. He had not removed his greatcoat. "I daresay I've icicles growing from my ears," he mumbled. "Beastly cold out there."

"Then I'm flattered you've braved the weather to call on me."

He turned and gave her a sly smile. "As much as I adore you, my dearest, I would not brave this damnable weather for you. As it happens, I was returning from my aunt's in Hampshire and haven't been home yet. Trust that when I do arrive at my abode I shall not leave it." He came to sit by her on the sofa. "Ring for tea. I must have something hot to drink. I'm positively freezing."

Fiona got up and rang, then returned to her seat.

"Feel my head," Trevor said. "I daresay I'm coming down with a fever."

She placed her hand to his forehead. "You feel fine."

He sighed. "There's nothing fine about me. I fear I'm taking a lung infection."

Fiona suppressed a smile and spoke gravely. "I pray that you're not." For as many winters as she had known him, Trevor courted every possible ailment but had never contracted a single one—much to his displeasure. "I'm so happy you've come, Trev, for I've been so low since Miss Birmingham left yesterday. And Nick's left, too," she added solemnly.

"Then that was him I saw! Did he leave on Tuesday?"

Her eyes widened. "How did you know?"

"'Pon my word, I saw him on the road to Portsmouth, traveling at some great haste."

"That couldn't have been Nick. He said—" Her chest tightened, her stomach dropped. Nick must have lied to her. He had told her he was going to Essex, which was in the total opposite direction from Portsmouth.

Trevor's eyes narrowed. "Where did he say he was going, darling?"

"To Essex."

"Now that I think about it, the man couldn't possibly have been your husband. The man I saw was . . . much shorter than Birmingham."

Dear Trevor. Her eyes became suddenly watery. "Thank you, Trevor. You're such a good friend, and I so desperately need one now."

For once Trevor was at a loss for words. His gaze shifted from Fiona to the table where she had placed the doll cape, then he lifted the cape by its tiny ermine hood and held it up. "I know you've not been eating properly and are growing thinner each time I see you, but really, darling, this is much too small for you."

She giggled through her tears. "You goose, I'm sewing it for Emmie's doll. As a Christmas present."

He turned suddenly somber. "There's something else you could give the child—something less tangible but even more welcome than a fur-draped doll cape. . . ."

"Yes, I know," she said solemnly. Now the tears spilled. "I want her to be mine. I was going to tell her to call me Mama, but she's not mine. Were I to . . . leave Nick I could not take her with me." She drew in a deep breath and whimpered a sob. "So I ca-a-a-n't allow her to become attached to me because of the teetering state of my marriage."

Trevor's eyes narrowed. "Surely you're not think-ing of returning to Windmere Abbey?"

"My thoughts have been far too jumbled to take clear form. I would like to go to Camden Hall for Christmas." She shrugged. "I don't know what Nick wants, though I daresay he would not mind being rid of me."

"I think you misjudge your husband," Trevor said in a grave voice.

"Your high regard for me influences *your* judgment."

"I think not. Birmingham's besotted."

"Nicholas Birmingham has a mistress."

Trevor's eyes rounded. "I make it my business to know everybody's business, and I'm sure you're wrong there, my sweet. Where did you get your faulty information?"

She rubbed her gloved hand to her eyes to staunch the flow of tears. "Wife's intuition."

"What you need, my dear pea goose, is to sit down with that husband of yours as soon as he returns . . . from Essex and be honest about your feelings for him, about your doubts."

She shook her head. "You know why he married me. I can't pretend to own him. He should be free to . . . fall in love with another woman."

Trevor took her hand and squeezed it. "Allow him to fall in love with you."

"Oh, Trevor, if you only knew how I've humiliated myself for the pleasure of his touch."

Trevor clapped his hands to his ears. "I beg that you say no more. You will put me to the blush." When she made no response, he redirected their conversation. "So, what about your brothers? Will you see them at Christmas?"

"I've had no communication with Randy." Then she brightened. "But Stephen's coming. It's been over a year since I've seen the scamp."

"I daresay I'd hardly recognize him. The fellow gets bigger—and more decidedly muscled—every time I see him."

"Then you must come with us to Camden Hall for Christmas and see for yourself how much Stephen's grown."

Biddles brought the tea, and Fiona quickly poured Trevor's, adding extra sugar. "I'm sure a hot cup of very sweet tea is just what the doctor would order for you, Trev."

"I tell you my very bones are icy." He sighed. "I only hope I'm well enough to travel with you to Camden Hall, and I simply won't go if it's as cold as it is today."

After he finished his tea, Trevor stood and gazed down at her. "I must go. My bed beckons." He rolled his eyes and spoke in a martyred voice. "I pray my valet doesn't discover my lifeless body tomorrow morning." Then he wrapped his muffler several times around his neck and halfway up his face, donned his gloves, and left.

As soon as he was gone Fiona called for her coach to be brought around, then she donned her own pelisse and cape and scurried to the conveyance, making a mental apology to Trevor. It *was* beastly cold. She directed the coachman to take her to the Birmingham's bank.

Through bleary eyes she watched out the window as they sped toward The City. It was so utterly gray today, a perfect match to her gloomy mood. Only the raggedly dressed children with cheeks rosy from the cold seemed oblivious to the frigid weather as they frolicked on the pavement, a few of them pausing to gather around the chestnut roaster.

When she arrived at the bank, she stuffed her hands into her muff, leaped from the coach, and hurried into the lobby, then went directly to Adam's tastefully decorated office.

He stood when she entered. He looked so much like his brother it made her heart ache. "My dear lady, Nick would not at all like your being out on such a wretched day, and I promised him before he left that I would look after you. Please take a seat." He indicated a throne-style chair that was swathed in a pumpkin-colored silk.

"I'm not staying. I merely wished to ask you a question."

One dark brow arched in the exact manner as Nick's.

"Where has my husband gone?"

He did not answer for a moment. "To Essex," he finally said.

She didn't believe him. "To interview the new foreman?"

"Yes. I expect he's already on his way back to London by now."

"You've told me what I wanted to know." *No, not what I wanted.* She turned to leave, tears clouding her vision.

"My lady!" He started after her.

But she did not stop.

She wept all the way back to Menger House. Nick had lied to her when he said he was going to Essex to resolve a labor dispute. How careless of him not to apprise his brother of his lies. Now he was found out.

But no matter. She would not be at home when he returned. He would be free of her. Free to cavort with his mistress in any way he wanted.

She was such an utter failure at everything, from the estrangement with her brother, to her unfulfilled promises to Verity, to her inability to win her husband's affection.

As the coach glided to a stop in front of Menger House, Fiona took a long look at the classically styled mansion that had always filled her with pride. This wasn't her home after all. Windmere Abbey was her home. How she longed to go there, to have Randy and Stephen and Mama and Papa all together again. To be surrounded by her own family. But, of course, that was impossible. Mama and Papa were dead. Randy did not desire her company. Besides, even if Windmere Abbey was her home, she was married to Nicholas Birmingham. She was his property. If she must leave London—and she must—then she would have to go to Camden Hall.

How she had looked forward to going to Camden Hall for Christmas, to taking Emmie with her to gather the holly and berries and mistletoe. Now she would go alone. As much as she wished to take Emmie with her, she couldn't. Nick would never give up the child.

Inside the house, she ordered Prudence to pack her things for Camden Hall, then she trudged up the terrazzo stairway to find Emmie.

The child was playing in the nursery with her favorite doll—one Fiona had given her—when she looked up and saw Fiona. "My Lady," she exclaimed, running to Fiona and throwing her little arms around her.

Fiona held her close. Such a precious little being. "Oh, my little pet, I'm going to miss you so much."

Emmie's face clouded as she looked up into Fiona's equally clouded face. "Where are you going?"

"I have to go to Camden Hall. I must ensure that all our cottagers and the loyal servants receive their Christmas packages. I do hope you and your papa will join me for Christmas."

"I want to go with you!"

"Oh, pet, I wish you could, but your papa will be lonely when he returns, and he'll want his little girl here."

"Then I must stay, but I'll beg him to take me to you."

"That would make me very happy, love."

Losing Nick was the worst pain she'd ever experienced, and now added to that was the sting of leaving a piece of her heart here in the Menger House nursery.

Chapter 27

His thirst to see Fiona was so great he had not stopped to sleep, or to change his clothes, or even to shave. The aching anticipation of seeing her helped to dull his constant fear for William's safe return. Nick repeatedly consoled himself that by having enlisted Yvonne's help, he had stacked the deck in William's favor. If anyone could secure William's release, it was Yvonne.

But the situation was grave.

His dusk arrival at Menger House—bone weary but exhilarated—could not have been timed better. Fiona would surely be home. No evening engagement would have started this early. "Where is Mrs. Birmingham?" Nick casually asked Biddles as he divested himself of his greatcoat and heaped it on the butler's proffered arm.

Biddles's face was inscrutable. "The lady has gone to Camden Hall."

Profound disappointment slammed into Nick. Though Fiona had mentioned her desire to spend Christmas at Camden Hall, he had allowed himself to believe she would be waiting for him at Menger House, as anxious to see him as he had been to see her. Her passionate response to him that last night had fooled him into believing that she cared for him. But, of course, if she cared for him, she would be here now.

He disguised his disappointment. "She took my daughter?"

"She went alone."

How strange. Fiona had shared with him her plans to include Emmie in all the holiday preparations.

Then suddenly, as quick and painful as the strike of a cannonball, he realized his wife had left in anger.

His stomach churned and his heart drummed as he mounted the stairs to the third-floor nursery. Had Fiona thought herself a deserted wife? Had, God forbid, she returned to Warwick's arms? He had but to ask her guards to know if she had met with Warwick. But he would not do that.

Dazed by his own grief, he eased open the door to the nursery.

"Papa!" a smiling Emmie said as she flew into his arms.

He gathered her close and just held her. He loved the feel of her, the sweet smell of her.

Her little arms tightened around him. "I'm ever so glad you've come back. I was so afraid you'd not return. Like My Lady. Please, can we go to her?"

What if she doesn't want to see us? But he could not voice such a suspicion to his daughter. "We'll go there for Christmas," he said firmly. *And heaven help me if she sends me away.*

"I wish My Lady were my real mother."

"I do too, love. I do too." *And I wish she were my real wife.* "Go get your hat and coat. We're going to buy My Lady a fine Christmas present."

It was Christmas Eve and Nick hadn't come. She had been right. He was glad to be rid of her. Now he could channel all his attentions on his damnable mistress. Was she Hortense? Or could it be he was still seeing Diane Foley—regardless of what Trevor had told her?

Dear Trevor. She smiled to herself. At this very moment he had ensconced himself beneath a rug in front of the fire, where he sipped steaming tea and cursed the foul weather. He had begged off gathering the Christmas greenery, leaving that task to Fiona and Verity. Thank the heavens for Verity. The daily intercourse with her sister was the only thing that made leaving London—and Nick—almost tolerable. Almost.

"Here you are," said Verity as she strolled into the morning room and set down her basket.

"What have you there?" Fiona asked.

"Presents for my loved ones."

Fiona sighed. "A pity Nick and Emmie won't be coming."

Verity's eyes softened as she peered at Fiona. "It's not Christmas yet. I believe Nicky will come."

"You've brought him a present?"

Nodding, Verity began to rifle through the basket. "I found him the nicest copy of Blake's poems—to replace what he gave you last Christmas. I know how dearly he loved that book."

As Fiona loved it. "Would that I'd thought of that. Not that I expect to see him, of course." She shrugged. "It's exceedingly difficult to find a gift for the man who has everything."

"What about giving him a miniature of yourself?"

Fiona gave a bitter laugh. "Miniatures are to be given to those who love you." *And Nick most certainly does not love me.* She spoke with false brightness: "I must show you the miniature of my eldest brother. 'Tis one of my most treasured possessions." She went to her reticule, withdrew the miniature of Randolph, and gave it a quick glance. "Of course he's changed vastly

since he had this made for Mama a decade ago."
She presented it to Verity.

Verity's face went white as she took the oval in her
shaking hands.

"What's the matter?" demanded Fiona, who rushed
to Verity's side and settled her hand at Verity's waist.

"This is y-y-your brother?"

"Randolph, Viscount Agar." Fiona nodded. "I wish
you could have met him."

"I have."

Fiona stared at her sister. Then everything became
so clear. "You mean . . . he's the man from the park?"

Verity nodded.

"Oh, my dear sister, this is wonderful! You're the perfect wife for Randy. I must write to him straight away."

Shaking her head, Verity grabbed Fiona's arm.
"You'll do no such thing! Your brother has no more
desire to marry a Cit's daughter than he desires his
sister be wed to a Cit."

Fiona stiffened. Of course, Verity, in her infinite
wisdom, was right. As much as Fiona loathed to admit
it, her brother had proven to be a terrible snob—and
such behavior was at tremendous odds with the
person she had thought him to be.

She had no reply for Verity. In the span of a few seconds she had swung from an incredible high to a de-
spairing low.

Verity handed the miniature back to Fiona.

"No, I want you to keep it. I think no other woman
will ever love my brother as you do."

Her cheeks were still red from gathering the berries
and evergreens, and her hands were numb from the
cold as she fastened sprigs of holly to the foggy win-
dowpanes in the front parlor. Off in the misty distance
she saw smoke curling from the chimneys at Great

Acres. The sound of Verity's and Trevor's laughter came from the next room as they contrived to make a Christmas bough. Stephen was in the wood selecting a yule log. At least Fiona would not have to spend Christmas completely alone.

Her thoughts drifted to the last Christmas Eve. Her wedding day. She could not look fondly upon that day. Everything had been too new, too bizarre for her to have enjoyed that first day she had become the bride of a stranger. Would that she could have understood then how precious that time was. Looking back on it now she was filled with a bittersweet sadness. How fortunate she had been then to have Nick, to share his bed. She would give all that she had to be able to go back now and recapture that night.

She heard the clopping of a lone rider before she looked up to see him, her heart hammering wildly in expectation of seeing Nick. But Nick would not come on horseback. He would come in his fine carriage. Her hands stilled, her pulse pounding in her throat, as she watched the rider draw closer. It was difficult to tell who it was because he was so heavily bundled against the cold.

Even as he dismounted some twenty feet from her, she could not tell who it was. Not until he shook off his hat and she saw his blond hair. It was Randy!

She dropped her basket of holly, ran to the entry hall, and swung open the door to greet him with the broadest of smiles.

His eyes narrowed, he cocked his head to one side. "Forgive me?"

She answered by flowing into his arms.

After they had affectionately embraced, she rushed him to the front parlor. "Come stand beside the fire. You've got to be frozen. I shall be most vexed that you came by horseback on such a frigid day—but, of course, I'm too happy to be vexed."

After taking off his damp greatcoat, he removed his gloves and waved his hands in front of the fire.

Turning somber, Fiona asked, "Did you know that she's here?"

His brows squeezed together as he regarded his sister. "Who?"

"Miss Birmingham. The lady from Hyde Park. The woman you're in love with."

He whirled around, his eyes wide. "My lady's . . . Miss Birmingham?"

"Indeed."

He cursed himself under his breath. "Of course Birmingham's sister would be all that is refined. A pity I've alienated her."

Fiona's voice softened. "Did you not tell her you didn't care whose daughter she was?"

"I did."

"Did you mean it?"

He did not answer for a moment. "I've done many stupid things—things that have hurt those I love most, but I want you to believe me when I tell you I had to hit the bottom before I could rise, before I could see how dearly my beastly pride has cost me. Rank no longer matters to me. All that matters is those I love." He turned around and faced the fire again. A moment later, his voice thick with emotion, he asked, "Do you think she'll have me?"

"You shall have to ask her yourself." Fiona came to link her arm through his. "Come, allow me to introduce you to the woman you love."

Despite that Nick had not come and that William was God-only-knows-where on the continent, Verity took comfort in Fiona and in the knowledge that Adam would be there that night to celebrate Christmas with his family. She found that she was rather enjoying

Christmas Eve. It was much merrier than she had expected, especially given the bleakness of her own romantic future. Trevor Simpson and the delightful, if quite youthful, Stephen Hollingsworth contrived to keep a smile on her face throughout the making of the kissing bough.

One moment she was laughing at Stephen Hollingsworth; the next moment she was gazing up into the handsome face of his elder brother. She felt as if a bolt of lightning had struck her.

"Hey, brother," Stephen exclaimed, "I didn't know you were coming. By Jove, we could have ridden together. I arrived only today myself."

But Randolph was not attuned to what his brother was saying. His eyes were on her. His blond locks were in disarray, his cheeks bright red from the cold, but Verity thought she had never seen a more handsome man.

"I wish he *would* have ridden with you," Fiona said. "Our foolish brother came on horseback all the way from London in this wretched weather." As Fiona gazed affectionately at Randolph, Verity thought she had not seen her sister so cheerful in a very long while. "Come, you must stand by the fire," Fiona told him, "but first I must present Miss Birmingham to you."

Verity's chest pounded, and she was quite certain she was trembling like an octogenarian—and even more certain that Lord Agar's presence had rendered her speechless. She showed a great interest in studying her lap as he strolled to her, took her hand, and brushed his lips across it.

Then she allowed herself to gaze into his eyes.

Had there been a hundred people in the room, she still would have felt as if she and her blond lord were the only two people on earth. If the eyes were the windows to the soul, then Lord Agar was as deeply affected by her as she was by him. She suddenly recalled

Fiona's talk about destiny. Nick was Fiona's destiny; Lord Agar, Verity's.

She was only vaguely aware that Fiona was asking Mr. Simpson and young Hollingsworth to assist her in hanging the kissing bough, but she was keenly aware of the door closing behind them, of being alone with Lord Agar.

"So you're Miss Birmingham," he said, still hovering over her chair.

"And you're Lord Agar," she said breathlessly.

He just stood there looking at her as if she had sprouted angel's wings.

"You must be chilled to the very bone, my lord. You came on horseback?" Thank God she had not lost her voice.

He nodded. "Allow me to say that any discomfort I experienced was well worth the reward of seeing my sister—and seeing you once again, Miss Birmingham."

She stood and moved toward the fire. "I beg that you come warm yourself by the fire."

He came to stand next to her, zigzagging his hands in front of the flames. Neither of them spoke for a moment. A rush of memories flooded her. Memories of him.

"When you quit coming to the park," he said solemnly, "it was one of the blackest times in my one and thirty years, but now I'm glad it happened."

Her stomach dropped, her pulse accelerated. So he wasn't her destiny after all. She wanted nothing so much as to flee the room ahead the torrent of tears that was threatening.

Then he continued. "For most of my life things have come easily for me. Until the past two years. My father died. Our family fortune was gone. Then I lost you." He turned to her, his eyes full of warmth. "I had to reach rock bottom before I could climb back. That night at Vauxhall I was too proud to ask for your hand when I had nothing to give you in return. Now I realize my deuced pride has kept me from that which is most important to me—you. I've been tormented that you'd find someone else."

Then he did still care! She melted into his arms and found his lips crushing against hers, his tongue thrusting, his arms tightening against her back. She exulted in his touch. Being here—in his arms—was her destiny. It was foolish to fight it.

After he had thoroughly kissed her, he settled her head against his chest and combed his fingers through her dark hair. "I can't let you get away from me again. Not ever. I vow if you will but honor me with your affection I will work harder than any man has ever worked in order to be worthy of you, to restore the Agar properties."

"Is this a proposal, then?"

He swallowed. "I have nothing to offer now, save my name and my heart."

"Your heart is all I could ever desire. But . . . you know my family background—"

"Were you the spawn of a stable hand, I would still love you. I will go to my grave loving you. It's I who am not good enough for you."

"There's no one else I could ever love."

He held her at arm's length and peered into her face. "Then will you honor me by becoming my wife?"

"I will."

The next kiss was far more tender than the first. When it was finished, he asked, "Pray, my love, what is your Christian name?"

"Verity."

He smiled. "Lovely. Just like you. I beg that you call me Randolph."

Then they heard the sound of the front door opening. She placed her hand in his. "Come, my dearest, that must be my brother, Adam. We must tell all of them our good news."

When they walked into the hall they saw it was Nicholas Birmingham, not Adam, who had arrived. His black eyes on the kissing bough over the door to the drawing room—and on Fiona who stood beneath it—he strode the length of the hall, then pulled his wife into his arms and settled his lips on hers.

Chapter 28

A man besotted over his mistress did not kiss his wife as Nick had just kissed her.

Still reeling from the powerful kiss, Fiona held Nick's hand to ground herself. She was possessed of the most dismaying feeling that she had taken flight. Nick was here! Nick had kissed her with deep passion. Nick had *chosen* to spend his Christmas with her. He'd even brought Emmie. No Christmas could ever be so wonderful!

She was far too happy to wipe the smile from her face as she gazed up at the husband she adored.

"Happy anniversary, my love," he said, squeezing her hand.

My love! Could any Christmas gift be more welcome? "I'm very touched that you remembered." Then she turned her attention to Emmie, who stood in the hallway with one hand clutching the doll Fiona had given her, the other stuffed into the ermine muff. "Come, love, you must allow your mother and father to kiss you beneath the kissing bough," Fiona said.

Squealing with delight, the child scurried to them and climbed up into Nick's arms as both her parents kissed her rosy cheeks.

Fiona wished to savor this moment of complete happiness surrounded by all those she loved. Her gaze swept from Trevor to Stephen, then to Randy and Verity, who looked every bit as happy as she. She knew at once that Verity had accepted Randy's offer. "Is there to be an announcement from my brother?" she asked, her smile impossible to dispel.

"Indeed there is," Randolph said. He met Nick's gaze. "I would be honored to have your blessing."

Nick gave him a quizzing look.

"Your wonderful sister has done me the goodness of accepting my offer of marriage."

"But . . ." Nick glanced from Verity to Randolph. He had not been aware that the two of them knew one another, but to look at them was to know that they were deeply in love. "You, of course, have my blessing. We can speak later, Agar."

As the others collapsed around the betrothed couple, Nick watched Fiona stroke Emmie's warm brown hair. "I'm so glad you've come, pet," Fiona said. "You can help your mama decorate the windows with holly."

"Could you give me a hand with a yule log?" Stephen asked Nick.

Nick's eyes glistened with happiness. "It will be my pleasure."

His heart swelled as he watched Emmie and Fiona hurry off to the front parlor.

Just as he lighted the log a few minutes later, Adam arrived with Nick's mother. "Happy Christmas, Mother. Come sit near the fire where you can get warm," he said with concern.

He could hear Fiona's and Emmie's laughter in the next room, and he glowed with the happiness of knowing he was surrounded by all his loved ones. Save one. His worry over William marred an otherwise perfect Christmas.

Once he helped the females wrap the bannister in a garland of fresh boxwood, all of them sat around the fire of the yule log and conversed amiably. Even his normally cranky mother was exceptionally hospitable. "I've brought the child a gift," she said gruffly. Turning to Emmie, she said, "But you can't open it until the Lord's birthday tomorrow."

"Thank you, Grandmama," Emmie said in a wispy voice. "This is my favorite Christmas ever."

As it was Nick's. Even if William wasn't here. Damn but he worried about the fellow.

It was just past ten when Trevor bid everyone good night. "I'm utterly fatigued."

"But you've not left your cozy chair all day!" Fiona teased.

"You forget, my sweet," Trevor answered, "how delicate my health is."

After Simpson left, Nick could barely manage the wait until his own bedtime, when he could be alone with the woman he loved above everyone.

Taking the cue from Trevor, Adam rose and offered his hand to his mother. "I'd best get you back to Great Acres. It grows chillier by the hour."

"And I need to show you to your room," Fiona said to Randy.

Just when Adam opened the exterior door to leave, Nick looked up to see William standing there under the portico. "Happy Christmas!" William said.

Now, thought Nick, *it will be a perfect Christmas.* The happiest ever.

After Nick had spoken privately with William in his library and learned the details of his brother's release, William left for Great Acres. And Nick mounted the stairs to Fiona's room, drawing up to her door and tapping it with his knuckles.

"Nick?" she asked softly.

His heartbeat tripped. "Yes."

"Come in."

He stepped into the dark chamber that was lit by a yellow circle of light from a bedside candle, relieved that her maid had gone. His gaze traveled to his beautiful wife. She sat on the edge of the bed, covered only by her thin lawn nightshift. The room was cold, so cold that her fair skin twinged blue and her nipples pricked the soft gown. "I hoped you would come to me," she said in a husky whisper.

At no moment in his life had he ever been filled with more happiness. His very loins ached with the realization that she wanted him to make love to her. He moved to her, never taking his eyes from her. "I wish to make love to you," he said as he came to stand before her and peer down at her loveliness, "but first we must talk."

He sat beside her and drew her hand into his, her left hand with its simple golden band. That she chose to wear so plain a symbol of their unity filled him with pride. "I think perhaps you were upset when I so hurriedly left London?"

It tore at his heart to see her eyes begin to water. "Even more upset when I learned you did *not* go to Essex."

"You were right to be angry. Husbands and wives should not have secrets from one another. I was concealing something from you, my darling." He paused to brush away a tear that spilled from her eye. "Not another woman. Never that."

She looked up at him with reddened eyes. "Then what?"

"I had vowed to never reveal the nature of William's work for our Foreign Office. That's why I was forced to lie to you. When I so suddenly left London, it was because William's life was in peril."

"The French?"

"Yes."

"Surely you know I would never reveal a confidence. Especially if it would jeopardize your brother."

He fingered her golden wedding band. "I do now. I realize I've made a huge blunder with our marriage."

"Me too."

Her words gave him hope. He withdrew a small velvet box from his pocket.

"I don't want any more jewels, Nicholas Birmingham."

"But this one's special." He opened the box. There on a bed of satin was a diamond pendant shaped like a heart. He handed it to her. "Happy Christmas. I want you to take my heart. Even if you still love Warwick, I'm begging that you give me a chance to earn your love."

Her eyes widened. "Warwick? You can't possibly believe I love him."

Nick frowned as his pulse accelerated. He would have to confront her. Even if it was Christmas Eve. Even if it was their first wedding anniversary. "I saw you together one afternoon in Whitehall. When I asked you about it that night, you lied."

She collapsed against him, sobbing. "For-for-forgive me, my love, for lying," she whimpered between sobs. "I'd merely gone to Warwick to learn Randy's direction." She drew in a deep breath. "I lied because I did not wish for you to know of my estrangement from my brother."

His hands traced sultry circles on her back. "Because I was the cause of it?"

She nodded.

"Sit back up, my love. I want you to wear my heart." He fastened the pendant's chain around the smooth column of her neck, then drew in a deep breath. "You truly *don't* love Warwick?"

"Truly." Her soft blue eyes caressed him. "I stopped loving him before we married."

"I regret that I never told you how much I love you. Will you give me the chance to win your love?"

A sweet smile softened her somber face. "You can't possibly win it."

His heartbeat stampeded.

"You already own it." She gazed lovingly into his eyes. "I've been in love with you for a very long time, Nicholas Birmingham."

"A very long time?"

"I think perhaps since that night at the theatre. Before I asked you to marry me. It took me all of a month after that to realize I'd completely lost my heart to you."

He tugged her to his chest, wrapping both arms around her. "I have a confession to make myself."

She stroked the dark stubble of his cheek. "What?"

"I knew I loved you that day in my office."

"The day I proposed?" she asked with a laugh.

"That very day. Once I kissed you, my passionate love, I knew for sure."

No Christmas had even been more magical. A grin pinched into her cheeks. "Then I suggest you prove it, Mr. Birmingham."

And he eased her back into the mattress.

ABOUT THE AUTHOR

A graduate of the University of Texas—and, yes, she loves those Longhorns—Cheryl Bolen enjoyed careers as an award-winning journalist and as a public school English teacher before she turned to writing historical romances. Her first book, *A Duke Deceived*, was published in 1998 and for it she was named Notable New Author. *One Golden Ring* is her eighth book, and she has also published one novella with Zebra.

Now having exchanged pantyhose for sweats, she's thrilled to write full time. Her other thrills come from her professor hubby, their two sons who claim to be grown, and keeping the needle on her bathroom scale from going up.

More Regency Romance
From Zebra